THE MYSTERY *OF*

THE VENUS ISLAND FETISH

By Tim Flannery

Minotaur Books
A Thomas Dunne Book
New York

A THOMAS DUNNE BOOK FOR MINOTAUR BOOKS.
A imprint of St. Martin's Publishing Group.

THE MYSTERY OF THE VENUS ISLAND FETISH. Copyright © 2014 by Tim Flannery. All rights reserved. Printed in the United States of America. For information, address St. Martin's Press, 175 Fifth Avenue, New York, N.Y. 10010.

www.thomasdunnebooks.com
www.minotaurbooks.com

Designed by W. H. Chong

The Library of Congress Cataloging-in-Publication Data is available upon request.

ISBN 978-1-250-07942-8 (hardcover)
ISBN 978-1-4668-9215-6 (e-book)

Our books may be purchased in bulk for promotional, educational, or business use. Please contact your local bookseller or the Macmillan Corporate and Premium Sales Department at (800) 221-7945, extension 5442, or by e-mail at MacmillanSpecialMarkets@macmillan.com.

First published in Australia by The Text Publishing Company

First U.S. Edition: February 2016

10 9 8 7 6 5 4 3 2 1

To my father

INTRODUCTION

by Tim Flannery

The Butterworth manuscript was discovered in rather unusual circumstances. The initial finding was made by Margot Fitzgerald, an education officer at the museum. Her classroom is a last stop for stuffed animals no longer needed by the scientists. The exhibits end their days there, petted by small hands until baldness, burst seams or an increasingly whimsical appearance consign them to the incinerator.

On the day of the discovery Margot heard a group of boys sniggering as they clustered around a taxidermised baboon which I had recently brought her.

'That monkey's got a cigar sticking out of its bum,' she heard a boy say. Since I had recently transferred the mount to her care, Margot contacted me. When I arrived to investigate I found that the hide of the creature had shrunk, and it had become almost bald. A scroll of paper, its tip yellowed with age, could be seen protruding from its posterior.

I could just about make out a few typed words on the outermost sheet, one of which appeared to be the name of a retired staff member. Animal skins are normally stuffed with kapok or cotton wool. Could this be a lost manuscript? My heart skipped a beat. I took the decrepit mount to the taxidermy workshop, where George Bowridge extracted one hundred and thirty-five sheets of government-issue, wartime foolscap paper, tightly rolled and covered on both sides with single-spaced type. In Bowridge's opinion they had been inserted at the time of stuffing, some fifty years ago.

He said that in his experience museum staff are notoriously averse to discarding anything. Some curators he knew had accumulated great balls of string originally used to tie packages sent to them, while others hoarded boxes full of worn-out shoes. He'd been told that in times past requests had been made of taxidermists to secrete objects, which might better have been destroyed, into animal mounts. Who, I wondered, would have selected the anus of an ape to secrete a manuscript? And why?

Authorship of the pages is attributed to a Miss Dido Butterworth, curator of worms (retired), but a search of the museum archives revealed no employee by that name. I can only guess that Dido Butterworth is a pseudonym. But for whom? I suspect Hans Schmetterling, curator of worms between 1936 and 1955. Strangely, a character by that name features in the manuscript.

I could learn little of the real Hans Schmetterling. Evidence of his activities as curator are sketchy to say the least, and the museum archivist noted that, despite the excellent standards maintained by her department, several key papers relating to his employment could not be found. A search of births, deaths and marriages also came up blank.

Others may disagree with my supposition that Schmetterling is the author. I'm convinced by the numerous, detailed and often lyrical references to worms in the work that whoever wrote it must have had an intimate knowledge of the annelida.

I have no idea whether *The Mystery of the Venus Island Fetish* presents fact or fiction, but it is a gripping tale and something of a window onto a lost world. In that spirit I offer it to the reader.

My duties as editor have been light. Some of the dates and events referred to are clearly erroneous, but I felt it best to leave things largely as they are, for fear of sowing further confusion. The only substantial alteration I've made is to delete the numerous (and often tediously lengthy) descriptions of worms.

Melbourne, 2014

THE MYSTERY OF

THE
VENUS
ISLAND
FETISH

Chapter 1

Archibald Meek watched from the canoe as the muscular form of his adopted brother Cletus dived through the water, coming to rest atop a submerged coral bommie. Cletus stilled momentarily, then thrust his arm into a hidden cavity. A black cloud erupted, leaving only the man's legs visible. *Agame.* The giant Pacific octopus. Archie's eyes followed Cletus as he swam to the surface, the beast's tentacles waving wildly.

Cletus bit into the animal's head as he broke the surface, then flipped the lifeless mass into the canoe and catapulted himself aboard. Then he froze. For a moment Archie thought he'd glimpsed the great hammerhead shark that had been hunting the lagoon of late. It was longer than Cletus' canoe and it moved hypnotically, as if to the throb of an invisible kundu drum—

seeing all, sensing all. But it was not that. Cletus pointed with his lips. On the western horizon was the faintest of black streaks.

How long since a steamer last anchored in the lagoon? Long enough that Archie had begun to feel that steamers were things you saw only in dreams.

He had been living outside time, at least as it is measured by clocks and calendars, for almost five years. But that smudge of smoke announced that a ship was coming to restore him to a land where time is doled out in precise units.

The canoe ground into the sand and Archie leapt ashore. He ran to the beach-side hut that he called home. Crates filled with pickled fish, birds and lizards occupied one wall, while from the thatched roof hung all sorts of artefacts, from grass skirts to spears and knobkerries. He sat on his ribbed, wooden sea-trunk, its rusty lock long untouched, and remembered the day he'd arrived.

Then, as today, Archie sat on the trunk. It was midday, and the sun beat down on the deserted beach like a hammer. The sailors remained silent as they offloaded his cargo of preserving jars, reference books and butterfly nets. He had told them what he had half-convinced himself was true: that museum anthropologists had studied and collected on most of the islands of the Pacific, and that very few had come to harm. But the sailors' eyes said it all: they were sure they were leaving the young scientist to be killed, and most likely eaten, by savages.

As he watched the crew row back to the schooner he erected an umbrella, and waited. Soon, the sounds of the wind in the palms and the chirruping of insects filled his consciousness. As the sun was sinking into the lagoon a man strode out of the shadows, took his hand, and led him to the hut he sat in. Months later Archie learned how lucky he'd been. By sitting and waiting on the beach until being welcomed by the village chief, a man called Sangoma, he'd unwittingly followed protocol, and had been accepted into the clan.

But God, how difficult those first months had been! Archie was as useless as an infant. No, worse. He had the mind of an infant, but the body of a man. He could not light a fire or prepare food. In fact he could hardly tell what was edible and what was not. He unwittingly stole fruit from people's trees because he did not know that the forest was owned. He transgressed into the women's menstrual huts and stomped through sacred sites, simply because he did not recognise the many warning signs placed around them. He killed tabooed creatures, defecated in taro gardens (which he took to be the bush), and generally made a nuisance of himself. All the while, Sangoma had made excuses for him, paid compensation to those wronged, and explained that Archie knew as little about life as a child, or a savage.

At first his only use was as a beast of burden—to carry firewood and suchlike. But he was soon participating in communal activities. One morning the men of the village set out to clear the bush for a new garden. Archie swung his axe until he was in a lather of sweat. When the tree he was hacking at finally fell, a great rat slithered out of a knothole in its trunk, and Cletus expertly flung a stick after it, striking it on the head. Archie scrambled to collect the animal, thinking that it might interest his friend and curator of mammals at the museum, Courtenay Dithers. Cletus' younger brother Polycarp had mimed that the creature was unclean, but Archie persisted in carrying it back to his hut and pickling it. For weeks afterwards, whenever they met, Polycarp would repeat the mime and walk off laughing.

Ever so slowly, Archie had grown proficient at things. He loved fishing best of all because the hooks and line he had brought, along with the experience of a childhood spent fishing around Sydney Harbour, made him moderately competent. But he could not manage a canoe, so needed someone to come with him. It was during his hours fishing, most often with Cletus, that he made most progress with the language.

As Archie realised how ignorant he'd been, he suffered agonies of embarrassment. When he felt competent enough to speak, he decided to broach a subject that he felt might gain him some kudos: the Great Venus Island Fetish, as the mask was known among anthropologists, was the work of a stone-age genius and quite the most famous Pacific Islands artefact in the world. The size of a dinner table, it took the form of a monstrous and stylised heart-shaped face, around the margin of which were attached thirty-two human skulls. It had been taken from the Venus Islands in 1893 by the crew of HMAS *Adelaide*, during a punitive raid in reprisal for the massacre of the passengers and crew of the *Venus*. Its loss had been more devastating to the islanders than the shelling of their village, or the destruction of their gardens. Archie was familiar with the fetish because it was a prized exhibit at the museum where he was employed.

Before its removal to Sydney, the fetish had resided on a deserted sandy islet—one of the five islands that made up the Venus Group. Only under the most exceptional of circumstances would the most senior men dare to visit it. To them, the mask was the embodiment of pure evil. Remove just one skull from the cordon of thirty-two sacrificial heads that surrounded the ghastly face, it was said, and the door to an age of depravity, madness and murder would open.

'Do you remember the great mask?' Archie asked Sangoma one day as the chief worked carving out a canoe.

Sangoma put down his adze, fixed Archie with a fierce gaze, and said, 'Such things must never be spoken of while we work. Wait for the story time.'

That night, as the coals died down and the young men drifted off to sleep, Sangoma and a few of the village elders refilled the yangona bowl, and began to whisper about the great mask. They told of its creation by a mad genius who was eaten by an enormous shark on the very day he completed his work. Only the spirits of warriors, which resided in their skulls, would be strong enough to contain its malignant power. But how difficult it was to get those skulls! The Venusians were few, and their enemies too fierce and numerous to make easy victims. So the islanders had lived for years in terror while the protective skull fence was in the making. Then, one day, a godsend came to them. A floating island, full of white-skinned warriors, had run aground during a storm and the survivors had straggled ashore. Exhausted, they seemed to give themselves willingly to the bamboo knife and man-catcher. In a single day the skull fence was completed, and the villagers slept soundly for the first time in years.

'I know the fetish. I look after it now.' Archie had boasted in the silence that followed. Eyes flashed in the darkness. Then all the elders started whispering at once.

'It survives!' Archie heard. 'But where? Where is it?'

'In my village. Sydney.'

From that day on Archie was treated with new respect. Old men took him under their tutelage. Things were shown to him that were revealed only to youths of great promise. One morning, an elder asked what his tattoo should be. Archie was not sure he wanted a tattoo, but sensed that his choice would be significant. Just then a platoon of frigate birds cruised past. Black and red, bent of wing and forked of tail, the enormous creatures flew in a strict V-formation, like some piratical, futuristic flying machines. '*Alaba*. The frigate bird.' Archie replied. Only later did he consider the possibility that the old man had waited until he saw the birds approaching before asking his question. The tattooing had been painful, but afterwards Archie looked with pride at the image of the bird decorating his forearm, knowing that it was Sangoma's clan symbol.

At some moment he found hard to identify, Archie stopped collecting things, and practically stopped making field notes. He had slipped from being the observing outsider to one of the clan. It was only as the final stage of his initiation approached that he took up his journal again. He had both personal and professional reasons to record the event. Circumcision had seemed a high price to pay to hear the sacred stories that were essential to his full comprehension of the culture. But after a few swigs of yangona the cut of the bamboo knife hadn't been as painful as he'd anticipated. As Archie watched his blood drip onto the sand, Uncle Sangoma told him that he was now a man, and a true Venus Islander.

After the ceremony, Archie, Cletus and the other lads had stretched their foreskins into discs, which dried to a parchment. As was the custom, they then tattooed them with their totems. Archie's frigate bird was beautifully executed. No proposal of marriage would be taken seriously in the Venus Islands unless a man presented his girl with a tattooed, parchment-like disc made from his foreskin. The youths whispered that the objects were infallible love charms. If a girl received one, she would be powerless to refuse the giver anything. She would signal her acceptance of the marriage by softening the parchment in coconut oil, rolling it into a ring, and wearing it on her finger.

The Venus Islands had made Archie a man in more ways than one. He had learned how to carve a canoe and make a bow and arrow. He could catch a tuna or a wallaby as adeptly as anyone. And he had seen five yam festivals, with their moonlit nights of lovemaking and fertility rituals. He was now a man of consequence among the islands. A man in his prime.

Archie's meditations were broken by a bugling sound. Sangoma was blowing his shell trumpet, his muscular chest rising and falling with the effort. He was magnificent, with his prominent nose, dark eyes and full, greying beard exuding authority.

'Launch the great war canoe! Launch the war canoe,' he

shouted between notes. 'Load it as well. Load it with Aciballie's cargo. All the cargo!'

Cletus, Polycarp and the other lads were already at the door, ready to carry Archie's crates to the beach. Outside, Archie could see that preparations were being made to launch the canoe he had purchased. As the boys puffed past with boxes and chests, Cletus mimed that he was carrying an extraordinarily heavy crate, and quipped, 'I don't know why you bothered collecting all those poisonous and useless creatures, Aciballe. They'll break my back!'

Archie grinned and covered his nakedness with a bark lap-lap. Then he dashed out the door. He was headed towards the yam gardens, his bare feet beating a frantic tattoo on the burning sand. Round one last corner and he saw her. She was bent almost double, and with each thrust of the yam-stick her withered breasts flapped against her chest.

'Auntie Balum,' he cried as he saw the woman who had cared for him as tenderly as any mother could. Balum stretched upright, one hand in the small of her back while she steadied herself with the stick. She'd been a beauty in her youth. Even now her almond eyes, delicate nose and shapely mouth were arresting. For a few moments her tattooed face remained blank, as if she couldn't understand why he was there. But then her sweet visage collapsed with grief.

'My son. My son is gone,' she wailed. 'My son is gone, gone from my sight!'

It was the traditional dirge for a young man slain in battle.

'Auntie. I must go home. I told you that when I first arrived. But I will be back.' Archie's eyes filled with tears as he cradled her slight body in his arms. He knew he was lying.

An hour later the steamer was inside the lagoon. It was time for Archie to go. He was desperately sad to be leaving his island family. It felt like a sort of death. But if he didn't leave now he would never see his fiancée Beatrice again. He had written to her at every opportunity. Letters had piled up waiting for a passing vessel. And she had written back. He imagined her beautiful face concentrating as she crafted each sentence, her glorious blonde locks flowing over her shoulders, her exquisite hands delicately holding her pen. And with every loving letter he'd received from her, his confidence had grown. In his last missive, sent by canoe and then native runner to the nearby mission, he had proposed marriage. He felt certain of a positive response. But just to be doubly sure he had enclosed his foreskin love-token with the letter. And now, in just a few weeks, he would fall into her arms, and a new life would begin.

'Get yer arse aboard!' the bosun screamed above the creak of the windlass. 'The fuckin' tide's turned. If we don't shift now we'll be spending the night with the bloody cannibals!'

The island lads were warily clambering up the rope ladders slung over the side of the SS *Mokambo*, somehow balancing Archie's crates on their shoulders as they went. At the rail, equally wary sailors took the crates aboard. The great war canoe had already been winched out of the water. As Archie climbed a rope boarding ladder its outrigger swung wildly, threatening to knock him back into the water. There was no time to say goodbye. He barely had time to wave before he heard the shout 'up anchor', and the tramp steamer began moving, leaving the cluster of outriggers and their forlorn paddlers in its wake.

By dusk Great Venus was a mere smear on the horizon, and West Venus Atoll, home of the famous fetish, was close a-starboard. In the gloaming Archie could just about make out the ceremonial path, lined with the ochred valves of giant clam shells, leading in from the beach. There was not a light to be seen on the place: the Venus Islanders would rather die than set foot there after dark.

The last of the tropical twilight faded, and Archie went to his cabin. A small mirror hung on one wall. What he saw in it shocked him: a brown man, muscular, trim and tattooed, dressed in nothing but a skimpy loincloth. The trunk containing his clothes had been placed beside his bunk. He opened it for the first time in years, took out his suit, felt its fabric, and at once remembered his nickname—Beanpole Meek. That, and his brothers' habit of pointing out his 'Bondi chest' (far from Manly) had been perpetual humiliations.

Archie dropped his loincloth and struggled into his trousers. He tugged at them and heard a ripping sound. His right thigh had burst through the seams. Next he struggled into his shirt. It seemed to belong to a child. Surely a fellow couldn't change that much between nineteen and twenty-four? Perhaps the fabric had shrunk. In any case, the captain's wife might be able to help.

'I can put gussets in them, but there's not a lot of spare fabric,' she said dubiously. Her gaze drifted from Archie's body to the suit and shirt lying in her lap.

'Do you think you could try? I mean, I can't arrive home looking like this.'

'You're not too hard on the eyes. But I suppose you'll need clothes in the city. Leave it with me. I'll fix up something.'

The captain invited his passenger to dine with him most evenings. Archie was surprised at how difficult he found it to have a conversation. He just couldn't find the words he wanted—in English at least. The captain seemed taken with a young cricketer called Bradman. Even though Archie followed cricket keenly, the name meant nothing to him. And both the captain and his wife kept talking about 'the crash'. He assumed they were referring to some terrible rail tragedy, until it became clear that it was about money. Lots of money.

Ten days later, with Archie only dimly aware of changes in the wider world, the *Mokambo* steamed into Sydney Harbour. She passed through the heads in the dead of night, and the first Archie knew of being home—if that's indeed where he was—was the stench of coal smoke. He sat on deck in the predawn darkness, observing the city lights through the grimy atmosphere.

It had been, he recalled, Professor Radcliffe-Brown who'd encouraged him to go to the Venus Isles. He had the ear of both the museum's director, Dr Vere Griffon, and Cecil Polkinghorne, the museum's anthropologist, to whom Archie had been apprenticed. And so, just four years after having arrived at the museum as a fifteen-year-old cadet, Archie was granted study leave to go to the islands.

The Venus Isles had a bad reputation. But in 1911 the Reverend E. Gordon-Smythe had brought Christ to the natives, and it was generally believed that headhunting had been curbed, if not entirely eliminated. Most families would have been concerned to see their son shipping for such a place, but the Meeks were a hard, unsympathetic people. He couldn't remember hearing a kind farewell from his parents, or from his four brothers.

'Study the culture, Archie. Note everything, and bring a rational, detached mind to your work,' Radcliffe-Brown advised. It only now dawned on Archie that, instead, he'd lived the culture. But he *had* done one important thing. He'd made a collection. And what a collection it was!

Chapter 2

As the sun rose over South Head, Archie made arrangements to clear his collection and personal effects through customs, and he set off in his ridiculously small, patched suit, on a leisurely meander towards the museum. After five unconstrained years his feet were so broad that his shoes pinched him wickedly, forcing him to adopt a strange, limping gait. People stared as he passed. Brown-skinned with hair uncut, he felt—and looked like—a stranger in his own city.

Had he forgotten, or perhaps never realised, how bleak it all was? There were no trees—no plants but weeds to soften the bare asphalt, dilapidated houses and overhead tangles of poles and wires. Even Hyde Park looked naked, its southern end turned into a morass by construction works for a new war memorial. He remembered the endless fundraising and planning for the monument, and was glad to see that building had commenced.

In front of the stately Burns Philp building stood a slender figure, balanced on short sticks and with a dead bird perched on its head. Its face was flawless, as pale as a corpse, and its fingernails and lips were as red as if dipped in fresh blood. Unnervingly, its eyes were surrounded with a strange purple glow. It took Archie a moment to realise that she was only a very fashionable young lady, albeit heavily made up, wearing high heels and a bird-of-paradise hat. He wanted nothing more than to grab Sangoma and shout, 'Look at that, Uncle! You think you look fine with a pig's tusk stuck through your nose and a few tattoos on your face. Well, it's we Sydney people who really know how to dress up! Just look at that young woman. Now, she *is* flash!'

The more Archie saw, the more he became amazed. In Macquarie Street there'd been a noticeable shift from hansom cabs to motor vehicles. And the men, in their grey suits and fedoras, moved like autumn leaves before the storm. He saw a banker with an expensive briefcase, a doctor with his trademark Gladstone bag, and a ritual leader in his black cassock.

At last Archie reached the museum. He paused before its column-flanked entrance. The place was a temple to nature, modelled along classical lines and constructed in a golden age when upstart colonies had vied to impress the motherland. Its doors, tradition had it, were tall enough to admit a brontosaurus, and wide enough for a blue whale.

Archie's eye caught a movement. A sparrow hopped in the

roadway, its confidence and smart black bib making it as much a city slicker as the banker with his briefcase. The bird looked Archie brazenly in the eye, then plunged its beak into a steaming pile of horse shit. 'You cheeky fellow!' Archie said as it flew off with its tidbit. Introduced birds—sparrows, starlings, blackbirds and rock pigeons—were everywhere. But hardly a native was to be seen.

Archie stepped over the threshold and strode the black-and-white tiles of the great hall. Slanting beams of light from a roof lantern caught the dust and transformed it into a glittering fog. The galleries were not yet open to the public. The high, empty space echoed with his footfalls.

The day was setting itself up to be a scorcher and the hall was filled with the scent of what most would gloss as *eau de museum*. Archie savoured the old preserving alcohol with its fruitiness, aliquot of cloying formaldehyde, and fishy high note given off by the pickled sea creatures immersed therein. The tang of lacquer from the stuffed Murray cod registered on his palate, while the dun dustiness of old bones coated his throat. But what was that other smell? The smoky, sweaty aroma of the inside of a stone-age hut coming from the New Guinean artefacts was so familiar that it went almost undetected.

He passed under the skeleton of a great whale suspended from the roof, its vertebrae strung on a straight iron rod. On hot days the oil that mottled its bones liquefied. Sometimes a splash would materialise—like a drop of blood from a holy statue—on what was claimed to be the skeleton of the last Tasmanian. The remains hung beside the bones of a gorilla and a chimpanzee, each suspended from a wire that passed through a hole in the top of its cranium. Their arms hung limply by their sides, their toes pointed earthwards. They looked like gibbeted criminals.

In the middle of the hall was a cylindrical glass bottle refulgent in a shaft of light. It contained the cigar-sized egg-case of a giant Gippsland earthworm. Archie could see the solitary embryo floating in its exquisitely translucent, golden case. Unborn, it was already twice the size of a common worm. Nearby stood a glass cabinet that lacked the accumulated grime of ages. It had not been there when he'd left. Inside were minerals, one of which formed a white, silken sheet that resembled the décolletage of a young woman, across which were scattered a soupçon of pea-sized, rose-red crystals. Its beauty held him spellbound. Surely the display was the work of that indefatigable curator, Dr Elizabeth Doughty. Her looks and energy had frightened him when he was a cadet. But then he heard her rhapsodising in the tea room about the beauty of tourmaline and the intricacies of malachite, and she became in his eyes the paragon of what he hoped one day to become—a museum curator.

He had once thought the exhibition the grandest thing in the world. But now it seemed forlorn. Bull roarers, bones, barnacles, butterflies and boomerangs all in random proximity—objects enough to make the tremendous space look cluttered. What, he wondered for the first time in his life, was it all for?

Then he remembered Cecil Polkinghorne's words when giving his new cadet a tour of the institution. 'Here,' he had spluttered, gesturing grandly towards the collection, 'lies the collective memory of our people. Objects may languish unstudied or forgotten for a century or more. But rest assured that one day, in response to the needs of the times, a curator will take up an object, and in it trace indisputable proof of the way things once were. Here, history finds its physical testimony.'

Archie arrived at the director's office before he was fully prepared. He hesitated, trying to recall the speech he'd practised on the boat. Just as he raised his arm to knock, the door swung open. Dryandra Stritchley, the director's secretary, flinched, seemingly horrified by the nut-brown stranger with his right arm elevated as if holding a knobkerrie. Her bearing was as upright as a sergeant-major's, and she was as slender as ever. Her elegant if slightly severe face, grey eyes and sensible clothing were all unchanged. Only the knot of greying hair hinted at the time passed. When she recognised him she quickly regained her composure. 'Meek. It's you at last! The director's waiting for you. He's been waiting for some time. Two years to be precise,' she said archly. 'And don't dare show your face here again before you get a new suit. And a haircut.'

She led Archie through the boardroom. The space was spectacularly large, almost ballroom-sized. The director's desk sat on a raised platform at one end. On the lower level stretched an oval cedar table surrounded by thirteen chairs. One—the chairman's carver—was ornate and twice as tall as the rest. Moving briskly forward, Miss Stritchley failed to notice that Archie had stopped mid-stride, his mouth agape. He was staring at something on the wall.

'The Great Venus Island Fetish,' he whispered.

Painted in white, red and black ochre, the heart-shaped face was carved with crazed, spiky lines that told of its maker's dangerous insanity. The nose, with its wide-open nostrils, sat above a great slash of a mouth filled with jagged, blackened, pigs' teeth. But these were not what one first noticed. It was the eyes. Bloodshot. Manic. Hypnotic. They had been fashioned from pearl-shells smeared with red ochre, the irises blackened spirals made from cone shells. They pulled at Archie's soul as powerfully as a vortex.

Among the thirty-two human skulls decorating its margin were the last mortal remains of the passengers and crew of HMS *Venus*, which had run aground on the uncharted islands during the great cyclone of 1892, and, incidentally, given them their European name. The object had caused quite a stir when it arrived in Sydney. Legend has it that the Anglican bishop thundered from the pulpit that it should be burned, and the skulls sewn onto it given a Christian burial. It was only the popular notion that the heads belonged to heathen Chinese, bound for the Queensland goldfields, that had allowed it to go to the museum, skulls attached.

Archie was unaware that, all along, the director had been watching him. Vere Griffon had shed his jacket, removed his bow tie, and undone the top two buttons of his shirt. But the spats remained in place, as did his starched collar. The slightly dishabille look, he felt, suited his Grecian physique. This mattered to him, even when alone. He could certainly afford the look in the presence of an inferior. On the desk before him were a dozen perfect red roses in a vase. As he watched Archie, he recalled the worst day of his life—the fundraising dinner of six months earlier.

Griffon never thought he'd need to beg for money. When he arrived in Sydney in '23 he'd been hailed as 'the wizard of Cambridge', and there'd been no end to government largesse. But all that finished with the stock-market crash. After that, his only hope of keeping the museum afloat lay in courting wealthy patrons. The trouble was, every cultural institution in the city was chasing the same small clique of philanthropists.

Chumley Abotomy, a new board member, had offered to host a dinner. In his late thirties, ruddy-nosed, paunchy and hairy-eared, Abotomy was an archetypical colonial country squire. He was rough, coarse, loud, and very nouveau riche. His small eyes had a sparkling elusiveness that made them transfixing. Vere Griffon had been seated next to Abotomy's fiancée, the divine Portia Clark. He studied her image, reflected upside down in his silver soup spoon, before deciding that her wistful expression bore a striking resemblance to that of Botticelli's Venus on the half-shell.

Abotomy sat at the head of a splendid table, lit with candles and laid with entreés of jellied trout and devilled eggs. Griffon wondered why Abotomy had seated Lord Bunkdom rather than him on his right. Most of Sydney had suspicions about Bunkdom's title. But there he was, goggle eyes swivelling madly as Abotomy held forth about his country estate.

As Griffon listened to Abotomy big-noting himself, his

bonhomie began to evaporate. By the time dessert was served, it was clear Abotomy would *not* invite him to speak on the urgent need for donations to complete the new hall of evolution. Nor would he turn the conversation towards the institution's many other pressing financial requirements. With his jaw clenched so tightly it hurt, Griffon scanned the table. Elizabeth Doughty, whom he had invited in the hope she might inspire Sir Hercules Robinson to donate some valuable gemstones, had come in a hunting hat and tweed trousers that were a positive parody of femininity. She *might* be coaxing a donation, but judging from her claxon-like tone and Sir Hercules' twitching moustache, she was more likely elaborating on the deficiencies of the museum's administration. As a board member, Hercules could do damage with such information.

That left only Dithers, his curator of mammals. Patrician, with impeccable manners, a Cambridge man. He never failed to charm with his tales of derring-do among the African big game. He was seated next to the evening's principal target, Mrs Gladys Gordon-Smythe. Wrapped in a fox-fur stole, the widow was on the wrong side of sixty. Griffon watched as Dithers fixed her with his soulful black eyes, his kind mouth forming the most sympathetic of shapes. The widow's titterings and fast-emptying champagne flute indicated that she was enjoying the attention. Then something broke the spell.

She raised her lorgnette and pointed her powdered face directly at Griffon. 'Director. Director! Have you any news of that young curator of yours, Mr Archibald Meek? I am most anxious to learn what he has done in the Venus Isles. Perhaps his collections of artefacts will complement those made by my dear, late husband. He was martyred bringing the gospel to the savages, you know.

'Perhaps,' she added coyly, 'if Mr Meek's collections are good enough, one might be motivated to fund a gallery of Pacific cultures to exhibit them.'

Griffon sat in silence, all eyes upon him. Blast Meek! The man had simply vanished. A year and a half overdue, and his director had no idea where he was. Off digging gold in New Guinea, no doubt, or in the thrall of some dusky maiden. Would the fellow never return and live up to his responsibilities?

'Nothing but early reports, Mrs Gordon-Smythe,' he replied at last. 'But they are quite encouraging. As you know, the Venus Isles are pretty much the most remote and uncivilised spot in the entire Pacific. Communications are slow. But I'm sure Meek will return soon, and in triumph.'

At that moment, Griffon would have loved to kill Archibald Meek. Along with the rest of his useless curators. Then he could start over, and build the finest museum in the Empire. One worthy to have him at its head.

As he watched Meek, Griffon let none of this show. He lay inclined, plank-like on his chair, his hands folded behind his head. Until he began stroking his hair, he'd been as still as a mannequin. 'Ah, the prodigal curator returns!' he murmured. 'Alas, after the stock-market crash, the museum budget no longer extends to a fatted calf. Welcome back, Meek.'

Archie wrenched his gaze from the mask. He had heard about the crash aboard the *Mokambo*, but none of it had made any sense. Not that he'd ever taken an interest in such matters anyway. But, at that moment, not even news that the plague had returned to the city would have made an impression. Only one thing mattered to him: the Great Venus Island Fetish. It unnerved him to see it removed from the locked and darkened storage chamber where he had left it on the eve of his departure. It seemed to him that the evil thing had been set free.

'The fetish,' he stammered. 'It really should be in the collection area, where it will be safe. There's a great danger. I mean of borer and dermestid beetle, not to mention fading.'

'Meek, have you forgotten your place? You come here two years late, dressed like an imbecile, and all you can talk about is the decor?' barked Griffon.

'No, sir. Sorry, sir,' replied Archie, automatically losing five carefree years.

'The board and I felt sure we'd never see you again. Thought you'd gone native. You were given three years' study leave in the Venus Islands, not a day longer. Your reports were laconic, to say the least, and we've had none at all for the last two years. You're damn lucky, Meek, that you've got a position to return to. Good Lord! What's that?'

Archie's suit revealed far too much shin and wrist, and the director's gaze was fixed on his employee's left forearm.

Archie squirmed. How could he explain his initiation and tattooing, and the absolute necessity of undergoing it? 'Er, a tattoo, sir,' he mumbled, pulling his sleeve over the image of a frigate bird.

'A tattoo!' thundered the director. 'A tattoo? God damn it, man. Have you gone completely mad? A curator, in my museum, gone bloody native! My God, how will you explain that to our donors? What will Mrs Gordon-Smythe make of that? She's been asking after you, you know, and is keen to fund a new Pacific gallery. But, my word, man, if she sees that damn thing on your arm she'll take her money straight to the art gallery!'

In all his years Archie had never heard Vere Griffon raise his voice. The director was a martinet, no doubt, but his style ran more to intimidation with tones indicating the slenderest restraint upon a cauldron of emotion. The young man felt crushed. Maybe he had gone native. But he had done great things as well. His only hope of mollifying his director lay in enumerating them.

'I've made a wonderful collection, sir, and I've already drafted a very comprehensive report.'

'A collection?' said Vere Griffon, his voice betraying a flicker of interest.

'A collection, sir. Of everything found on the Venus Isles, from the plants, worms, fish and insects to the artefacts made by the islanders. I've even got a set of spirit masks and a headhunting canoe, though the Venus Islanders were most reluctant to part with them.'

'Perhaps the prodigal has redeemed himself,' Vere Griffon murmured under his breath. His expression softened to the extent that Archie felt he could return to the most urgent issue.

'Sir, the Venus Island Fetish is a most delicate artefact.' Moving closer, he could see now that several of the skulls were tinted orange rather than their original smoked-brown colour.

They were, he decided, beginning to lose their patina, perhaps because of exposure to sunlight. Then he spied a small object lying on the floor beneath the mask. He bent down and picked it up. It was a human incisor. Archie slotted it carefully into an empty socket on one of the discoloured skulls. The fit was perfect.

The skull that had lost the incisor had terrible buck teeth— the worst he'd seen since Cecil Polkinghorne had waved him off at the docks five years earlier. Despite the fit, Archie couldn't reattach the tooth in its socket. Without adhesive it would simply fall out again. So he placed it in his pocket, intent on returning with some glue.

'Would you allow me to care for the fetish while it's here, sir? Otherwise its pigments will fade, and bits will drop off—'

'Balderdash!' Vere Griffon shot back. 'Bumstocks inspects it weekly. He may be only a taxidermist, but he's more than capable of basic maintentance.' The director composed himself and continued. 'We must do all we can to engage the board of directors, and surrounding them with treasures from the collection keeps their minds on what's at stake. Their personal donations are all that's keeping us above water at present.'

Vere Griffon sat up and cleared his throat. 'My dear Archie, you've been away a long time. And you do seem quite lost. But you need to get a grip, man.' Griffon smiled. 'I've put together the best collection of curators in the colonies in this institution, and it's vital that we all pull together. We cannot have dissent, or disloyalty. Not now. Go to your office and take up your work. I'm afraid that we've had to move you into a rather smaller one. But I think it will do for the time being.'

Dryandra Stritchley ushered Archie out the door.

'Phew,' said Archie. He slumped against the doorjamb. The worst was over. He composed himself and walked back into the great hall. It was just after nine and the first visitors of the day were trickling in. As he approached the stuffed orangutans he slowed to eavesdrop on a pair of elderly women who stood looking at the creatures.

'Ain't he the spitting image of my Clarrie?' one quipped.

'Yairs,' the other replied. 'I can see the 'semblance—'specially round 'is eyes. But Clarrie's teeth are dirtier. And there's less of 'em.'

Archie left the cackling women, and walked towards the unmarked wooden door that led to the curatorial offices. Amid the clutter of the exhibition it was easy to overlook. He inserted his antique key in the lock, and as it turned he heard that satisfying 'thunk' which heralded his admission into the bowels of the institution.

The walls of the narrow corridor were crowded with books and journals. Archie was on his own turf now, and his heart began to soar. How long had he waited for this day? In a few moments he would see his Beatrice. Surely she had accepted his proposal of marriage.

Chapter 3

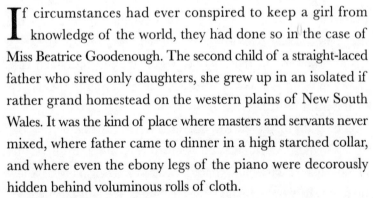

If circumstances had ever conspired to keep a girl from knowledge of the world, they had done so in the case of Miss Beatrice Goodenough. The second child of a straight-laced father who sired only daughters, she grew up in an isolated if rather grand homestead on the western plains of New South Wales. It was the kind of place where masters and servants never mixed, where father came to dinner in a high starched collar, and where even the ebony legs of the piano were decorously hidden behind voluminous rolls of cloth.

Her childhood memories consisted of time passing slowly: she and her younger sisters dressing dolls; the parlour with its heavy drapes and ticking grandfather clock, its chimes marking what seemed an unvarying eternity. Just once, something extraordinary happened. She had gone to the kitchen, a realm forbidden to her, when a knock sounded at the back door. Cookie, as the children called her—a rotund woman in her fifties—rose and opened it.

And there stood a near-naked Aborigine, a nulla-nulla in his hand.

'Mi laikim tukka, missus. Cuttim plenty piaiwood.'

Cookie slammed the door shut. She noticed Beatrice and shooed her away. But not before that momentary glimpse of the wider world had both terrified and thrilled the young girl.

Beatrice was schooled by her mother until she was twelve, and then packed off to stay with an aunt and uncle at Mosman on Sydney's north shore. She would be 'finished' at the Methodist Ladies College. Her custodians, she was dismayed to discover, were even more Victorian in their attitudes than her parents. Beatrice felt that the only reason they accepted her was the generous stipend paid them by her father. With few diversions, she devoted herself single-mindedly to her schoolwork. Unsurprisingly, she matriculated with the highest encomia.

Despite her obvious intelligence, her teachers worried about young Miss Goodenough. Miss Sodworthy, the Latin mistress, summed matters up when, on the eve of Beatrice's matriculation, she warned the girl that her combination of naiveté and rather rapturous temperament would get her into trouble.

'You're an intelligent and diligent student, Beatrice, but you're hopelessly romantic—and flighty to boot. To avoid, er, let us say, distractions, I suggest a job in a quiet environment. A museum, for example. There are always lots of labels to be written in such a place, and your calligraphy is excellent. There's a new director at the natural history museum. From Cambridge, I hear. And so handsome.' A dreamy quality crept into her voice. 'Perhaps Headmistress can make inquiries on your behalf.'

And so it was that in 1926, at the age of seventeen, Beatrice's glorious copperplate secured her the position of registrar in the museum's anthropology department. Archie, a year older, was in the final year of his museum cadetship. Gangly, pimply, pale and small for his age, he was awkward in the way only teenage boys can be. A careful observer, however, might have noticed in his hazel eyes, fine nose and well-defined mouth the makings of a handsome young man.

The anthropology department occupied the entire basement of the museum. At one end, tall double doors opened into a capacious room used to unpack collections and curate oversized objects such as canoes and carved trees. This space opened onto the registration area. At its centre was an imposing oak table, upon which sat, on an angled bookstand, a great, leather-bound register. Beside it was an inkwell, a fountain pen and blotting paper. A stool, and a tall wooden cabinet against the adjacent wall, in which were stored specimens upon which the registrar was working, completed Beatrice's realm.

A few chairs, scattered about a bench set below a high window, occupied most of the remaining space, which acted as a sort of anthropology common area. Four doors opened from this room. Three led to offices of varying size, while the fourth opened onto a dank corridor which led deep under the building. Light switches along its length lit up only three bulbs, while simultaneously turning off the three behind, so as to leave darkness before and behind the visitor. Heavy wooden doors, resembling those of prison cells, opened off it. Behind each lay a storeroom crammed with objects for which there was no space in the exhibition, or which were considered unsuitable for public display. Painted wooden plaques indicated the category of the objects therein: Egyptology, Oceania, Osteology and so on, into the far darkness.

In his early days at the museum Archie wandered the storerooms, familiarising himself with the contents. The walls of the osteology room, he discovered, were fitted with wooden racks, while coffin-sized crates, stacked almost to the ceiling, occupied the centre of the room. The boxes held skeletons, the racks, skulls. Hundreds of them. Each shelf was labelled: 'Solomon Islands', 'British New Guinea', 'New Hebrides', 'New Zealand', 'Tasmania', 'Victoria' and so on. The largest area was 'New South Wales', every shelf of which was crammed with skulls. Some had jaws, but many did not. Some were stained brown with soil, indicating a long time buried, but others were fresh and white from the dissection table. One day Archie took a skull in his hands. It looked like it had been burned, and he noticed that there was a neat hole in its side, just large enough to accommodate the tip of his little finger. 'Myall Creek, Female' had been inked across the brow. He put the skull back in its place, wondering how the perforation had been made.

By the time he entered the next room the minor mystery had been forgotten. 'Oceania' was long and rectangular, much larger than 'Osteology'. The walls were festooned with shields, spears and clubs, while dozens of canoes, fish-traps and doors to spirit houses were slung from the ceiling. On the far wall, lying like a funnelweb spider in its lair, was a terrifying mask, surrounded by skulls—the Great Venus Island Fetish. Archie backed out, shut the door and vowed never again to enter the room alone.

On the rare occasion that Archie emerged into the registration area, Beatrice hardly noticed him. As a cadet he was a general dogsbody, and, except when she needed a heavy object moved or something brought up from the storeroom, Beatrice ignored the painfully shy young man. But from the moment Archie laid eyes on Beatrice, he'd been ensorcelled. As she sat, straight-backed on her stool, with the great register open before her, her blue eyes fierce with concentration, her blonde locks cascading around her face, she became his goddess.

Beatrice would never admit it, but despite her romantic flights of fancy she was probably the one person on earth more shy and awkward with the opposite sex than Archie. The merest intimation of anything to do with real boys had her melting in an agony of embarrassment, which perhaps explained why her taste extended only to pale, skinny, academic types—and then only in her dreams.

It was some time before Archie plucked up the courage to speak to his idol. It happened at the museum Christmas party, after they had each drunk two glasses of punch.

'Miss Goodenough, are you musical, at all?' he blurted. 'I mean, do you like music—that sort of thing?'

Somehow, Archie's mirroring of her own internal anguish put Beatrice at ease. Or perhaps it was the punch. In any case she responded in a rather breathless way about the glories of Brahms and Schubert, and the virtues of Elgar, then blushed violently.

Desperate to sound cultured, Archie had drawn his question

from thin air. He knew nothing at all about music, and was trapped by a rising sense of panic. He was about to slink away, a self-confirmed failure, when he remembered the posters advertising a recital at the town hall.

'Would you come to a concert with me?' he stammered.

'I'd love to,' said Beatrice, somewhat surprising herself.

Archie made a feeble excuse that he was needed at home, then rushed into the street to find out exactly what the poster advertised. To his horror, he saw that it was not Brahms or Schubert, but a Salvation Army hymn night. But he was committed now. Just have to make the best of it, he said to himself. It was, after all, the season for such things.

The more Archie thought about the concert, the more daunting the whole thing became. What does one do with a young lady on a first date? Was it even a date? And what to wear? He confessed his worries to his best friend, the mammalogist Courtenay Dithers.

'Just kiss her,' Dithers replied airily. 'Politely, on the cheek. Or the lips if you must. That's all that's required on a *first* date, Archie. But you must pass muster, clothes-wise, old man. Do you have a suit?'

'Maybe I could borrow my brother's,' Archie replied doubtfully.

'Don't be ridiculous. You'd be swimming in the thing. Better ask for Nev at the Maori's Head. He'll sort you out.'

That lunchtime Archie detoured via the Maori's Head Hotel. It was the museum's local. Nellie, the barmaid, pointed out Nev, a slight, furtive-looking man who was smoking in a darkened corner of the public bar. He was, Archie felt, the kind of bloke who'd vanish at the first sign of trouble. And, judging by the look on his face, trouble was never far off.

'Suit, is it?' Nev said, as he mentally measured Archie up. 'Formal? S'right? See me out the back at four, and bring a tenner. Nine bob as surety you'll return it on time.'

At the appointed hour Archie presented himself in the dank laneway at the rear of the Maori's Head. Nev materialised out of nowhere. The fug of smoke around him thickened, courtesy of the durry hanging at a corner of his mouth. He was carrying a large parcel wrapped in newspaper.

'It'll fit yer like a glove,' Nev said. A smile revealed gappy, nicotine-stained fangs. 'Just get it back on time. Tomorrer, 7 a.m. Don't be bloody late or yer'll do yer dough!'

Archie untied the package to reveal a pair of black and grey striped stovepipe trousers and a splendid tails coat that hung halfway down his calves.

He cornered Dithers. 'Nev gave me a mourning suit! I'm going to a bloody Salvo's concert,' Archie wailed, 'not a state funeral.'

'It will all be all right, Archie. Never hurts to dress up. Just don't be too public in it.'

'Why not?'

'Well, Nev runs a little sideline. He works for a dry cleaner up the Cross, and rents out clothes overnight. Then he cleans them before the shop opens in the morning. As long as nobody knows, no harm is done. Wouldn't do for the suit's owner to see you, though.'

'This is a bloody nightmare,' Archie mumbled to himself as he waited for Beatrice on the steps of the town hall. She was surprised to see him so smartly decked out. Perhaps the concert was a formal one? If only she'd known, she said to herself. She wore a knee-length tan skirt and bolero jacket, which broadened her shoulders, and an elegant green velvet hat with a fine net over her forehead and eyes. Despite the hat, she now felt distinctly underdressed.

Archie must have looked like he needed saving, because the ticket seller had given him front-row seats. As they entered the grand hall they saw that the stage was decorated with red flags. In the centre of each was a yellow star on which the words 'blood and fire' were emblazoned. Archie and Beatrice had only been in their seats a few moments when a crisply dressed man in a military uniform strode onto the stage. He introduced himself as Brother Amos, leader of the Salvation Army in Sydney, and announced that this was a charity night in aid of homeless families. 'The three S's! Soup, Soap and Salvation. That's what we are here for tonight!' he shouted as the brass band and choir mounted the stage.

The announcement added to Archie's worries: he was down to his last few shillings, and the thought that Beatrice might consider him a skinflint convinced him that he must part with all he had. The band and choir gave a peculiar salute, their forefingers pointing skywards, and shouted, 'Hallelujah!' When they launched into 'I Will Follow Jesus', Archie risked a peep at Beatrice. She looked glorious. And, he noted with relief, she seemed to be enjoying the hymns. He began to relax.

'Brother, come pray with us,' a voice boomed. It was Brother Amos. He was pointing directly at Archie. 'It's easier for a camel to pass through the eye of a needle than for a rich man to enter the kingdom of heaven. Hallelujah, brother. We are delighted to have a gentleman such as yourself here tonight! You are a beacon to your class. Please do honour us by joining our choir for "Onwards Christian Soldiers"!'

There was no choice. Wishing that he might vanish, Archie dragged himself onto the stage. He did his best with the hymn, but his wavering voice couldn't be controlled, and he found himself slipping up an octave.

'Sounds like a billy goat pissing in a tin!' a rough-looking chap in the centre of the third row shouted derisively.

He was, thought Beatrice, probably a member of the 'skeleton army', knockabouts recruited by publicans and paid in beer to disrupt teetotal gatherings.

'Tune don't suit, that's all,' said a more sympathetic voice, but all Archie heard was 'suit'. Was the owner of his splendid outfit about to mount the stage and strip him of it there and then? His throat tightened, and he lost his voice entirely.

It was a terrible moment. Archie felt as if the eyes of the whole town hall were on him. Then, to his astonishment, he saw that Beatrice was beside him, singing the hymn in a beautiful soprano. She had amazed herself. In all her life she had never done anything quite so public, or so brazen.

At last the band stopped and Beatrice and Archie stepped down from the stage. Archie emptied his pocket into the collecting tin. Then Brother Amos asked if they would help out in the soup kitchen.

'Of course,' Beatrice replied. 'That's why we came tonight. Wasn't it, Archie? To help those less fortunate than ourselves.' She looked up at him and caught his eye, for the first time without blushing.

Beatrice took to the soup ladle with gusto, while Archie handed out the bowls. They had settled into a splendid rhythm, until a gent whose filthy pants were held up by a rope round the waist held out his bowl to Beatrice. 'Best tits I've seen since I worked in the dairy!' he smirked, setting the entire line of men laughing.

Somehow, this upset Beatrice's soup-serving rhythm. Before she knew it, instead of filling a bowl, she was emptying a ladle full of hot soup straight into Archie's lap. It all seemed to happen in slow motion: the steaming soup cascading towards Archie's trouser-front, his yelp of pain, his sharp leap backwards upsetting the piles of waiting soup bowls, and his agonised clutching at his sodden trousers.

'Heavens to Betsy!' Beatrice squeaked as she dashed forward. She averted her eyes from the actual site of the stain, and dabbed ineffectively with a petite lace handkerchief at Archie's chest. The homeless men were in gales of laughter. 'Best prayer meeting ever, Pastor, having that Charlie Chaplin bloke and his girl entertain us. Well worth a hallelujah next Sund'y—just for the laugh.'

Beatrice and Archie walked towards the ferry in the gathering dusk. The scalding had left Archie feeling distinctly uncomfortable. Beatrice, he knew, must be feeling uncomfortable too, though in a different way. 'Don't worry, Beatrice, please,' he said. 'It was a simple accident.' He recalled Dithers' admonition that a kiss was required. By the time they reached the ferry he'd still been unable to summon the courage to deliver it. So he boarded with her, though he had not intended to do so. Beatrice led him to the bow, where the waters of the harbour lapped in the moonlight. Archie, feeling that time was running out, made a rather unexpected lunge. Beatrice had never been kissed.

Instinctively she turned away, causing Archie merely to brush her lips before landing his kiss on her ear. Or rather in her ear. The explosive sound made her squeal. She was always squealing, she told herself sternly. She must stop it.

'Tickets, please.' They were now halfway to Mosman. Archie had not a penny.

'Ah, sir. I'm here by accident,' Archie mumbled.

'I don't care if you're here on behalf of Billy Hughes hisself, mate, you need a ticket,' barked the inspector. 'Now where is it?'

'I haven't got a ticket. I got on by accident.'

'Don't be a smart-arse with me, son!'

'But I've got no money!' Archie almost wailed.

'You look well enough dressed to me, mate,' the inspector said. 'Flash as a pox doctor's clerk, I reckon. Now pay up or I'll slap a fine on yer!'

'Please, inspector. Give me two singles to Mosman.' Beatrice handed the inspector a shilling. When they alighted she swiftly turned, kissed Archie on the cheek, and vanished into the darkness.

It had not occurred to either of them that Archie had no way of getting home. He walked to the ferry at Blue's Point and cadged a lift, promising to pay the pilot on the morrow. As the ferry crossed the calm waters, Archie looked up and imagined what the great bridge might be like when it was completed. The pylons on the north and south shores were already taking shape. He imagined the arches reaching towards each other from either shore. One day they would be joined, and the bridge would be complete. Would he and Beatrice ever make their own arch?

Chapter 4

Now, over five years later, and despite Archie's proposal of marriage by letter, that question was still unanswered. As he walked towards the anthropology offices, intent on finding Beatrice, Archie felt nervous and unsure. He reminded himself that he had been initiated into manhood in the Venus Isles. He was now a fully competent adult in the world, cured of all silly shyness and prudery.

He turned the corner into the anthropology department and saw her, bent in silent concentration over the great leather-bound register. She was wearing a white blouse and knee-length grey skirt which revealed her perfect legs and accentuated her slender waist and full breasts. Her curling blonde hair cascaded almost to her waist, and her posture, even while seated, was perfectly upright. He stole up behind her, not wishing to break her concentration. She was holding an elegant fountain pen, from which flowed line after line of exquisite script. The register entry—as much as the artefact she was registering—was a work of art.

'Beatrice. Darling.'

Despite his best efforts at self-control, Archie's voice was breathy, less manly than he'd intended.

She turned to face him. For a moment her exquisite blue eyes were kind, if inquiring.

'Archie Meek, is it—you? How dare you,' she half screamed. 'How dare you send me that…that…that THING. You—you—BEAST!' She squeaked as she flung down her pen and fled out of the room.

Archie was stunned. He looked at the register. An ugly ink-blot was spreading across the otherwise immaculate page. The top line, yet to be engulfed, was still legible: 'Love token, Venus Islands. Don. A. Meek. December 15, 1932.'

Archie felt puzzled. 'Love token'. Could that be his foreskin? If so, her entry stated that he had donated it to the museum. Had there been a terrible misunderstanding? Or was this a rejection? As the implications of the entry sank in, blind rage surged. How could his fiancée tag and number his foreskin—his own flesh—which he'd sent as a pledge of his commitment to her, and so make it the property of the government of New South Wales!

No, she was not his fiancée. In treating his sacred love token so foully she had ground his love and trust into the dirt. Yet he could hardly believe that a girl as tender and intelligent as

Beatrice could act like that. And why had she fled as if he were the devil incarnate? After all her loving letters, her promises, had his Beatrice really turned into an unfeeling monster?

Archie needed to sit down. He looked about and saw his name on a door. He pushed it open and groped in the gloom for a light switch. When the naked bulb flicked on, Archie discovered that his new office was barely larger than a broom cupboard, and windowless. In fact, he decided, it was a renovated closet of some sort. A desk and chair all but filled the space, and his small library of anthropology texts was stacked on the floor.

Beatrice Goodenough was already stomping across Hyde Park. 'How dare he call me *darling*!' she muttered. 'How dare he send me that—thing!'

Archibald Meek had caused her the most severe embarrassment she had ever experienced. No, he had ruined her life. Beatrice flopped on a bench and began to sob.

It was some time before she looked up and saw the half-completed war memorial. It reminded her of how many women had waited in vain for the man of their dreams to come home. She cried some more at the thought. She had not recognised him at first. He looked ridiculous in that ill-fitting suit. Yet at the same time he seemed so brown and grown-up. That had scared her and dismayed her all at once. Mixed with her fierce anger at him was another, deeper emotion. She feared that Archie had experienced a great deal during his time away. He was now a man and she felt a mere girl. Had he left her behind?

Despite herself, she remembered the letter she'd written to her sister Betty shortly after attending the Salvation Army concert. She'd omitted the unfortunate incidents.

'But, oh Betty, he is a most interesting young man,' she wrote. 'He's not so tall and rather thin, but he has expressive hazel eyes and he seems so pale and wan that I'm certain there's something quite spiritual about him. He doesn't say much, which makes me feel sure he is wise and kind. Last night we attended a concert. He dressed splendidly, and gave all the money he had to feed the poor. He'll soon be going to the islands to complete his studies, so we can communicate by letter, which will be easier and more satisfying, I feel, than if he were here. I don't know whether he has the sort of vim that Father would like to see in a young man, but I am rather fond of him, Betty, though please don't tell anyone.'

Beatrice was thrilled that Archie wrote to her so often from the Venus Isles. When she opened his last letter, her heart swelled to bursting. She loved him, loved him, loved him, she told herself over and over as she read its opening words:

Beatrice. Would you be mine? My wife. Forever and ever?

Her brave Archie, who had gone all alone to the islands! How happy they would be with their house on the North Shore and a growing band of children. Of course, she would have to leave her job at the museum, as all female public servants must do upon marrying. But Archie would support her, and the children. And she would help him with his work.

She was desperate to tell someone her good news. The only

person in the whole museum who seemed to care about her since Archie left was Giles Mordant, the Cockney taxidermy assistant. A flash dresser, young Mordant possessed a forced sophistication that sat well with his sallow complexion. He had a way of joking that made Beatrice feel like a younger sister, though it often seemed to her that she was the only one who didn't get the joke. Mordant had the kind of face, she decided, that could be either handsome or viciously ugly, depending on his mood. She was struck, too, by the terrifying vacancy that could play over his eyes when he felt he was unobserved.

Beatrice ran across Mordant in the great hall, where he was tinkering with an exhibit. 'Giles, I'm engaged to be married!' she blurted.

He didn't seemed particularly pleased. She showed him Archie's letter.

'Blimey, Beatrice, what's this?' he asked, picking up the small object folded within it.

'Oh, that,' she said, trying to sound knowledgeable. 'It's a foreskin. Archie says it's an infallible love charm.'

Mordant was almost choking. 'Beatrice, you do know what a foreskin is, don't you?'

'It's the skin of a *fore,*' she lied, desperately trying to hide her ignorance, 'which is a kind of frog found in the islands.'

Giles burst into high-pitched laughter, attracting the attention of a group of schoolgirls. 'Beatrice, that bloody thing is the end of Archibald Meek's cock, his penis, in other words, which some savage has chopped off with a stone knife!'

The schoolgirls began giggling. One of them mimicked Giles: 'The end of Archibald Meek's cock!' This unexpected announcement caused a vicar, who had been examining an exhibit of seashells, and an elderly couple standing by the stuffed lion to evacuate the gallery. Beatrice was convinced that both gave her dirty looks as they fled. She felt herself turned to stone, unable to shift from the spot.

The schoolgirls stared gleefully at Beatrice, and everyone seemed to be hooting in derision. All of a sudden it was too much. Beatrice ran to the women's toilet, in tears. She sat in the cubicle a long time, holding the offending object between the pages of the letter, as she considered flushing the horrid thing down the pan, along with Archie's letter. A hard streak of spite arose in her. No, she thought. She would not flush it. Instead, she would register it in the collection, where future generations could read of horrid Archibald Meek's perfidy!

Beatrice returned to the anthropology store, filled out a label, and threaded a needle with a length of cotton. She then stabbed the foreskin savagely, pulled the needle and thread through, and attached a label to it. Holding it by the label so that it dangled at her side, she walked to the cabinet where she kept the newly registered objects and opened a drawer labelled 'Pacific Islands: Charms and Fetishes'. Archie's foreskin was slapped down next to a sorcerer's bag filled with bits of bone and claws, and Beatrice slammed the drawer shut.

She was still standing by the cabinet when Giles Mordant visited. He said he wanted to apologise to her, and seemed sorry for what he'd done. Could he see the object again? Beatrice pointed at the drawer. Giles opened it, picked up the foreskin, and put it in his pocket.

'I think you should have labelled it "Archie's cock-end: an

exceedingly tiny specimen!"' he said. 'Tell Archie-boy when you next write to him that I've got his cock-skin in my wallet, and, blimey, I intend having some fun with it!'

Chapter 5

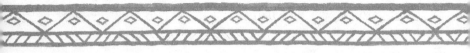

By morning tea Archie's office was beginning to feel like a cell in the insane asylum. It was impossible for him to think. He needed air. Could Beatrice have been frightened by his uncouth appearance, he wondered? It wouldn't hurt to buy a new suit and get a haircut. Then he'd go to the Maori's Head for lunch with whatever colleagues he found there. Perhaps they could shed light on why Beatrice had changed. But first he needed to set up an experiment—one he had devised as he'd walked away from the director's office that morning. He went to the collection store and returned with three bones—the leg bone of a kangaroo, the rib of a dugong and the jawbone of a human. They had been kept as trophies in native huts, and were stained brown with smoke. He arranged them on a windowsill in the anthropology common area, where they would be exposed to sunlight for several hours each day. Then he placed a piece of cardboard, on which he had scrawled 'Do Not Touch', across one end of the bones.

The heat of the midday sun was baking the city. The place was largely deserted, except in the shadows. Archie, now the very picture of tonsorial and sartorial elegance, strolled down Bourke Street and into Woolloomooloo. Despite lying between the museum and the up-market suburb of Potts Point, the dockland area, known locally as 'the loo', had earned a reputation as being the most dangerous part of Sydney. The muddle of narrow lanes between tiny half-derelict terrace houses were the haunt of sailors, where cheap rum and women were easy to be had. It was far grimier than Archie remembered it. Tin lean-tos had been set up in every nook and cranny, and the rags that served as bedding for those sleeping rough lay everywhere.

Prostitution had always flourished, but now there seemed to be a girl loitering in every doorway. Some, who were not so young, looked so unhappy that Archie decided they'd been put there by their husbands. And the street urchins! They'd increased from a smattering to a persistent cloud. One particularly dishevelled lad was carrying a bowl of soup to a tired-looking whore—a sight that simultaneously touched and revolted Archie.

'Mister, got thruppence?' The scrap of a specimen looked up at Archie imploringly. His shaved and scabby head hadn't seen a mother's care for weeks. Archie handed over a shilling, and suddenly the street was filled with kids scrambling for the coin.

At the boxing club on Dowling Street there was a commotion. Archie peeked in. Someone had given two scrawny runts gloves, and a crowd of men was egging them on as they clobbered each other. The smaller boxer, who must have been all of eight, already had a split lip, and tears were welling in his eyes. 'And they call the Venus Islanders savages,' Archie muttered as he pushed his way through the crowd, grabbed the larger boy and walked to the door. 'Find a bigger kid to pick on,' he shouted. He stopped in the street and put the boy down. 'What's your name?' he asked as he untied the boxing gloves.

'Louie Lopes,' the boy replied. 'My mum's dead.'

Archie forked out another bob.

It was only when he got to Dago Joe's fruit barrow, and the old Italian greeted him as if he'd been gone five days rather than five years, that Archie began to feel at home. 'Some lovely bananas today, Mista Mik?' Joe cried.

'Not today, Joe. Maybe tomorrow. Good to see you again, though!'

'*Buon giorno*, Mista Mik. Good onions.'

'Good on you too, Joe.'

Joe had a genius for mishearing the King's English. But he was also the most successful fruiterer in East Sydney. His barrow was perpetually surrounded by a gaggle of women. He had once told Archie the secret of his success.

'Don't serve anybody until there's plenty customer around. Tell the good story, and make de lady's eye. That way they stick about, and even more come!'

Walking had cleared the cobwebs and given Archie a keen appetite for the cheap and cheerful kind of counter lunch the Maori's Head offered. He decided that he would not ask anyone directly about Beatrice. That would be too embarrassing.

But he would keep his ears open.

The bar was sparsely furnished, dark and cool. White tiles covered the floor and extended halfway up the walls.

'Archie Meek? Been a while hasn't it, love? Where'd ya get the tan?'

Nellie had always had a soft spot for him, but before it was because he was a sweet kid. Now, Archie sensed, she might develop a different kind of appreciation. He was about to reply when a stentorian voice hailed him from the gloomy interior. It was Courtenay Dithers.

'Archibald Meek! Long time no see, old chap! How were the Venus Isles? I hope you cadged me a bat or two, and some of those giant rats the place is famous for?'

When Archie first arrived at the museum he idolised Dithers. A decade and a half older than Archie, the curator of mammals carried his Cambridge polish lightly. His handsome face, with its aquiline nose, looked almost patrician to Archie, while a tinge of sadness around his dark eyes revealed a deep empathy with the world. After lunch, Archie would seek Dithers out for a private conversation about Beatrice. He saw his old friend as an oracle on all things—but especially women. Much later, Archie would think how strange that was, since Dithers had lived alone as long as he'd known him.

Archie's eyes grew accustomed to the gloom. Dithers was taking lunch with some colleagues. Around the table sat the artificer Roger Holdfast and his idiot son Gerald. They were responsible for constructing exhibits, and mounting specimens within them. Holdfast's crew cut made his head look like a bristly brush. Below it his eyes were haunted and his lips set hard and thin to the point of vanishing. Gerald followed his father around like a puppy. Just now he was staring at Nellie, open-mouthed, as if she were dancing the cancan.

Next to Gerald sat Eric Sopwith, the retired curator of molluscs. His watery eyes and ruddy nose testimony to a long-standing romance with the bottle. And Giles Mordant was there too, wreathed in the brittle arrogance of a man whose ambitions outreach his abilities. Mordant had disliked Archie from the moment they met, and the feeling soon became mutual. You'd never guess from the look of him, Archie thought, that he made a living stuffing rats and lizards. Such a flash dresser. Everyone said he had tickets on himself. He even wore those newfangled vulcanised India rubber gloves as he gutted and skinned.

All those present, except Giles, greeted him warmly.

'My shout,' said Eric. 'What'll it be, Archie? Your old favourite, Castlemaine? Bet it's been a while since you've wet your whistle.'

It had indeed been so long since Archie had drunk anything but yangona that he was quickly tipsy. Between them, Dithers and Sopwith had seen more Pacific islands than Archie had had hot breakfasts, and they were soon roaring with laughter at Archie's accounts of the predicaments he had got himself into. But when it came to the effects of yangona, Eric became serious. The drink was made from the roots of a shrub, which were chewed by village virgins and spat into a large wooden bowl. There, the saliva and juice fermented into a frothy grey liquor. It was a curiously intoxicating drink.

'I hope ye didn't have too much of that stuff, laddie,' said Eric. 'It has a strange effect on the mind. Ye ken that Kidson went stark raving mad with it in the Feejees? Became paranoid in the end: swore the Methodists were out to get him.'

At first, Archie had been revolted by the brew. It looked and tasted like old sock water. But it wasn't possible to live in the Venus Isles without drinking huge quantities of the stuff. At every hut he'd visited he was required to swill down a half-coconut shell of it, and when the men told stories at night, the yangona bowl never ceased doing the rounds. Eventually Archie had become quite fond of it. And he *had* noticed that the world seemed different after a yangona party.

Giles Mordant sparked up. 'The Venus Isles have made you quite a man, haven't they, Archie? Though not a complete man, I suppose. Just a *bit* off, eh, old nakker?'

Mordant's smarmy superiority irritated Archie—it was as if the assistant taxidermist had something over him. After all, Archie hoped soon to be a curator, and Mordant was a mere technician. Moreover, he had no idea what Mordant was talking about, and evidently neither had anybody else. The conversation reverted to Archie's island adventures.

Dithers asked whether Archie had anywhere to stay. 'Doss down with me, old chap, if you like. I've still got the room in Stanley Street, and I'm hoping to go to Africa to study big cats before too long. Got a grant application in with the National Geographic Society, and could be away some time. If I get the funding you're welcome to look after the place while I'm gone.'

By the time they'd eaten lunch and were onto their second round of shouts, Archie was asking about the museum.

'You should know that Polkinghorne's vanished,' said Dithers with some emphasis.

Vanished? Cecil Polkinghorne was Archie's supervisor. It was to him that the painfully shy teenager had applied for a museum cadetship. He was a queer old coot, sure enough, but Archie had grown rather fond of him. Polkinghorne had started out as a museum guard, and there his career might have ended if he hadn't developed a fascination with the Egyptian room. Enthralled with antiquities, he took a course in classical archaeology, following which he applied for a curator's job.

The museum had its own reason for wanting to move Polkinghorne on. He was without doubt a diligent guard. But a purple growth had sprouted on the tip of his tongue and swiftly swelled to the size of a cherry. Not only had it given him prodigious buck teeth, but it left him incapable of speaking without spraying his listeners with saliva. When Vere Griffon arrived he'd experienced the problem firsthand. The guard, who was somewhat in awe of the new director, had drawn himself up at his approach, saluted, and sprayed out, 'Cecil Polkinghorne, sir. At your service!'

Complaints from the sprinkled and befuddled had been accumulating, and it was with some relief that the director had, upon Polkinghorne's graduation, assigned him to a role away from the public—as curator of archaeology.

'What do you mean, vanished?' asked Archie.

'Just what I said. Around three years ago. He left work one evening and never came back. The most popular theory is that he fell off a ferry and drowned. But no one saw anything, and no body was found.'

'There's summat rum about it, Archie. I fear the worst.' Eric Sopwith shook his head, his eyes more watery than ever.

'Utter rubbish, Sopwith,' exclaimed Mordant contemptuously. 'Bumstocks saw him getting onto the ferry that night, and he didn't disembark at Balmain. No doubt about it. Polkinghorne drowned and his body was eaten by sharks. The harbour's full of them now that the abattoir at Homebush dumps blood and offal into the water by the ton.'

For a moment silence reigned. 'I best be off,' said Roger Holdfast. He and Gerald rose from the table as one. 'The skeleton of the giant sloth needs articulation, and work for the new exhibition is falling behind.' Dithers announced he had a report on giant rats to complete.

Mordant seemed to find the diminished company not to his liking. As the assistant taxidermist stood up he got out his wallet with a flourish, and winked at Nellie. 'There's a few treasures in here, love. How would you like to be paid?' There had been no tab. Nellie looked confused as she peered into the open wallet. Mordant snapped the wallet shut and turned to Archie. 'Welcome back to the happy ship HMAS *Museum*, Archie. Consider this my homecoming present.'

Archie, concluding that there was something seriously awry with Mordant, was about to rise too when Sopwith laid a hand on his arm. 'How about staying for another'un, Archie? I've a few things I need to tell ye.'

Archie got in first. 'How could Cecil Polkinghorne have disappeared? It beggars belief, Eric! I still remember the first day I came to work. There was the director in the centre of the long table, sipping his tea, with the curators lined up on either side. Polkinghorne was immediately on his right. It looked like Michelangelo's *Last Supper*.'

'Aye, those were the days!' enthused Eric. 'The institution'd be a far better place if the director had continued taking tea with his staff, rather than locking himself up in that great office of his.'

Mind you, it hadn't all been fun working with Polkinghorne, Archie recalled. When they were alone in the collection, the older man would sometimes become rather too excited, especially when he was explaining the process of mummification and how the bowels were removed with a hook via the anus. The salivary spraying was one thing, but the way Polkinghorne would stand rather too close, his hands groping about as if trying to insert a hook into his young cadet, was quite another. Nothing untoward ever happened, but in those first few years Archie sometimes felt that it might.

'Could it have been anything else?' Archie asked Sopwith. 'Could he have…offended somebody?'

'Laddie, take my word for it! There's summat suspicious—mighty suspicious—about Polkinghorne's vanishing. I saw the man on that very day. He was not happy; had a falling out with the director, they say.'

'But not bad enough to top himself, surely?'

'This place is mighty changed, Archie. And so is our director. He's become angry and domineering. And he's rifling the collections for their treasures. After Polkinghorne went, he shipped off the two best mummies to America, to be sold. I tell ye Archie, there's summat mighty rum goin' on.'

Beer disappeared down Sopwith's throat like water in desert sands, especially as the cry 'last round' rang out. To his shock, Archie realised that it was nearly 6 p.m.—way after closing time at the museum. He was more than a little unsteady on his legs as he meandered back to his office. It had been a momentous first day back.

The sun had sunk low by the time Archie left the museum, but it was still stinking hot and the road reeked of molten asphalt. Dithers' rooms were only a few hundred yards away, behind the museum, and Archie decided to go on foot. His trunk had been delivered to the museum, and he struggled to get it across Yurong Street and into the cash and carry, where he bought some biscuits as a gift for Dithers. He was covered in sweat as he dragged it along the street and up the narrow stairs of the boarding house to Dithers' room.

The white walls and ceiling were stained yellowish-brown with tobacco smoke. A narrow barred window, which was nailed shut, ornamented the far wall. 'Put your trunk down there, Archie,' Dithers said, pointing to a tiny clear space at the foot of one of two narrow beds that took up much of the room. He was absent-mindedly puffing on a durry while reading a scientific publication on the diversity of Australian bats, and seemed not to notice the heat. Archie could reach the space indicated only by stepping around and over piles of dirty clothes and books. Dithers was notorious for his chaotic office, but it was a paragon of tidiness compared with this. It dawned on Archie just how cramped life would be until Courtenay left for Africa.

Dithers put down his publication, pulled a whisky bottle from under his bed, and groped about in a pile of soiled shirts before coming up with some shot glasses. 'We must have a dram to welcome you home!'

It was the last thing Archie felt like, but he took the proffered glass, sat on his trunk, and downed it in a gulp.

'How does it feel being back, Archie? A bit queer, I'd venture.'

Something in Archie collapsed. 'Very hard,' he said. 'Beatrice is acting quite bizarrely. She has refused my proposal of marriage. She stormed out when she saw me.'

'Oh, Archie! My dear, poor old fellow. Five years, you know, is a very long time. You're a different man now, and Beatrice is quite possibly a different woman. I know how you feel, though. The war cost me dearly in love. And trust. But I'm sure things will work out. Give her some time, Archie. That's what she needs. After all, your return must have come as quite a shock. Now, have another tot.'

Archie found himself unable to say anything else about Beatrice. Everything was so confusing that he seemed to be in a dream.

'Courtenay, I can't thank you enough for this,' he said. 'I can see it will be quite a squeeze with two of us staying here.'

'Not at all, old chap! Delighted to have you doss down with me. A man needs company at times. I'm out late at least one night a week with the Society for the Preservation of Native Animals. They've just appointed me treasurer. And with any luck I'll be off to Africa before too long.' Dithers rolled and lit another cigarette.

'What will you do there?'

'Oh, I'll study the fauna. That sort of thing. But I also hope to answer some questions that have been with me for quite some time—since 1918, you know. Africa's the last place where the cold-blooded killers thrive—the lion, leopard and the hyena.

Our stone-age ancestors lived among them. I want to understand how the prospect of being eaten alive impacts the psyche. It might account for the devil in us.'

Archie was stunned. This was so uncharacteristic of the genial, untroubled Dithers he thought he knew.

'The common washroom is down the hall. Just one thing, Archie. I don't always sleep well. If you hear me yelling and carrying on, take no notice.'

Dithers flung a towel over his shoulder, and disappeared out the door.

As Archie arranged his belongings he developed a severe headache. Was it the beer, the whisky, a malarial attack—or the effect of Beatrice's rejection? Before he could decide, he collapsed onto the bed beside his trunk, and was instantly asleep.

He found himself back in the Venus Isles, in the head-hunting days. Polkinghorne had been captured by cannibals, and a ritual leader approached with a bamboo beheading knife. The curator screamed, and his buck teeth lunged forward, as if to bite at Archie's face.

Buck teeth! Archie sat upright in his bed. He had a crushing headache, was covered in sweat, and was shaking. He went to his jacket pocket and took out the incisor that had fallen from the fetish. He looked at it. 'Don't be so bloody stupid, Archie. It's impossible,' he said to himself.

'Go back to sleep,' Dithers drawled from the adjacent bed. 'There's a good chap. It's just a bad dream.'

Chapter 6

Archie had slept badly. He struggled into his new shoes for a second time. His suit was damp and musty with sweat, and he disliked putting it on. 'In the islands, a loincloth is haute couture,' he thought wistfully as he limped to work. Jeevons, the museum guard, was waiting for him in the foyer. The man had, by his own account, seen a torrid war. His own limp seemed to come and go with his retelling of the battle of the Somme. But Archie had to admit that John Jeevons really looked the part in his polished shoes, military-style uniform, and cap, with its magnificent three-inch wide, shield-shaped badge, proclaiming 'Museum Guard'.

'There's somebody waiting that I hope you might speak to, sir,' Jeevons confided with a knowing look. 'He arrived early, and I must say I think he's rather queer.'

'I see,' Archie replied wearily. His headache was increasing, and the last thing he felt like was dealing with an inquiry from a member of the public. Jeevons led him to the guard room, where a man sat slumped in a chair. Beside him was a parcel the size of a golf bag.

'Good morning,' Archie said. 'How can I help you?'

The man leapt to his feet. 'Are you the curator of artefacts? You see, I've got a priceless treasure.' He started unwrapping the parcel, and soon the floor was covered with sheets of newspaper. Still, the fellow unwrapped, until the parcel was reduced to the size of a large cigar. As the last sheet came off, Archie saw that it contained the point of a spear.

'This, professor, is the spear that killed Captain Cook! The very one!' The man thrust the object under Archie's nose.

'I see,' Archie said, nursing his head and stalling for time. 'How do you know that this is the very spear?'

'Oh, that's definite, prof. I got it from my grandfather, who was given it by a sailor who'd been to Hawaii, and he bought it off the chief who ate Captain Cook's leg. Said he found it in the flesh of the inner thigh. Near broke his teeth on it, he said. Anyway I've looked at the painting—'

'What painting?' Archie managed to interject.

'The one of Captain Cook's death in a book my sister's got. There's no doubt about it. You can see the spear going in, and I reckon I can even see the tip breaking off. How much will you give me for it, it being a family heirloom and all?'

'If it could be authenticated—'

'Whaddya mean, authenticated? I told you, my grandad got

it off a sailor, who got it off the dirty cannibal wot ate Captain Cook's bloody leg. What more proof do you want! You know that the council's going to put a statue of Captain Cook in the park outside the museum, so I'm sure people'd want to see the spear that killed him when they come in.'

'Well, this really is a weighty matter,' Archie said, biting his lip. 'I'd need to discuss it with the highest authorities. It might take some time.'

'That's all right,' the man said, sitting down. 'I can wait. But how much time? And how much money?'

'Oh, it could be months. At least. Might even be years. And the money. Well, that would be up to the museum board.'

'In that case, young fella, I'm going to offer it to another museum, one that might appreciate it!' He grabbed a handful of newspapers, wrapped them roughly round the spear point, and stomped out.

'Well, sir, that's one for the books,' Jeevons said as the fellow disappeared. 'But as you'll probably soon be a curator, you'd better get used to it. We get at least one duffer a week wanting to sell some priceless relic or other. Last week it was a bloke who claimed he had the wireless radio that Abel Tasman took to New Zealand. Sure enough it had "1642" engraved on the back, but poor Dr Doughty had to tell him it was a serial number, not the date of manufacture. Fellow got so upset he smashed the radio on the spot! We direct all the rum'uns her way. A lot of the other curators just won't turn up for an inquiry.'

'Thank God for Dr Doughty!' Archie replied. He remembered her as being a distinctly academic type with little interest in anything beyond her minerals. The fact that she'd been performing such a valuable service on behalf of the institution raised her even higher in his esteem.

When Archie reached his office he was dismayed to discover that Beatrice was not at her desk. He could not go on without clearing things up, even if it did end with another rejection. He was about to go looking for her when the phone rang. He picked up the handpiece and listened to the prim tones of Dryandra Stritchley. 'The director requires your presence on the second floor, Meek. The old skeleton gallery. Please be there at two o'clock sharp.' Before Archie could reply, he heard the dial tone. She had hung up.

At 1.59 p.m. Archie was in the public galleries, ascending the ample staircase leading to the second floor. The entrance to the old skeleton gallery had been temporarily blocked off with a pair of enormous, paint-flecked tarpaulins. Behind them could be heard much hammering, sawing and shouting. Archie ducked through the gap between the sheets. The old skeleton exhibit, which had occupied the hall for many years, was being dismantled to make way for a new display.

'Step aside, please, sir!' a strained voice warned. Almost immediately the skull of a great whale, borne aloft amid clouds of dust by half a dozen workers, came within a whisker of Archie's head. The men had evidently been hired from the boxing gym: arm muscles on them like Popeye, he mused. And cauliflower ears to boot!

The dust cleared a little and the light improved. Much of the hall was already vacant. In the middle of the great vaulted space a shaft of sunlight from a roof lantern pierced the gloom. In the centre of the beam stood Vere Griffon. He was dressed immaculately as always, in white shirt, bow tie and spats, and a black suit which was dusted at the shoulders. In that light, Archie thought, he looked like a figure out of a Rembrandt painting. Then he noticed that Vere Griffon was not alone: on the periphery of the beam crouched, or rather stooped, another figure. Dressed in a leather apron and a striped blue butcher's shirt, it seemed the embodiment of a goblin from a fairytale. But, of course, Archie knew the man. He was Henry Bumstocks, the museum's chief taxidermist.

Bumstocks' situation seemed somehow appropriate. A creature poised on the border of lightness and dark. He was almost a caricature of a man, and had certainly deteriorated while Archie had been away. His long grey hair was falling out in clumps, perhaps as a result of exposure to the chemicals used to prepare hides. His greasy beard reached almost to his waist, and his eyes were so deep-set they couldn't be seen, leaving his hairy eyebrows and beak of a nose to dominate the wrinkled face.

'Welcome back, Archie,' Bumstocks mumbled through his thick lips, revealing irregular yellowed teeth. He gave an obsequious nod and offered a hand whose skin was so scabbed from contact with acids and alkalis, and whose nails were so deformed by constant exposure to formaldehyde, that they resembled mottled claws.

'Good day, Henry.' Archie forced himself to touch the proffered hand. 'I must say it's good to be back,' he lied.

'Afternoon, Archie,' Vere Griffon said stiffly. He consulted his watch. 'This is the site of our grand new venture: a gallery of evolution. In the great European institutions of learning Darwin's theory has become the dominant paradigm, though,

60

regrettably, here in the colonies it's been rather slower in achieving ascendancy. An exhibition of the key fossils—ancestors and missing links—will do much to educate the public on the matter. It may even, over the long term, result in increased funding for science. You, Archie, have a key role to play in this enterprise. Which is why you are here today.'

Archie looked around. The skeleton hall was the museum's most opulent exhibition space. Its roof was supported by rows of fluted columns, each carved of a different rock type: creamy sandstone, black basalt, royal purple porphyry, pure white marble. Perhaps it had once housed an exhibition of minerals, he thought. In the golden days, before the 1890s depression, there had been huge interest in mineral wealth, and money was no object. The upstart Australian colonies were desperate to import culture and to show that they were the equal of the British in everything, from the sciences to sport. Extravagances such as this hall had been commonplace: they placed the museum, for a few decades at least, as one of the finest in the world. Back then it was routine for the museum's agent to outbid all comers for specimens collected by the greats, such as John Gould, Wallace, and Humboldt, even Charles Darwin himself.

'Now, Archie, this new gallery will house many of our greatest treasures,' Vere Griffon continued. 'Wallace's orangutans, for example, and our gorilla, one of the first brought out of the Congo, you know. We shall tell the whole story of the evolution of life, from the ancient fishes of the old red sandstone right through to modern times. But it's the evolution of the human race we will focus on. Some months back Professor Radcliffe-Brown gave a most interesting lecture on the evolution of our species, from Pekin man to Heidelberg man, and of course our very own Piltdown man. I'm determined to illustrate all stages of development, and am delighted to say that through the kind offices of Sir Arthur Woodward, who as you may recall is the retired curator of geology at the British Museum, I've been able to obtain an excellent cast of that inestimably important missing link, Piltdown man. Sir Arthur has even taken a personal interest in our new exhibition. He has intimated that he might be induced to make a trip to Sydney for the opening, health permitting, of course, as part of a farewell tour, so to speak, of the geological curiosities of the Antipodes. Under his guidance Bumstocks has been undertaking a full reconstruction of the Piltdown man, which will form a centrepiece of the new exhibition. The model is well advanced: and a splendidly barbaric creation it is!'

Vere Griffon marked a line in the dusty floor with his shoe.

'Your input will be required from here on. Eastwards to the far wall, it's all man: modern man, the story of our ascent from a state of savagery to the pinnacle of human development—the English race. Your job, Archie, is to find striking examples to illustrate the ladder of human development, starting with the degraded state in which mankind exists in nature. The black fellow must figure large: he's an immensely important human document, so to speak. The Venus Islanders clearly belong with him, on the lowest rung of the developmental ladder. Warfare, cannibalism, idolatry: that's the sort of thing we'll need to show if we're to get the point across. Your first task is to provide me with a list of objects suitable for the exhibition. Have them ready for inspection before the end of the month. I'm not sure yet what we'll use to illustrate the superiority of the English. But I feel certain it will come to me soon.'

For once the director seemed happy. But Archie was flummoxed. He'd never thought of the Venus Islanders as being at the bottom of the human totem pole. On the contrary, during his years among them he had learned how sophisticated their canoes, gardening and social relationships were. What's more, Auntie Balum and Uncle Sangoma had fed and educated him— indeed, taken care of him as if he were their own child. He was more fond of them than he was of his own parents, who, he reflected bitterly, had not sent a single letter while he'd been away. Archie silently vowed that the Venus Islanders would *not* feature as savages in this new exhibit.

'Meek,' Vere Griffon added. 'You have come back at the right moment. I have one more task for you. I'd like some savages to perform at the exhibition opening. It would bring the display to life. Arrange for a troupe of Venus Islanders to travel to Sydney and perform for us.'

For a moment Archie was silent. Sangoma would surely want to see the fetish. What would he make of the four orange skulls? Griffon looked at him demandingly. 'Yes, sir,' he said reluctantly as he turned and made his way to the entrance. As he walked away, it occurred to him that it might not be such a bad thing to have Uncle Sangoma visit Sydney. He could see civilisation, and he might take some useful ideas back to the islands. Archie would write to him via the mission, asking for a dance troupe. He would protect them, and make sure the islanders had a damn fine time of it during their stay.

Archie headed straight to Dithers' office. The mammalogist

had dozens of flying-fox skulls arrayed on the desk in front of him, and was evidently considering a knotty problem concerning their classification. 'Have you seen Beatrice today, Courtenay?' Archie asked.

'No. I heard she's on sick leave. But, as I said, give her time, Archie. You'll do more harm than good chasing her around before she's ready.'

'But I don't understand it, Dithers. I get the feeling she abhors me. Do you think she's found someone else?'

'I don't think so, old chap,' Dithers said, his mind on his studies. 'Mordant's been giving her a bit of company lately, but—'

'Mordant! My God! Surely not!' Archie exclaimed. 'I mean to say—she wouldn't stoop that low. No, not Mordant, Courtenay? That nasty, mediocre little ponce!'

Dithers immediately regretted his injudicious words. He did not for a moment think there was anything between Beatrice and Giles.

'Archie, listen to me. I'm certain that Beatrice has waited for you. Just give it time, man. If you go off half-cocked now you'll lose all chance of winning her over.'

Archie felt as if he were about to explode, a feeling made worse by the knowledge, deep down, that Dithers was right. He must be patient. With a supreme effort, he told himself that his thoughts would be best directed elsewhere. And, heaven knew, he had enough distractions to keep him occupied.

As he left Dithers' office, Archie looked back. The mammal department was a scene of chaos. Dithers had created a niche in one corner by lining up his specimen cabinets. Behind them were mountains of papers on the floor and desk. Laboratory benches and cabinets occupied the remaining space, but they were covered with objects. Hippo skulls tangled with stuffed tree-kangaroos, and hyena jaws jousted with babirusa tusks in a great confabulation of stuffed, pickled and skeletonised specimens. How Dithers ever found anything—or indeed got anything done—was a mystery.

Archie decided to avoid his own tiny office and instead walked towards the 'old men's room', a space in the museum's attic reserved for retired curators who wished to continue with their studies. The corridor which gave access to it passed by most of the curators' offices. A few of the doors were open. He passed Elizabeth Doughty at her desk. She was reading a journal article, her face rigid with concentration. A second desk in the same room was occupied by the registrar of minerals, a thin, feeble-looking type who was vacantly picking his nose. The office of the curator of jellyfish, Dr Abraham Trembley, was so enveloped in darkness that Archie couldn't make out what was going on. The only evidence of life came from a lamp, barely visible behind a stack of filing cabinets. Then came Clive Wrigley's den. Archie flinched as he peered in. The place was crammed with terrariums, in each of which lurked enormous, hairy spiders. Wrigley himself stood before a terrarium. Its lid was open. On the back of the curator's hand sat a fat, black funnelweb spider. Archie shivered and hurried on.

The old men's room was tiny, and barely high enough to stand up in without knocking your head on the exposed wooden beams of the roof. Half-a-dozen desks had been assembled there for the use of the retired curators, who worked in a voluntary capacity. As Archie anticipated, Sopwith was in residence. The old curator was bent over his desk, upon which he had arranged several dozen ginger-spotted cowrie shells in neat rows. When he lifted his eyes, his face brightened. Visitors to the old men's room were infrequent, to say the least.

'Ay, Archie! What do ye say to a wee snifter? I'm sure the sun's over the yardarm somewhere in the Empire, and I'm tiring of my cowries. There's a new species to be found, for sure, in this *Umbilia* complex, but it has me defeated for the moment.'

'Sorry, old chap, I can't today.' Archie touched the back of his still-aching head. 'But I did want to ask you something. Do you know how many curators are away or on long-term leave?'

'Aye, but that's a strange question, laddie.'

'I was just wondering how the place changed while I was away.'

Archie wasn't ready to share his fears with anybody yet. He remembered Sopwith's warnings about the effects of yangona, and didn't want to be thought of as drug-crazed or having gone native.

'Well, let's see. Bray Hadlee, the bird man. Do you remember his work with cuckoos? He's been on sick leave for a year or more now. Very strange, it was. The director announced at a staff meeting that he'd be gone for some time. We never saw him again. Rumour was it was a nervous complaint. Wouldn't be surprised if he were locked up in a home for the mentally infirm, and I can understand his family wanting to keep *that* under wraps.

'Then there's Alan Jonah, the curator of parasites. He kept rough company, ye ken. One fella he got tangled up with swore he'd sew him into a chaff sack and throw him off the end of a pier! But that came to nothing. Anyway, he was none too careful with his dissections, and his body became riddled with flukes and parasitic worms of all sorts. The director heard from his family that he choked on his own phlegm. Then there was Andrew Dolt. I'm sure you remember the blowfly expert? Always buzzing around. Did ye ken he was one-eyed? The other was glass. He lost his vision altogether, they say, and went to stay with kith and kin in Victoria, at Nar Nar Goon. The first we knew about it was a letter that the director read out. But, all in all, Archie, most of the old crew are still about.'

'Hmm,' said Archie. 'That's four.'

'What do ye mean four? I just told ye, it's three.'

'I'm not sure, exactly, Eric,' said Archie. His heart was in his throat. Four absent curators, if you count Polkinghorne. Four orange skulls on the Great Venus Island Fetish. In his mind's eye Archie saw an image, close-up: a hand removed a skull from the fetish and replaced it with another. In the instant that a gap existed in the skull-fence, a torrent of pure evil rushed into the world. Archie forced the vision from his mind. It was too ridiculous for words.

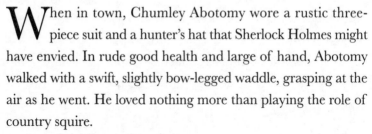

Chapter 7

When in town, Chumley Abotomy wore a rustic three-piece suit and a hunter's hat that Sherlock Holmes might have envied. In rude good health and large of hand, Abotomy walked with a swift, slightly bow-legged waddle, grasping at the air as he went. He loved nothing more than playing the role of country squire.

As he strolled towards the museum he was feeling particularly pleased with himself. He'd got the honeymoon over, and with any luck Portia was already bubbly. If he'd sired an heir, the family name would be assured. And, my God, the things he'd seen in Italy! Enough culture to last a lifetime. That old fussbudget Vere Griffon should bring a little of that culture to the colonies.

While Abotomy was striding down College Street, Dryandra Stritchley was arranging a bunch of white roses on her desk in the office antechamber.

'My God, Dryandra, you are a gardening wizard!' Griffon exclaimed as he drank in the exquisite scent. 'I don't know how you do it. Colonial roses are usually pale shadows compared with those from home. But these roses, well, somehow they transport me—to a green and pleasant land.'

Griffon's reverie was interrupted by a sharp treble rap. The director retreated to his desk, and Dryandra opened to Chumley Abotomy. The squire charged into the room, intent on marching straight into the director's inner sanctum. Dryandra had to insert herself between his imposing frame and the inner doorway to check the rhino-like charge.

'One moment, please,' she managed to gasp. 'I'll see if the director is available. Now take a seat over there, Mr Abotomy!'

Dryandra enjoyed the routine that she and Griffon had developed. Her gentle knock was followed by his low 'come in'. She found the director in his thinking position: heels on the floor, body stretched stiff, eyes gazing at the ceiling.

'It's the new board member, Mr Abotomy.'

Griffon murmured a Latin phrase under his breath. He relaxed into his chair. 'He insists on pronouncing it "Abumley", you know. After the French village his ancestors supposedly resided in prior to the Conquest. Ah, the nouveau riche. What would we do without them? Show the fool in.'

'Chumley, how perfectly splendid to see you!' crowed Vere Griffon as Abotomy waddled through the door. 'I trust the grand tour went well? Perfect time of year for Florence. What did you make of Michelangelo's *David*?'

'Not much, quite frankly, Vere. Supposed to be a statue of that chap who slew the giant. Jewish, wasn't he? Couldn't help but notice, though, that he's still got that bit of nonsense at the end of his tossle. Rum, if you ask me. Think the damn statue's been misidentified. But, my God, there were some good things in Rome! That Vatican Museum's a corker. Most interesting things in it are the Giglione goats. Spent half a day looking at 'em. You *do* know the Giglione goats, old chap, don't you?'

The director was having trouble keeping up. 'Not my bailiwick, old fellow. I trust you saw the Pantheon?'

'Saw a few old piles. Wife took notes. Useful in designing Abotomy Hall. But the goats, old man! Never seen anything like them. One of every sort, and the finest billies, most of 'em. Giglione shot them himself, you know. He's even got a Chilean mounteback. Last one in Tierra del Fuego, the professor says.'

At last Vere Griffon understood what Abotomy was raving about. Professor Giglione, the expert in early domestication at the Vatican Museum, was legendary for his collections of domestic livestock and their wild ancestors.

'Jeellionay, pleaaase!' Griffon ejaculated loudly, before regaining his self-control. If there was one thing he could not tolerate it was mispronunciation. Nor could he suffer fools, unless of course they were very rich ones. And even then his limits were narrow.

'What I said,' Abotomy shot back. 'Giglione's goats. We've got to have 'em, Griffon. My support depends on it.'

The director wasn't sure precisely what Abotomy meant but, given the dismal state of the museum's finances, his support could count for a great deal. Griffon sensed that he was becoming trapped, and he began to feel his way cautiously.

'Are you suggesting, my dear fellow, that we might borrow the collection?'

'Not at all what I had in mind. I'd like to have them here at the museum. Permanently. I'm sure the professor's willing to entertain the idea of an exchange. Took the opportunity of discussing it with him. Knew you wouldn't mind.'

'I see,' said Griffon unenthusiastically. 'I shall write to Professor Giglione this week. But such matters can be delicate, and there's no guarantee of success. Foreign institutions often expect the crown jewels in exchanges. Now, dear chap, would you mind leaving me to my labours? I've some serious issues with the new exhibition, which I must resolve today.'

When Dryandra re-entered the office, a slight wrinkling of the director's forehead and a look in his black eyes spoke of his distaste.

'Abotomy,' he said quietly. 'Most ridiculous man. If it wasn't for his donation potential I'd have him stood down from the board.'

Miss Stritchley shut the door and watched Griffon cradling his head in his hands. 'I'd have been spared these colonial bumpkins if I'd got the directorship of the British Museum. Only missed out by a whisker. Freakish unfair the way that relative of Lord Brenchley was given it…'

There was more than self-pity in his ruminations. In the deepest recesses of his heart Griffon feared that, despite his Cambridge education, he too was second rate. Fit only to be the Lord of Misrule over this colonial rabble. How he hated them! From the pesky and incompetent board to his errant curators. He'd get them into line come what may, and make a fine collection of them yet. Even if it killed him. Or them. But Abotomy's financial support was crucial. And if it hung upon acquiring Giglione's goats, by God, he'd get them. In fact, the venture might even assist in turning Abotomy into a useful tool to further the museum's needs.

Griffon turned to Dryandra. 'No help for it. I'll write to Giglione and see what he wants in exchange for his collection.'

'Which collection, precisely, director?'

'His damn stuffed goats. I'll dictate the letter to you. But for now come into the liquor cellar with me. I think we need to commiserate over a little Meissen.'

Abotomy had business to conduct in Oxford Street. No matter how much Portia begged, he'd resolutely refused to buy any 'knick-knacks' while on the grand tour. He didn't trust the dagos who were trying to sell them—and now it seemed that Portia would never let him forget it. To shut her up he'd promised to look into buying something antiquey in Sydney. He remembered Bunkdom from the fundraising dinner. He'd given the man the seat of honour, even though he made Abotomy's skin creep, in the hope that he'd provide some introductions in Europe. Bunkdom's shop was reputed to have the best collection of antiquities in the city, so he'd set aside his dislike and arranged a visit.

Abotomy rolled up the hill towards Oxford Street, grasping the air. What was it, precisely, that riled him so about the man? Bunkdom's goggle eyes and verrucose skin were certainly repulsive, but he'd never let looks put him off a chap before. If the cause of his dislike were to be summed up in a word, it would be unctuousness. Lord Bunkdom was so unctuous and cloying that Abotomy found him nauseating. Still, there was no help for it. If Portia was to be placated he needed to beard the revolting toad in his den.

Stopping outside Bunkdom's shop, Abotomy had to concede that the man did a good line in window displays. The shop-front was filled with elegantly placed antiquities and curiosities, from enormous yellow Chinese vases to classical figurines and paintings. As he pushed through the doorway, a bell on a coiled spring rang out. Bunkdom emerged from the shadows.

'Oh my goodness. Oh, my beard and whiskers! I am overwhelmed, sir! What an honour, sir! What an honour your visitation does my humble premises! Please, please come this way, into my inner penetralia, so to speak, and take a seat. I'm afraid there's nowhere in this shabby shop even remotely suitable for a man of your quality.'

Bobbing his head, Bunkdom retreated backwards to the rear door. Abotomy allowed himself to be led into a back room. A comfortable lounge chair with a small round side-table sat in a corner.

Bunkdom ushered him into the seat. 'Please take your leisure, sir. I insist that you partake of a cup of tea. I have the best Puer, which will be yours presently. I obtained it from Chinese Morrison's widow, in Devon, years ago.'

'The best what, man? I'm not here to buy your poo-jar, nor any sort of chamber pot,' roared Abotomy. He was finding Bunkdom's honeyed ways more cloying than shit on a shovel. 'I am here to look at those Roman bits and pieces you said you might be receiving.'

'Ah yes, of course. But please, give me a moment, sir. A man of your quality must be served tea.'

Chumley Abotomy demurred in an irritated sort of way. To his surprise he found that he enjoyed the smoky brew Bunkdom offered.

'It's fifty years old, you know. The best Puer is itself an antique,' purred Bunkdom. 'It really is most fortunate, Mr Abotomy, that you dropped by today. As you may know, I'm a late convert to Catholicism. Last year I took the opportunity of combining business with pleasure. I travelled to Rome to kiss the Pope's toe—and while there got my hands on some truly remarkable stock.'

'A left-footer, eh? And a convert. It's a rum business in my view, this popery jiggery pokery. Toe-kissing indeed! But each to his own. Now, man, show me these knick-knacks. I must be on my way.'

'Of course, Mr Abotomy. But if you opened your mind to the spiritual, I'm sure you'd find the rites of the Church of Rome sublime. They're my only enduring pleasure these days.' The antique dealer sighed.

Bunkdom disappeared behind a curtain, only to appear a few moments later carrying a half-sized marble statue of a naked woman, and a strange-looking bronze object.

'This statue of Aphrodite is a Roman copy, from a Greek

original. Possibly Praxiteles. But very fine in any case.'

'How do you know?' asked Abotomy suspiciously.

'Know what, sir?'

'That it's Roman?' Portia was particularly keen to have something from Rome.

'The toes,' replied Bunkdom. 'Greek statues have toes that decline evenly in size from the greatest to the least, while on Roman statues the second toe is longest.'

Abotomy was impressed.

'And this,' continued Bunkdom, holding up a curved bronze object about a foot long, 'is a most magnificent priapus.'

'Bunkdom. I mean, bunkum!' said Abotomy. 'Looks nothing like a platypus. More like a tossle, I'd say. Except for the wings.'

'Well, sir, it is indeed, as you say, a "tossle", but a very ancient one. It is reputed to have come from the ashes of Pompeii itself. The ancient Romans, you know, hung the *membrum virile* by their doors as a goodluck charm.'

'S'pose I could hang it in the smoking room. Might give the lads a laugh,' said Abotomy. 'How much do you want for it?'

'I can let you have them both, sir, for £299. But I beg you, not a penny less. I'll barely cover my costs at that price.'

'Done!' said Abotomy decisively. 'Have them sent to my city residence. And cover the delivery yourself.'

Chapter 8

A few days after his return, Archie's collection, having cleared customs, arrived at the museum. The pile of crates, trunks and oversized artefacts formed a veritable mountain on the floor of the anthropology store. With the help of Jack Gormly, the museum storeman, Archie laid the items out methodically and began to open them. As word spread through the great institution, staff gathered to see what Archie had secured in the little-known islands.

Soon, the unpacking had turned into a sort of curator's Christmas. Whenever Archie unwrapped a bird or a worm preserved in spirit, or a giant cockroach, cries of admiration went up from the relevant experts. So great indeed was the attraction that even gouty old Slederman, the herpetologist, who'd been virtually bedridden for decades, turned up. '*Rana arfuckiana!*' he crowed as Archie unveiled a massive frog floating in a glass jar. 'Never thought I'd live to see the day.' Slederman wiped a tear from his eye.

Not being expert in the amphibia, Vere Griffon suspected the old man of possessing a foul mouth. But on that day nothing could have dispelled his joy. For here, at last, was a truly worthy addition to the institution's holdings. One that, when studied and described in full, would carry the museum's name—and its director's reputation—into the glorious annals of scientific achievement.

Archie's own joy would have been unalloyed if it were not for one thing. Beatrice was not there to witness his triumph. She had taken annual leave to visit her family up country. Nobody knew when she would be back. He'd considered visiting her, but thoughts of her stern uncle, along with Dithers' advice to give her time, saw him procrastinate.

Amid all the hubbub, the director's gaze was soon fixed on a group of workers who were pulling apart a tall wooden scaffold. The prow of a magnificent war canoe could be seen emerging from the timbers. It was exquisitely carved and at least eight feet high, the wood blackened and decorated along its outside edge with hundreds of white egg-cowry shells. But what really caught Vere Griffon's eye was the figure crowning it. It was a homunculus, whose oversized head was resting in its hands. The thing was so expertly inlaid with mother-of-pearl that it could have been the work of the finest Renaissance craftsman.

'That headhunting canoe, Meek, is of a most superior type!' Griffon enthused. 'It could seat thirty paddlers, I'd guess, and the figurehead is the finest I've seen. It would make a splendid centrepiece for a gallery of Pacific Cultures. And it may help in gaining Mrs Gordon-Smythe's support. Congratulations on securing it! I just hope you didn't pay too much, funding being what it is.'

'Well done, old chap,' shouted Dithers as he held aloft the stuffed skin of a rather large rat. 'The *Mus carnivorans*. We don't have one in the collection, and this is the largest and most perfect specimen I've ever seen. Professor Stein in Berlin will be green with envy!'

By late afternoon the unpacking of the major items was complete, and Archie was left alone to sort the smaller objects. One of the last crates he opened was filled with fish and marine molluscs. It contained that rarest of shellfish, the golden cowrie. He wanted desperately to show it to Sopwith, but the old man was probably already at the Maori's Head. So he told Jeevons to let Eric know that an item of interest awaited him in the anthropology store. That way the old fellow could drop by at his earliest convenience.

Just one job remained before an exhausted Archie Meek could head home, and it was a messy one. The pickled fish had to be transferred from their temporary jars into permanent ones.

By the time Archie had finished it was almost eight o'clock. He was exhausted but also exhilarated. It really had been his great day. He had been back less than a week, and already he was the museum's golden boy. Even Vere Griffon had looked upon him with new respect. If he had passed the rites of manhood during his initiation in the Venus Islands, then here in the museum he had passed the rites of passage that mark one as suitable for promotion to curator.

When he got home there was no sign of Dithers. He was doubtless attending a meeting of the Society for the Preservation of Native Animals. Archie negotiated his way around the chaos, climbed into bed, and slept the sleep of the blessed.

When Archie awoke at dawn, Dithers was still snoozing. Archie dressed quietly, slipped out of the room and returned to the museum. It was well before opening hour, but he was eager to examine once more the haul of treasures he'd secured. He roused Jeevons, who was snoring in his guard box, and gained entry. He slipped through the wide doors of the anthropology department's unpacking area, and was surprised to see Eric Sopwith, bent over a crate on the floor.

'Ah, Eric. Didn't expect to see you here so early! What do you make of that golden cowrie, eh?'

Eric neither replied nor rose to meet him. Archie walked to his friend and looked into his face. Sopwith's skin was even more liverish than usual, and a gobbet of drool extended from the corner of his open mouth. The old man was, at the very least, not well.

A half-drained museum specimen jar, its lid removed, was on the floor beside the crate. The head of a pickled fish poked into the air. At seventy per cent proof, preserving alcohol is more powerful even than the navy's renowned hospital rum. It was not unknown for museum curators to develop a taste for it.

'My God, you've really been on a bender this time, haven't you?' Archie said. He tried to lift the curator to his feet. But Eric would not cooperate. He was as stiff as a board.

The young man was shaking uncontrollably as he ran back to the guard's room. 'Help,' he bellowed. 'Get a doctor! It's Sopwith. In the anthropology store. Dead!'

Archie was so upset that he could not stay in the museum. He walked round and round the block, then into Woolloomooloo. North of William Street the usual toughs were loitering by lampposts, while a few sharp-looking men in suits sat at tables outside terrace houses that might have been sly grog shops. Their faces were hard. One fellow had a fresh scar running from his left eye to his chin and the most chilling blue eyes Archie had ever seen. Archie turned up Crown Street into Darlinghurst, where he ran into Dithers, who was strolling to work.

'Good God, old chap!' Dithers exclaimed. 'You look half frightened to death! What were you doing in the loo? Not really safe these days, you know. Let's have a cup of tea before we go into work, and you can tell me all about it.'

Over a cup of sweet, milky tea, Archie told Dithers about Sopwith.

When he had finished, Dithers sat silent for a moment, then said, 'He was the best of men, Archie. Gentle, kind and generous. But we all had our suspicions. The preserving alcohol in molluscs was disappearing far too quickly for evaporation to be the only cause. Honestly, I don't know how anybody could drink the stuff. It's so full of formaldehyde and the stench of shellfish that it would put a dead man off. And he'd begun saying strange things, almost raving at times. He was nervous as well. Looking back, I think he feared that the museum was onto him, and that he'd be turned out on his ear. You know, Archie, once you start drinking that stuff, it kills you pretty quickly. He probably only had months left, in any case.'

'Bless you, Courtenay, for trying to ease my conscience,' Archie replied. 'But I can't help feeling responsible. If only I hadn't told Jeevons to let him know about the golden cowrie.'

'Come on. You've nothing to reproach yourself for, Archie. You've done the right thing.'

Dithers rose and placed a few pennies on the table. By the time the pair reached the museum the ambulance carrying Sopwith's body was pulling out of the courtyard. The mood was sombre, and as Archie walked by people fell silent. A golden boy indeed, he said to himself.

At his desk, Archie did not know what to do or think. He absent-mindedly picked up the latest issue of the journal *Eugenics*. Among its offerings was an article tracing the ancestry of the editor back to Roman times—through the male line. The Venus Islanders would have laughed at that, he mused, cuckoldry being what it is. At least the islanders were realistic about such things. And from the United States came another article proposing the sterilisation of the mentally feeble. It was a barbaric piece which claimed, among other things, that the American Negro was of subnormal intelligence. Disgusting, Archie thought. No, not just disgusting. Delusional.

Even these distractions could not shift the focus of his thought. What had Sopwith told him? The director had gone mad. Curators were disappearing. Were these just the ravings of a man in the grip of *delirium tremens*? Or...what? And whose skulls were they on the fetish—those four orange ones? Could his suspicions be true? Could they be Polkinghorne,

Hadley, Jones and Dolt? Buck teeth like those were a rarity, that's for sure.

Then it struck him: what if Sopwith's death hadn't been accidental. What if he'd been killed to shut him up?

Chapter 9

Vere Griffon tried to form his features into the sort of saintly, caring look that he imagined was appropriate in the presence of a corpse. His friend, the state pathologist Dr Leopold Upton, had greeted him warmly at the city morgue. Griffon had known him since their student days. Neat, mustachioed and discreet, Upton was, despite his profession, perhaps the most clubbable man in Sydney. Now the pathologist wore the solemn expression of one about to deliver bad news.

'All signs are consistent with poisoning, I'm afraid, Vere.' Upton and Griffon were standing in a cold room, and in front of them lay the body of Eric Sopwith, stretched out, arms by his side. A long criss-cross of coarse stitches held together an incision that stretched from groin to neck.

'Can't be sure without more tests, of course, but it looks very much like fugu poisoning. The active substance is found in the liver of toadfish. Quite a common species in the Pacific. Only the Japanese make a habit of eating it. Sometimes the sushi knife touches the liver—that's all it takes to see a diner off. Ran across a few cases in Tokyo during the international pathology conference in '26. The only question is, was it accidental or deliberate? I'm sorry, Vere, but the police will have to be called in.'

'Don't suppose it could have been alcoholic poisoning?' asked Griffon. 'He was our crapulous curator, after all.'

'Don't think so, old chap. By the look of his lungs the poor old fellow asphyxiated. Toadfish toxin destroys the nerves. The victim remains conscious while the lungs fill with fluid. Can't cough it up—or move, so they die slowly of suffocation. Terrible way to go, really.'

'I see. But can you give me a day or so to try to sort things out at our end? I'm sure there's an innocent explanation for all of this. I'd appreciate the chance to question certain staff. Besides, it wouldn't reflect well on the museum, having the police about the place just now, with all the fundraising that's needed for the new gallery. I think you can trust a Christ's College man to play with a straight bat, Leo.'

'Of course, Vere. Take your time, and I'll keep things on ice here, so to speak,' Upton said, looking dubiously at Sopwith.

Two hours later Giles Mordant, Archie Meek and John Jeevons found themselves standing to attention in front of the director's desk. Vere Griffon's eyes burned like coals. Between stroking the back of his head and staring at the ceiling, he quizzed them about the hours leading up to Sopwith's death with all the zeal of a prosecutor who'd scented blood.

'Jeevons. You saw and heard nothing on the night in question, even though you had the third watch? Is that right?'

'That's right, sir. Quiet as a mouse, the place was.'

'Are you saying you saw nothing of Sopwith that night? I hope for your sake that you weren't sleeping on the job! It will go very badly for you if you're lying.'

Jeevons flushed crimson.

'So how in the hell did Sopwith get into the museum without alerting the guard room?' Griffon fulminated.

'I think I can help there, sir,' volunteered Mordant. 'I met Sopwith that night.'

'Did you, Giles? Pray tell more.'

'Drunk as a skunk he was, sir, if you'll forgive the expression. He'd come up William Street, fair swaying, mumbling that he had to see Mr Meek's collection. Said he'd heard about it from someone at the Maori's Head, and couldn't wait until morning.'

'I did tell Holdfast that if he saw Sopwith, to let him know about the seashell,' Jeevons volunteered.

'Anyway, sir,' Mordant continued, 'I'd been working late on the model of Piltdown man, that stone-age coot, for the new exhibition. So I walked back to the museum with him and let him in through the taxidermist's entrance.'

'The taxidermist's entrance?' repeated Griffon. 'It's the only way into the building without passing the guard room. You know, Mordant, that it should only be used for moving large mounts. And removing your, er...effluvia.'

'I know, sir. But I felt sorry for the old fella. He seemed so keen to see the treasures, as he called them.'

Archie was astonished. So Mordant had taken Sopwith back to the museum. He knew that Giles was lying about wanting to help the old man. His hatred of the curator, who frequently ordered him to clean rotting seashells, was plain for all to see. Archie got the feeling that Giles was telling the director something he wanted to hear. He thought back to that day at the Maori's Head when Mordant had so vehemently contradicted Sopwith's assertion that Polkinghorne's disappearance was suspicious.

'Meek,' barked Griffon. 'You claim that you were sorting the pickled fish you brought back, and that you went home when you finished at eight o'clock? Can you prove that?'

'No, sir,' Archie replied dismally, recalling Dithers' absence.

'The jar on which Sopwith had, let us say, quenched his thirst, contained a small coral trout, did it not? An entirely innocuous fish, I believe. But Mordant tells me that the jar was labelled "giant toadfish". Do you think it possible, Meek, that you might have switched the fatally poisonous toad fish with the coral trout? Moreover, did you remove the toad fish's liver before pickling it? If not, its toxins could have leached into the preserving fluid, where they would have remained until our poor deceased colleague drank it.' Vere Griffon's voice had become almost triumphant. 'It would have been a simple mistake, Meek, in your tired state, to swap the fish.'

Vere Griffon was now looking at Archie as if beseeching him to accept the explanation. But Archie was as certain as he had ever been about anything that he'd not swapped the fish, or the labels. He'd always been extraordinarily careful to keep label and specimen together. The collection would have been useless without such care. But how could he convince anybody of that? Was it possible that the yangona had addled his brain a little?

Wearily, he conceded. 'It *could* have been the case, sir. But I have no memory of it.'

Vere Griffon's face broke into a great smile—the first of that magnitude Archie had seen on his director.

'Needless to say that none of what we've discussed today shall leave this room. Thank you, gentlemen. I'm sure the authorities will deal with this expeditiously.'

And indeed Griffon was right, at least in this respect. Within days the state pathologist brought down his verdict: 'Death by misadventure'. Despite the finding, and to Vere Griffon's intense irritation, the worst of the city's newspapers portrayed Sopwith's death as a sort of Agatha Christie mystery. For a few days gossip about 'the murder in the museum' flourished, but then the hysteria died down and the matter seemed forgotten. Just one loose end needed tidying up. Vere Griffon made another trip to the morgue, to see his old friend, Dr Leopold Upton.

'My dear fellow, thank you for handling poor Sopwith's demise so...sensitively. It was a great consolation to us all, at this delicate time, to know that the police wouldn't be traipsing through the place, alarming board members and donors. Not to mention staff. But I'm afraid that there's one other thing. Sopwith's solicitor came to see me the other day about the old man's will. It seems that Eric wasn't at all keen to leave the museum. In fact, it was his express wish that his skull be donated to the institution he had served for so long. I often heard him joke that the place was full of native skulls, but with "ne'er a

Caledonian to be seen", as he put it. I thought he was being morbidly jocular, but his will indicates that he meant it. The old fellow has no close kin. I suppose he thought of the museum as his home.'

'Hmm. An unusual request,' replied Upton thoughtfully. 'Unusual, but not unheard of. Descartes' skull, you know, resides in the Musée de l'Homme in Paris, along with those of a goodly number of curators who have served that fine institution. And, of course, in this state of New South Wales, many people donate their bodies to the university's anatomy department.'

'So donating one's skull to a museum is possible,' ventured Griffon, 'in a legal sense, I mean.'

'I think so. But there are practical things to consider. For example, the delicate matter of defleshing.'

'I've thought of that,' Griffon responded. 'Our taxidermy department is more than capable of doing the final cleaning, but it would be a great kindness if somebody here could do the decapitation and skinning. Not quite right, I feel, to ask a colleague to do that sort of thing.'

'I'll get an assistant onto it, but it might take some time. As you can see, it's pretty much full house here, and tonight looks to be inclement. I expect to take receipt of at least a dozen corpses by morning. Pneumonia and starvation, you know. And that means that this gurney will be needed.' Upton's hand came down on the stainless steel trolley on which Sopwith lay. 'Until we can get to the job, your curator may have to go into the freezer.'

'Probably best not to say anything of this in public, old chap, given the run we've had in the papers. And it might unsettle the staff if they hear about Sopwith's somewhat unconventional return to the workplace.' Griffon gave a faint smile.

'Of course, Vere. We must lunch at the club, say what? Next Tuesday is the seafood spread. All the great and the good will be there. Care to come along?'

'Very kind of you, Upton. See you at midday on Bligh Street.'

Griffon walked back to the museum. It was decent of Upton to have accepted his word on Sopwith's will, he thought. Otherwise he'd have had to explain how it was that he had entirely forgotten to bring the document with him.

Chapter 10

The letter was written in elegant Latin script and signed, with a flourish, *Professore Virgil Giglione, Curatore Principio dell' Archeologia, Musei Vaticani.*

'The bloodsucker,' Vere Griffon fulminated. 'This is extortionate! Three Tasmanian tigers—and in good condition! Doesn't the man know they're next to impossible to come by these days? We've had a standing order for a *Thylacinus* in with the Hobart zoo for years, and it's still unfilled. *And* fifteen Aboriginal crania. In perfect condition, he dares say! It would take the morgue years to supply such a number, especially if he insists on full-bloods. And getting them out of the collection will only cause trouble with the curators. My God! The list goes on and on. Look here: a desert rat-kangaroo! Well, the only place that's got one of those is London, and they're not giving it up, I can assure our dear professor Lily! *And* a Sepik River canoe and mask. And look at this: the man's got the gall to ask for the Bathurst meteorite! Dr Doughty would have *my* stones if I tried to wrest that from her! And all of this in exchange for a few mouldering, stuffed goats! My God, this is impossible. Just impossible.'

'Director,' Miss Stritchley interjected rather firmly. 'Do you think that Mr Abotomy might assist us in obtaining some of the exchange specimens? After all, this was his idea, and he has a very large run up country. All kinds of rare creatures doubtless abound on it.'

Dryandra! Where would he be without her? Vere Griffon promptly dictated a letter to Abotomy, inviting him to the museum to discuss the Giglione goat acquisition. 'Miss Stritchley,' he said, addressing her with unusual warmth, 'I think we've done enough today. How about a sweet sherry, and a moment with the Meissen? You deserve it.'

Vere Griffon opened the door to a sort of alcove at the rear of his desk. Behind it was a small room. Then another door belonging to a massive walk-in safe. It had been installed at great expense in the early days, when enormous gold nuggets were commonly exhibited at the museum. The director turned the lock, opened the heavy metal door, and ushered Miss Stritchley in.

Along one wall of the safe—more properly a strong room— stood a wine rack filled with bottles of Bordeaux and Burgundy, while in the middle stood a simple wooden table with two chairs. Elegantly placed on the table were a decanter and two sherry glasses. Beyond that, and occupying the rest of the table's length, were a dozen exquisite porcelain vases, teapots and figurines. They had been arranged with great thought.

Griffon filled the glasses. He and Dryandra savoured the excellent vintage.

'This damn country might have the finest clay,' Griffon said, 'but it will never produce Meissen or anything near it. In Europe everybody knows their place. Even the forest is cultivated to perfection. Just look at that,' he said gesturing at a vase. 'Bavaria in spring. How glorious! Australia is as ugly as sin by comparison. Flat, dry and as pathetic as the naked blacks that once roamed it. And it's still ruled by felonry rather than gentry. What a lot of galoots I've inherited here! I swear, Dryandra, I will bring my collection of curators to culture, order and discipline, even if it kills me.' The pair communed in companionable silence, admiring the diminutive painted figurines in their wigs and tricorn hats, yearning for a Europe that existed only in their imaginations.

Upon receipt of Vere Griffon's letter Abotomy dashed to the museum. 'No problem at all, old chap, with this lot!' the squire declared after hearing Giglione's demands. 'Admittedly, Tassie tigers might be a bit of a stretch, but Abotomy Park is riddled with wildlife. Damn parrots and kangaroo-rats everywhere! As for those skulls, Grandfather Ebenezer was a crack shot, you know, and I've got a fair idea of where the bodies are,' he said with a wink. 'You just take care of the tigers and the Sepik stuff. And that meteorite—I'll get the rest. By Jove, I know what I'll do,' Abotomy added. 'We'll have a *battué*. And a digging jamboree! That'll produce such a swag of specimens it'll knock old Giglione's socks off. Would you care to join us, Director?'

'Perhaps not,' replied Griffon, struggling to hide his disdain. 'But I'll think about who on staff might be useful to you.'

Vere Griffon walked Abotomy out of his office and onto the street. He leaned towards the squire. 'This is all very well, old chap,' he whispered, 'but there are certain, let us say, impediments, to me getting access to the objects Giglione requires. Curators need to be got out of the way—that sort of thing. It might require a bit of support from you—financial as well as moral—at our next board meeting.'

'You have me intrigued, Director. But it sounds like good sport—and those goats are worth any effort!'

Abotomy waddled off gaily down College Street. The fingers of his right hand twitched as if he was already pulling the trigger of his shotgun.

'Miss Stritchley, can I see my copy of the board papers?'

The board meeting was the most important event of the month for the director—the occasion on which his powers were tested against those to whom he reported. The board, and the board alone, could sack him, or order an investigation into any aspect of the institution he presided over.

In fact, the august position of 'Member of the Board of Directors of the Sydney Museum' was a sinecure—a special favour from the premier to those from whom he himself needed favours. As a result, the board was stacked with people who had no idea at all about how a museum should be run. Abotomy was a wonderful instance of this. There were only a few sly reynards, and Griffon fancied that he'd learned how to manage them.

But the greatest gift heaven had bestowed upon the director was his chairman, the Very Reverend Sir Crispin Jugglers, Anglican Primate of Sydney (and hence all Australia). He had held the position since the age of dinosaurs; his superannuated clothing hung on him like funereal garments on a mummer, and his slender black cane, doubtless once an elegant accoutrement, had long been an indispensible aid to perambulation.

The old gent spent much of each meeting asleep, his shiny bald head nodding to the rhythm of his breathing. Which was all to the good, because when awake his interventions were at best inappropriate, at worst dangerous. Vere Griffon still fumed about the long and tedious discussion that had followed Jugglers' opining what a great shame it was that public hanging was no longer in fashion. The enthusiasm with which the board members endorsed the death penalty for almost any offence had made the meeting run well over time, causing the director to be late for an important appointment.

Vere Griffon read through the agenda. 'Minutes, Apologies, Update on galleries. Ditto Science. Ditto collections. Donations, Finances. Request for funding. All very straightforward,' he announced to himself.

Listed among the donations were the seashells of a Reverend

Bloomingdale, who had gifted his collection, numbering three thousand specimens, to the institution. These days such donations were worth almost nothing, and were becoming monotonously common as the previous generation, among whom shell collecting had been a fad, died off. Worse, now that Sopwith was gone there was nobody on staff to curate the donated shells. But since it came from a member of the clergy the director saw it as politic to accept it.

The next donation was more interesting. A Mr Marchant of Double Bay had bequeathed his collection of antique coins. There was no numismatist at the institution, so the museum had no capacity to curate and catalogue old coins; but it would be handy to have the money. There was a danger that some smart alec might suggest giving it to the Nicholson Museum at Sydney University. Griffon made a mental note to prevent this potential occurrence.

When the grandfather clock in the hallway struck two, the board members began to make their way to their accustomed seats in the grand boardroom. An extravagant bunch of roses sat in a glorious porcelain vase in the centre of the table.

As usual, first through the door was Cedric Scrutton. Representing the state government, he was head of the Department of the Arts, which administered the museum. A grey man with pale blue eyes and a narrow face, Scrutton looked so prematurely hollowed out with worries and cares that he could already pass for an old man. Always businesslike and keenly interested in the museum's finances, he was sharp enough to pick up the smallest of irregularities, and therefore was Griffon's principal adversary.

Next to enter was Chumley Abotomy, the board's youngest member. Matters at Abotomy Park meant that he was a frequent apology, and this was only the fourth meeting he'd attended since his appointment. But now that they had formed an alliance over the Giglione goats he was, the director hoped, someone who could be relied upon. Then came Professor Harold Atleigh, a marine biologist from the University of Sydney. He could have been a danger, particularly in the scientific arena, but he was a timid fellow and Vere Griffon had learned long ago that he'd do almost anything to avoid causing a fuss.

Mrs Adora Frederick, wife of Sir Clement Frederick, the owner of Mark Frederick's department store, was doubly useless in Vere Griffon's opinion, for not only did she know nothing about museums, but in all the years she'd served on the board she'd never once dipped into her personal wealth to assist a project. Adora was followed by Sir Hercules Robinson, the war hero, then Jock Higgins, the state architect. Dr Lawrence Bullock, head of the state agriculture department, was an apology. 'No loss there,' Vere Griffon said under his breath as he read the note proclaiming the doctor's absence. 'He has about as many brains as the average steer.'

On a bad day, Vere Griffon had taken to fantasising about how, if the board fell into his power, he'd arraign its members. The setting was a cross between Dante's *Inferno* and the museum's taxidermy workshop. Bumstocks, who would make a suitable Mephistopheles, was busy administering punishments. Adora Frederick was being racked with great vigour, until streams of hitherto concealed pound notes flowed from her clothing. Bullock was being carved up, to be served as Christmas dinner to the starving staff, while Higgins was being crushed under a large stone inscribed with the words 'New Museum, opened 2030—if ever'. But it was Scrutton for whom Griffon's most fearful imaginings were reserved. He sat chained into a sort of iron throne, with a large accounts book before him. As a voice intoned the museum's ever-diminishing budgetary position, a large steel spike penetrated further into his rectum.

The board members were chatting among themselves when the chairman made his way into the room. They stood as one while Jugglers settled himself painfully into his ornate carver. Set above a high-collared shirt and black robe, his face bore, Griffon realised, an astonishing resemblance to the Venus Island Fetish that served as a backdrop. He must remember to get a photograph of Jugglers sitting below the thing before the chairman retired—for the wall of the boardroom—and perhaps as a gift to the departing chairman, who would be sadly missed.

Following his usual practice, Griffon guided Jugglers through the tedious preliminaries. There was nothing much of note, except for the retirement of Mr Jonas Blockhead, the museum's printer for thirty-three years.

'He's retiring to the Cook Islands,' the director explained, 'where we wish him many happy years of well-earned leisure. In honour of his long service, we felt it appropriate to present him with a fob and cufflinks, embossed with the museum crest.'

Scrutton looked up.

'To be paid for by staff donations, of course,' Griffon added. He couldn't resist baiting Scrutton.

'With permission, Your Grace?' Griffon warbled as he shuffled through his papers. 'I'd like to report on the new gallery.

Progress has been splendid. Many of the principal models have been completed, and the best of them are the equal of anything I've seen in the museums of the world. To my great delight I've had a letter from that most eminent of geologists, Sir Arthur Woodward, recently retired from the British Museum. You may recall that he's been acting as an advisor, and it now seems possible that he will travel to officiate at the opening. This would be a great coup for us!'

'Is this the new evolution gallery?' Abotomy seemed to be confused about precisely which exhibition was being discussed. Griffon had avoided the word 'evolution' for good reason.

'What's this evolution nonsense? Monkeys and suchlike? Thought Wilberforce knocked that on the head years ago.' Jugglers was having an ill-timed lucid moment.

'Your Grace, may I respond simply by pointing out that Mr Charles Darwin lies buried in Westminster Abbey. The church has forgiven him.'

'The abbey, eh. Very well.'

The effort seemed to have drained Jugglers, who, to Griffon's relief, was falling into slumber. He made a mental note to speak to Abotomy about sensitivities surrounding relations between the museum and the church.

'Any questions?' Griffon asked, before turning to the next item. 'With permission, chair, several members of the public seek to make donations. Seashells from a Reverend Bloomingdale; a numismatic collection from a Mr Marchant; the offer of a jacket once worn by Napoleon Bonaparte himself from a Miss Delacour; and a replica bust of Queen Nefertiti of Egypt from a Dr Ernst Wonderlicht.'

'Poor Bloomingdale,' mumbled Jugglers, his eyes closed, providing the director with an opportune moment.

'With the board's permission, I'd like to move that the donations be accepted, and, furthermore that Reverend Bloomingdale be elected honorary correspondent to the museum.'

'Entirely fitting given his lifetime of toils in the realm of malacology,' Adora Frederick responded. At least she'd got the department right, thought Griffon.

'Seconded,' said Abotomy, following which Jugglers moved his hand as if in benediction.

'Thank you, Your Grace. We shall have a letter drawn up with the assistance of Dr Ponders, our corals expert.' Vere Griffon nodded to Miss Stritchley to make a note.

Griffon may have appeared obsequious, even slightly bored, as he worked his way through the agenda, but mentally he was *en guard*. The critical item was fast approaching.

'Next item, gentlemen.' Somehow, Griffon often forgot to acknowledge Adora Frederick at such moments. 'We've had several requests for extra expenditure. I realise that in these straitened times such requests are generally not welcome.' Scrutton's ears pricked up, and a sour expression crept over his face. Vere Griffon ignored him, instead looking to the chair for permission to continue. Jugglers' eyes were closed, but after a few moments his head nodded.

'Thank you, Your Grace,' Griffon said as he returned to his papers.

The colour intensified in Scrutton's face.

'Miss Stritchley, could you leave off your minute-taking for a moment and tell Dr Doughty that her presence is required?'

Elizabeth Doughty was waiting outside the boardroom door. She was mad keen on fieldwork, and her plaid trousers, which she was wearing now, were a frequent sight in every quarry and cavern in the country. She was always scrabbling for funds, and had been delighted when the director asked her if she would personally petition the board for funding for her latest venture. This was her great opportunity—her moment to shine. Best to be no-nonsense and to the point, she told herself, as she strode into the room.

'Reverend Jugglers, board members,' she commenced in a stentorian voice, 'I wish to travel to Tidore, in the Dutch East Indies, to obtain specimens of two most splendid minerals recently reported from that island. The intrepid Count Vidua of Genoa, whose immortal expedition is, as we speak, steaming homewards, has written to me concerning a strange mineral growth, a kind of phyllosilicate clay, which he encountered in the caverns of the volcanic isle. From his sketches, I can only assume that the count has stumbled across a massive Dickite.' She wagged her forefinger back and forth like a school ma'am. 'It really is a most exceptional new mineral: the royal purple crystals are exquisitely shaped, and in this instance are of a most prodigious size. A *most* unique discovery, Director,' she said looking towards Griffon, 'and *most* exciting to the public! Ours could be the first museum to obtain a specimen, which might form the centrepiece of a *most* popular minerals exhibition. It's an opportunity not to be missed!'

Dr Doughty paused, searching the faces of the board members for traces of enthusiasm. Not put off by the puzzled looks, she plunged on.

'Count Vidua's notes also hint at the possibility that Isleby Cummingtonite may be had on Tidore. It's a rare new form of the mineral, known previously only from Isleby rock stack in the Orkneys. As you may recall, Director, the original mineral species was named after Professor Gaythorn Cummington, under whom I laboured most ardently at Oxford.' A spot of moisture appeared in the corner of her eye. 'With such rare minerals in its collection, to what heights might this institution not rise?' she concluded in rapture.

'I don't think…Isleby Cummingtonite?' Jugglers muttered confusedly.

'How much will it cost, Griffon, this little jaunt to the Spice Islands?' Cedric Scrutton was scowling at the director. 'You do realise, don't you, that thousands of homeless people are sleeping rough tonight all around this grand museum of yours, and that the government is most stringent in approving any new expenditures whatsoever!

Dr Doughty was astonished that such a weary- and worn-looking body could generate such a thunderous response.

'The total cost of the *expedition* is £300,' Griffon responded calmly. 'And if Dr Doughty does manage to get her hands on the Dickite, who knows what the result will be, my dear Cedric. We may be able to sell duplicates to other institutions for thousands of pounds.'

'Out of the question, Griffon. The premier would never approve the sum. Not in these straitened times, and not on such a speculative venture.' Scrutton was already turning to the next item when Chumley Abotomy raised his hand.

'Chair, if I may? As a new board member and a man of independent means, I would like to do something for this grand institution. Three hundred pounds is a large sum, I admit, but if the state could contribute £100, I'd be willing to foot the rest of the bill, as a tax-deductible donation to the museum.'

Scrutton looked warily at Abotomy. He knew that the squatter had the premier's ear, and as a public servant he understood the value of avoiding trouble.

'Very well. I'll take your proposal to treasury,' Scrutton said reluctantly. 'I can't promise anything, mind you,' he added, unable to hide his irritation.

'That will be all, Dr Doughty. Thank you for your most stimulating presentation,' said the director, looking to Miss Stritchley to usher the mineralogist from the room.

'I have just one further item under expenditure, Your Grace, if I may?' continued Vere Griffon. 'It concerns our splendid mammalogist, Dr Courtenay Dithers. You may recall that he's our star recruit—a Cambridge man with a first-class academic record. He had hoped to travel to Africa to study big cats. Unfortunately, we've had a communication from the National Geographic Society refusing his grant. Not that it was considered in the least unworthy. But, like us, they face straitened times. I haven't informed Dr Dithers of this yet as I don't want to disappoint the chap. A rejection may even incline him to return home, to Britain. He would be a great loss to us.'

'How much does he want?' Scrutton asked, his eyes narrowed to slits.

'Eight hundred pounds, for six months in the Kenya colony.'
'Eight hundred pounds so that a public servant can join some

upper-class flappers and their layabout gentlemen on safari in Africa! Out of the question!' Scrutton thundered, emphasising individually each of his final four words.

'Chair, if I may?' Abotomy had his hand in the air once more. 'Abotomy Hall is rising swiftly, and will soon need furnishing. A pair of stuffed lions beside the fireplace and a zebra-skin rug or three would enliven the place, I think. If the institution could see its way clear to have Dithers shoot a bit of big game for me, and if the museum could prepare the mounted specimens and skins, I'd be willing to underwrite the expedition—again as a tax-deductible donation.'

In the silence that followed Scrutton seemed to be gripped by an apoplectic seizure. The Reverend Jugglers once again nodded his head, though by this time it was clear he was fast sleep.

'Thank you, Your Grace,' Vere Griffon said. 'I believe that's the end of our business for today. Anyone for a cup of tea?'

Chapter 11

Archie Meek had now been back in Sydney a little over two months. Sopwith's death and the phantoms of missing curators haunted his imaginings, while his anxiety about Beatrice had increased in her absence. A few days after his 'trial', as he'd come to think of Griffon's inquiry into Sopwith's demise, Archie dragged himself to work after a sleepless night, feeling more dead than alive. And there was Beatrice, bent over the great register, concentrating intensely.

'Beatrice,' he gasped.

'Stay away from me,' she hissed.

Archie backed into his room, and shut the door. He sat down, a crumpled heap, while outside Beatrice shed silent tears onto her register.

'By Jove,' Dithers exclaimed when he saw Archie later that day. You look a bit queer, old cove. Are you unwell?'

'I'll be all right.'

Dithers' eyes were shining with excitement. 'I've got funding for my study of big cats! Almost given up hope, but look at this.' He waved a memorandum in Archie's face. 'It seems that Vere Griffon has intervened *personally* with the board on my behalf. And he's had a word with Mr Abotomy. The upshot is that they're willing to fund the entire expedition! All I need do is pot a few extra lion and zebra for Abotomy Hall—more a holiday than hard work, I'd say. What a splendid fellow our director is turning out to be!'

'Vere Griffon? Really?' Archie replied tartly.

'Archie, show the man a bit of respect, please! He is your director, after all, and he has a most difficult job at present.'

Vere Griffon, Archie felt, was now a closed subject between them. But should he tell Dithers that Beatrice was showing no signs of relenting? His friend was so jubilant that Archie felt there was no point in troubling him now. In any case he knew what Dithers' advice would be: 'Give her time, my boy.'

As things turned out, Dithers' departure for the dark continent was delayed by one misfortune after another. First, news arrived that the steamer *Zambesi*, which ran from Perth to Mombasa, had been wrecked on a reef somewhere in the Indian Ocean. No alternative could be found. Then there was an outbreak of sleeping sickness on the Masai Mara, and shortly after word came that Dithers' father had been taken seriously ill. Courtenay considered diverting via England to visit him, until a telegram told of a swift recovery, once again putting

Dithers' plans into disarray.

Through it all the mammalogist remained chipper. 'The big cats will still be there, Archie, when the tide turns in my favour.'

Thought of an overseas trip had Elizabeth Doughty salivating. Geologising on such a remote island was a rare opportunity. As soon as Abotomy's cheque for £200 arrived she left for Tidore, not daring to risk bureaucratic delay by awaiting the government's £100. She hoped she might just scrape by on the reduced sum.

It was an ironclad rule in the museum that curators were responsible for their collections. But while they were on fieldwork decisions could not be delayed indefinitely. So a convention had developed. While curators were in the field, authority over their collections fell to the director. Curators felt it was a convention more honoured in the breach. Indeed it was rarely invoked for fear of a curatorial backlash. But, under Griffon, things had begun to change.

On the very day that Elizabeth Doughty left for the Spice Islands the director ordered Giles Mordant to go to the mineralogical collection and bring back the Bathurst meteorite. Mordant was exultant. For once he had authority over the scientific staff. He found the registrar of minerals with his finger up his nose, puzzling over a box of rocks.

'I've come on behalf of the director. He wants the Bathurst meteorite.'

'What does he want with it?'

'That's none of your business. Now get it. Quick smart.'

'Dr Doughty will be most upset. I mean, this is most irregular.'

Mordant looked him in the eye. 'Hop to it! The director

himself has ordered this, mate, and if you disobey or say a word about it you will be taken care of.'

The meteorite in question had shot to fame some years earlier when it had streaked across the skies of the western plains and made a direct hit on the Church of St Barnabas the Sinner in Bathurst, which was all but vaporised in a tremendous explosion. The Protestants of the small community could not entirely conceal their glee. And there were rumours of celebrations at the local joss house, though in public the Chinese expressed their condolences, even putting on a charity yum cha for the churchless Catholics. News of the singular event travelled round the globe and was the subject of heated discussions in Rome. Which was perhaps how Professor Virgil Giglione heard about it.

Vere Griffon was surprised when he saw the reddish lump of iron. At fifty pounds' weight, the Bathurst meteorite hardly seemed large enough to destroy a church. But the oddest thing about it was its shape. Rather like a leg of lamb, Griffon thought. He ordered Mordant to store it in a wooden crate in the walk-in safe.

It had been a warm, sunny summer. The bones that Archie had placed in the windowsill on the day of his return had remained undisturbed. One April morning, when the staff decamped for morning tea, Archie stayed behind. He went to the windowsill and lifted the piece of cardboard on which he had written 'do not disturb' nearly three months earlier. There was no difference in colour between the shaded and exposed portions of the bones.

The skulls on the fetish had been exposed to far less sunlight. If fading had not altered their colour, then what else could have? Perhaps their smoking had been done differently from the rest. But they had not looked different when he left. Perhaps they were not the original skulls. He could hardly bear to think that they might be the remains of the missing curators. That seemed insane. Yet the idea would not go away. And if they were the missing curators, who had put them there?

As Archie walked past the entrance to the Egyptian room he ran into a small knot of visitors. The place had a reputation for terrifying the more gullible members of the public. It was poorly lit, claustrophobically small and crowded with Egyptian arcana, and its contents included the hands, heads and feet of mummies which, judging from their condition, had been roughly torn from their bodies. Even Archie had to admit that the place could be unnerving.

The gaggle at the entrance consisted mostly of ladies whom his mother would refer to as being of 'a certain age'. A theatrical whisper carried through the air. Archie recognised it as the voice of John Jeevons, the museum guard.

'I'll never forget what I saw that day, not as long as I live. He was lying in a queer sort of way, twisted up like a snake. The effects of the poison, me missus reckons. And his face…' Jeevons' eyes turned heavenwards. 'Black and puffed up like a Christmas puddin', it was. One eye was open, all staring and glassy. Chilled me blood to see it. But, my God'—he crossed himself—'the worst was his hand. I seen things on the Somme that'd turn a man's hair white overnight. But that hand! I never seen nothin' like it in all me living days. Like a mummy's claw it was, reaching out for the treasure.' He paused for effect. 'The treasure of the golden cowrie, which that young Mr Meek brought back from the cannibal islands.'

A collective shudder went through the crowd.

'Mister Jeevons,' a tremulous female voice inquired. 'The newspapers reported the death as a misadventure. Was poison really involved?'

'There are suspicions. Suspicions indeed, ma'am.'

Sopwith's death was clearly far from a closed chapter with the public, and Jeevons seemed intent on stirring curiosity to a fever pitch. Would he, Archie, end up in the tabloids, portrayed as the Lucrezia Borgia of the scientific world? he wondered.

Archie left the museum and walked automatically around Hyde Park, wondering what to do. There seemed little point in approaching Griffon about Jeevons' behaviour. No, best to pick the right moment, and speak to Jeevons directly.

As Archie walked back to the museum, he turned to his most unbearable problem. Beatrice had written him off, it seemed, and Dithers' strategy of giving her time was yielding nothing. Could she really be in love with Mordant? Archie had not entirely lost faith in Dithers as his 'Dear Dorothy', so he made his way to the mammalogist's office.

Dithers was bent over the stuffed skin of a large rat, a durry with a perilously long ashy tip hung from the corner of his mouth.

'Courtenay, I'm having no luck at all with Beatrice. No matter how much time I give her, she just ignores me,' Archie blurted out.

'Hmm. A difficult case. But I'm sure that she can be won over,

Archie. Might be best to speak to her, or write her a letter. Say you're sorry. Got carried away. That sort of thing.'

'But what about Mordant?'

'There is absolutely nothing in that, Archie. I was a fool to have even mentioned the thing.' Dithers turned his attention back to the rat on his desk.

Archie walked to Anthropology and found Beatrice. She did not look up, but he could feel her body tense at the sound of his footfalls. The words tumbled out of him. 'Beatrice. I am truly sorry for whatever I have done to offend you. I really am. I'm still mad about you. I meant what I wrote in my letter.'

Beatrice didn't even look up; she kept on writing. Archie crept back to his office, feeling thoroughly miserable.

The following day Archie thought he could discern the slightest thaw. When they found themselves alone, by chance, in the collection, Archie saw his opportunity. Apropos of nothing, and looking at nobody in particular, he said, 'I got carried away in the islands, Beatrice. Five years is a long time, you know.'

'It was horrible and embarrassing, Archie. But I forgive you,' Beatrice said with some effort. 'And I'm terribly sorry about Sopwith. I know how much he meant to you.'

Beatrice met his gaze. They both blushed, and Archie retreated to his cupboard. That evening Beatrice permitted Archie to walk her to Circular Quay.

'The place is so changed, Beatrice. And Vere Griffon frightens me. He has always been a martinet, but he never seemed unhinged, as he sometimes does now. With Polkinghorne missing, and Sopwith dead, there's a ghastly gloom over the place. I can't walk past the spot where I unpacked my collection without seeing Eric's face. He looked terrible, Beatrice. Just terrible! And to think I might have been responsible. I was as careful as could be with the labels, but I feel so out of touch with the world just now that anything's possible.'

'Archie, it's most emphatically not the same museum. Everything has changed since the stock-market collapse. I sometimes think that the worry of it *is* driving our director mad. At least, as you say, he seems to be so at times.'

Archie took a deep breath. 'Beatrice, could I ask you a favour? I don't like the idea of my, ahem, love token, being the property of the state. Do you think it might be deregistered and returned to me?'

Beatrice stood stock-still. Then she burst into tears. 'Archie! I waited so very long for you. And when your proposal of marriage came I was the happiest girl in the whole world. While you were away the only person who seemed to care that I existed was Giles. I told him about my engagement to you, and showed him the thing in the letter. It was he who told me what it really was. He laughed so cruelly about it, Archie! I was so embarrassed and upset—ashamed that I didn't know what it was, and that you could send me such an obscene thing. And Giles had been so very kind, letting me cry on his shoulder when I missed you.'

Beatrice fidgeted with her cuff, and looked at her feet.

'I can't give it back, Archie—because *he* has it!' she finally wailed.

Archie's face hardened. 'Good God! What are you saying, Beatrice! Do you mean that you gave that little ponce my foreskin?'

'Oh, Archie! Please don't! I knew you'd be upset. But you must know that I'd never do anything like that. He has it because he stole it! When I showed it to him in the collection, he reached down and snatched it out of the cabinet drawer before I could do anything. I couldn't go to the director, Archie, I just couldn't,' Beatrice wailed again. 'It was just too embarrassing.'

Archie had no idea how he found his way back to Dithers' rooms. He was so upset he could barely speak. Dithers, assuming that Beatrice continued to remain distant, and having run out of ideas, left Archie to his silence.

So it was true, Archie told himself. Beatrice *had* been seeing Giles while he was away. Had she kissed him? Or maybe gone further? He found himself shaking with rage. It was as if the top of his skull had been lifted off and a green poison poured into his brain. A poison that suffused his vision and coloured every thought and action. A poison that made Beatrice seem at once desirable and detestable.

To top it all off, the little ponce had his foreskin. A terrible suspicion began to form in Archie's mind. What could Mordant possibly want with the thing? Then he remembered Griffon. Did the director know of his circumcision? Was Mordant working for him, and might his foreskin end up on the fetish, with his skull to follow?

The only alternative explanation was that Mordant was out to embarrass him—to make Archie look like something out of a circus sideshow. He could just imagine it: 'Step up, step up and see the man who proposed to his girl with his foreskin!' Perhaps Mordant was displaying the thing to some squealing hussy right now. Or, horror of horrors, maybe he was showing it around the museum. The thought that the people he worked with could be gawking and pawing at it unmanned him. Archie choked with revulsion as he lay in his bed. Endless scenes of mockery played out in his mind. Perhaps even Nellie at the Maori's Head had seen it! It was all too much. What a total idiot he had been.

He knew he must get his foreskin back. But if his suspicion that Mordant was in cahoots with the director was correct, he would have to be very careful indeed.

Chapter 12

Abotomy found Dithers at his desk, examining a series of small bats through a hand lens.

'Understand you're a bit stuck, old fellow?'

Dithers sprang to attention. 'Yes, sir. A combination of unfortunate circumstances. But I'll soon be off to British East Africa to secure your lion and zebra.'

'As it happens, I could do with your help out at Abotomy Park. We're having a *battué*, and a fellow who knows how to do a little stuffing could be of use.

'A *battué*?'

'Shooting the fauna off the place, you know. For the museum.'

The news put Courtenay Dithers in a quandary. There was no doubt that the specimens could be valuable. Abotomy Park was located in one of the biologically richest and least explored regions of New South Wales. But what of his position as treasurer of the Society for the Preservation of Native Animals? Its members might look askance at his participation in a *battué*.

'Umm, Mr Abotomy…'

'It's Abumley, Dithers, but Chumley will do between us.'

'Thank you, er, Chumley, I'm a little unsure…'

'Man, don't talk twaddle! Vere Griffon insisted on your participation. He'll be severely disappointed if you don't come.'

'I see,' replied Dithers. 'How long do you think the *battué* will take?'

'Be away for a few weeks, I expect.'

'When do you leave?'

'Tomorrow morning. You can stay with me tonight. We'll set off early.'

That afternoon Dithers packed his bags and left a note on Archie's bed saying that he'd had to depart urgently, on director's orders, and would be away for 'some time'. He remembered that he'd booked tickets on a steamer to Cape Town the following week. Now he would have to delay his African adventure once again.

'You'll enjoy the crowd,' Abotomy said, as he loaded Dithers' luggage into his Rolls Royce Phantom II Sports Saloon. 'We country folk are a sociable lot, and I'm sure Portia will appreciate your company. She gets a bit glum up on the farm by herself.'

The sun was at its zenith as they drove through the Blue Mountains. An hour or two later, Abotomy pulled into the Hydro Majestic Hotel. Perched at the edge of a vertiginous cliff, almost on the summit of the mountains, it resembled a sumptuous palace.

Dithers stepped from the car and breathed deeply. Humus, oak. The crisp, cool mountain air soothed him. When he saw his suite, he was astonished. It consisted of a bedroom, lounge room and a most extravagant bathroom, all exquisitely appointed. He'd seen nothing like it since the Savoy years ago. By the bed he found a catalogue offering a range of hydropathic treatments. Drawings of languorous women, draped in nightwear or up to their necks in bubbles, adorned the pages. And there were advertisements, too, for various 'electric therapies' which were not illustrated, but were evidently meant for those with nervous complaints.

That evening, after soaking in the bath, Dithers met Abotomy in the Hydro's dining room. He mentioned the electric therapies.

'Well, you're most welcome to try one, Dithers old chap,' Abotomy said with a wry smile.

'Why, thank you, Chumley. But what are they?'

'Don't suppose you know much about farm animals, do you? More an expert on wild beasts. Well, if you leave a mare without a stallion for too long, she grows edgy. Same as a cow without a bull. Women are no different. And these damn quack doctors have got onto it. They get to work with a bit of electrical fiddling and before you know it the womanly nerviness vanishes! Damn cunning. And damn rum too, if you ask me. I'd never let Portia near the place, though she's at me often enough for a holiday here.'

'How the other half live!' thought Dithers as he blushed into his soup.

First light saw the Phantom again heading westwards, the great vista of the inland plains open before it. Dithers had not appreciated how far beyond the black stump Abotomy Park was. Or how poor the roads of the outback were.

'It stretches on forever,' Dithers gasped. He had no idea of the extent of the country.

'Yes, indeed. And the soil's pretty good in parts. If it weren't for the droughts it would be the best country in the world, my grandfather used to say.'

As the countryside drifted by, Abotomy explained to Dithers how the museum intended to make an exchange for the Giglione goats. Prudently, he omitted mention of the thylacines. It seemed to Dithers that Abotomy was a splendid sort of chap, truly passionate about science and the welfare of the museum. Abotomy even took a keen interest in the distributions of Australasian bats—a subject Dithers was working up a report on, and which hitherto had aroused little curiosity, even among his fellow curators.

'Are there any dangers in the outback?' Dithers asked, thinking it best to have a little local knowledge.

'We have our fair share of spiders and snakes, but nothing a man of your experience couldn't handle.'

'Spiders?' echoed Dithers. Since childhood he had had a phobia about them: he could front a charging lion without blanching, but there was something about large, hairy spiders that terrified him.

'You don't like them, Dithers? Don't worry. There are very few at Abotomy Park.'

Dithers was keen to change the subject. 'Has the director

told you how he plans to exhibit the African mammals I'll bring back?'

'No, nothing as yet. Old Vere's been a blank page on that. What do you think, Dithers?'

'I did have visions of a grand diorama. Perhaps as part of a new mammals hall.'

'What do you mean, a diorama?'

'Have you ever seen the exhibits of fauna at the museum in London? Their lion are displayed magnificently. The pride sit on a grassy slope below a kopje. The rocks in the foreground are real, but those behind are painted. You can't tell where the real grass and rocks end and the painted ones begin. Looking at it, you really feel you're there on the veldt.'

'I see what you mean, old chap. A great maned male in the foreground, female and cubs at his feet. Yes, it could be very stirring.'

'There's a real trick to making a diorama, Chumley. In them, you'll never see animals as they are in nature. You might see a pride of lion on the veldt, but you'll never see the hyenas as close to them as they are in a diorama. Or the warthog and gerenuk. Dioramas beguile you into believing they represent the wild as it is. But they present things as we'd like them to be. They're as much artifice as science.'

'Hmm. I wonder if Vere would be interested in a diorama of Abotomy Park?'

'Well, the creatures of the western plains are fascinating. And fast disappearing. I imagine that if you mentioned it to him, he might.'

'If he did, I'd like to include myself and Portia in the work.

Perhaps painted into the background. Portia should be shown eight months bubbly, and myself with my shotgun. Might be fun.'

'Is Portia pregnant, Chumley?'

'Yes, dear chap. Sorry I forgot to mention it. Early days, but we're hoping for the best. After all, she's from excellent stock. The Clarks have a great pedigree, and Portia is a Yarck Clark. Seat of the family. True currency aristocracy. Not a broad arrow or touch of the tar-brush as far back as they can trace. Purity of race, Dithers. Tremendously important in breeding. One must guard it with one's life.'

'Congratulations! Excellent news, old fellow,' said Dithers, deciding to ignore the last part of the conversation. 'I just hope that Portia doesn't resent the intrusion of a stranger at such a time.'

'Don't worry about that, Dithers. All will be taken care of.'

By afternoon Dithers was beginning to tire. The plains were so endless and bleached that it felt to him as if the car had been crawling over them like an ant across a tabletop. When he asked how far it was to Abotomy Park, he heard himself sounding like a child on a long journey.

'A while yet, old chap. Should reach the place by tomorrow afternoon. Can't drive at night in these parts, you know. Too many kangaroos. We'll pull up at Barrunbuttock.'

Just before dusk the Rolls swerved off the road and down a track towards a low, ramshackle homestead. Two date palms stood in the middle of what had once been extensive flower beds. A flight of decayed wooden steps led to a verandah, on which swung a painted wooden board bearing the property's name. From the cobwebs and dust, Courtenay could see that the front door was never used. Chumley guided him towards a rear entry, explaining as they went that Barrunbuttock was the ancestral pile of the Bastion family.

A flyscreen door led directly into the kitchen. In the galley stood Horatio Bastion himself. Fifty-something, dusty, lean, and with hollowed cheeked, he was dressed in bowyangs, a checked shirt and a battered fedora. He'd clearly come in from a hard day's work.

The men seated themselves at an unadorned dinner table boasting three plates of boiled potatoes and corned beef. A kerosene tin with its top hacked off, which might once have served as a vase, was the room's only ornament—apart from a pair of muddy hobnail boots by the door. The place hadn't seen a woman for some time, Dithers concluded.

'Hard work breeding sheep out here,' Bastion exclaimed. 'Between the pear, the fly strike and the pizzle rot, I've lost half my flock this year. It's no fun handling maggoty sheep and slitting pizzles on my wethers. The poor bastards can't piss, the rot's that thick. I tell you, Chumley, it's not fit work for a man of my position. But I've got no money to pay wages, so what bloody choice do I have?

'The worst of it, though, is the blasted pear. Bloody thing's just about got me buggered. It won't burn, and not a thing'll eat it. The growth's that thick over the home paddock I can't get a horse through it.'

Dithers was confused. Talk of pears had brought to mind scenes of orchards and pleasant country arbours. But Horatio could not be talking about that kind of pear. Then he remembered the *Opuntia*, known colloquially as the prickly pear. It was a kind of cactus that had been imported from South America as a garden ornamental because it bore sweet, fig-sized, very prickly fruit. It had found Australian conditions very much to its liking. So much so that it had become, alongside the rabbit, the greatest plague the country had ever seen.

Horatio Bastion had stopped eating. His eyes filled with water and his face flushed. 'Honest, mate, I'm that far down on my luck that even the bloody Abos have taken to pitying me. "Close-up flyblown, that one," they say as they walk past with their fingers stuck up their nostrils—as if I were a stinking fly-struck sheep!'

Bastion looked at his plate, then filled his mouth with corned beef. 'How's the pear up your way, old son?'

'Doesn't seem to thrive in the river soils. Hard to believe that a damn cactus could be such a menace.'

'You just wait till you spend your evenings pulling spines out of your backside, like I do. Then you'll know how bloody bad it is.'

'So sorry to hear it,' said Abotomy, avoiding Horatio's eyes.

'Ah well, nothing that can be done about it anyway. Leastways not this evening.' Bastion gave the faintest of smiles. 'But I must say it's good to have company! The wife's off in Sydney, spending my last pennies, no doubt. Maybe even pennies I don't have. And bloody good riddance to her.'

After dinner they retired to what had once been a fine drawing room. Bastion struck up a pipe, while Abotomy offered the port he'd brought from Sydney.

'Haven't enjoyed a port since you were last through, old

chum. By God, it's good to see you! It can get lonely out here.'

'And good to see you too, Horatio. Very kind of you to put us up.'

'You know, Chumley, my great grandfather, Elias Bastion, could have had that river frontage of yours. Legend has it that he drove his flocks into what is now Abotomy Park, but the river blacks wanted to fight him for it. He wasn't hard enough to clear them off. In fact, Grandad told me that Elias liked the blackfellas. Always treated them decently. So when the Jigalong tribe suggested that he settle with them, he came here to Barrunbuttock.'

'Less sensitive types tried to clean the place up after your great-grandfather left,' said Abotomy, 'but the blacks kept disappearing into the brigalow. Stuff wouldn't burn, so they couldn't flush 'em out. You know how Grandfather Ebenezer dealt with that, don't you? Hired a hundred convicts, organised the black police to visit, and then starved the warrigal blackfellas out. The family records say he shot well over a hundred off the place before the remnant agreed to go to the mission.'

'We stand on the shoulders of giants,' said Horatio, with only the slightest hint of irony. 'At least some of us do, anyway.'

Dithers was shocked. Was Abotomy describing mass murder? He said nothing as he refilled his glass and rolled another durry.

Later that evening Horatio explained to Dithers how the Bastion family had originally come up country from Wagga Wagga, telling the curator that the town was named after the call of the crow. '*Wgaar, wgaar*,' he warbled slowly—assuming the cry would interest a man of science. But Dithers was tired with a weariness far deeper than that born of travel. Thoughts of the country's terrible history flowed about him like the first muddy waters of a great flood. He made his apologies and went to bed, leaving the squatters to the last of the port.

Dithers awoke, as if emerging from the abyss, to the sound of a distant hum. It was, he eventually concluded, caused by the rising sun as its rays heated the plains. He wearily pulled on his trousers and socks, then tried to get his shoes on, but, inexplicably, they seemed to be several sizes too small. He just couldn't get his heel in.

After several attempts he heard a giggle at the door. Looking up, he saw Abotomy peeking through a crack. Dithers reached into his shoes—and extracted a crumpled ball of newspaper from each. By the time he'd tied his laces, Abotomy had vanished.

Dithers decided to say nothing. He climbed into the Rolls, and when he opened his eyes after a brief nap, the plain still stretched on forever. It was as if they were standing still: the shadows of the gums shortened, then lengthened again, but nothing else changed.

As the sun sank low, a glint of green appeared on the horizon. Abotomy turned the Phantom off the dirt road, through a gate, and up a track lined with a splendid white post-and-rail fence and an avenue of newly planted elm saplings that cast shadows across the road. At the foot of a line of low hills Dithers could make out a habitation. As they neared it he beheld a scene of great industry. A mansion was rising in classic grandeur from the Australian landscape, and around it lakes, lawns and pleasure grounds were all taking shape.

They had reached Abotomy Hall.

Chapter 13

Dithers got out of the car and stretched his cramped legs. One wing of the mansion was already complete, and on its expansive verandah sat Portia Abotomy. Barefoot and in a white, ankle-length dress, from a distance she reminded him of an odalisque from a romantic biblical painting. As he neared, he could see that she was hot, bored and just beginning to show. She smiled shyly at the dashing visitor.

'How's things, old stick?' said Abotomy.

It was clear that he was not going to introduce Dithers. The curator turned to Portia. 'Madam, I'm Dr Courtenay Dithers, mammalogist at the museum. Congratulations on your news. Chumley told me in the car. I assure you that I'll be as little bother as possible.'

'Grab your luggage, old chap.' Abotomy opened the boot, retrieving two parcels wrapped in cloth. 'Now, what do you make of this statue, and this rather queer piece? Thought it might provide a bit of fun for the men after dinner.'

Dithers felt that the statue was mediocre—possibly a recent copy of the Venus de Medici. The bronze, though, was an exquisite piece of workmanship, if rather obscene.

'Oh, darling, you remembered! How very thoughtful!' exclaimed Portia, doubtfully eyeing the phallus.

'Not entirely sure I got a good deal. But I'm glad you like them, dear.'

'I'm no expert,' Dithers chimed in. 'But if you would like a valuation the best fellow is Harvey Herringbone-Trout, professor of classical archaeology at Sydney University. I'm sure he'd be delighted to assist a member of the museum board.'

'Hmm. I'll take them back to town so he can have a look,' said Abotomy.

The dining room was grand, with a high ceiling and curtained sash windows along the wall opening onto the verandah. On the opposite wall a low walnut crockery cabinet formed a shelf at waist height. Above it hung elaborately framed, rather poor copies of Elizabethan and Restoration portraits.

'Meet the family,' Abotomy said, gesturing towards them.

'I had no idea you could trace the line back to the sixteenth century,' exclaimed Dithers.

'Right back to the Conquest, actually. Some of the gents in the paintings may not be in the direct line, exactly, but they give the general idea. Picked 'em up on our honeymoon.' He winked at Dithers.

Portia served an excellent roast lamb dinner, complete with vegetables from the garden. The wine had evidently been sourced on the European tour.

'I haven't eaten like this since mother cooked for us before the war,' Courtenay said wistfully.

'Mr Dithers, did you grow up in London?' asked Portia.

'We had a London house, but Kent was really home.'

'So your family had an estate?' Portia asked.

'Not a great one. But we never lacked for anything. And my parents—one couldn't have asked for better, really. But that all changed with the war, as I suppose it did here.'

'I lost more uncles and cousins than I can bear thinking about, Mr Dithers.'

'And I brothers,' said Dithers. 'All three of them. My parents never got over it.'

'Our family got off rather more lightly,' Abotomy broke in. 'Someone had to supply the meat. And the wool. Crucial part of the war effort, you know.'

After dinner, Portia led Dithers to the guest bedroom.

'I'm sorry that the guest bathroom is not yet plumbed. So it will have to be the outhouse, I'm afraid.'

Dithers removed his clothes, fell into bed, and was instantly asleep. He woke soon after dawn, deeply refreshed. After removing the balls of newspaper from his shoes, which were becoming a fixture, and enjoying a fortifying gasper, he walked across the frosted grass towards the ancient bark dunny, which Portia had euphemistically called the outhouse. Set among discarded tin sheeting and timber in the home paddock, it was accessed by a path the length of a cricket pitch. He closed the door. The walls were made of bark, and the toilet seat was roughly cut from an old hollow log. He unhitched his trousers and sat on the throne, and something caught his eye—a slow movement on the inside of the door. It was the leg of a great, hairy huntsman spider, camouflaged against the wood. Aghast, Dithers realised that it was the size of a dinner plate. As his eyes adjusted to the gloom he saw that every surface was covered with the creatures. There were dozens of them. He hitched up his trousers and fled, unaccomplished.

After breakfast, Dithers asked Abotomy if he might explore the area.

'Best not to go too far from the homestead, old chap. The brigalow, wilga and leopardwood are thick hereabouts, as are the taipans and tiger snakes. I can't spare a man to guide you. You'd be doing me a great favour if you stuck to the home paddock. Portia's got an interest in birds. Maybe you could do a bit of birdspotting with her?'

That afternoon a rather costive Dithers set out across the paddock with Portia, who was armed with an enormous pair of binoculars. The bush behind the homestead was badly knocked about. Barbed wire and other rubbish made the going a little hazardous. But there were plenty of birds. Quite near the house they saw a family of blue wrens, the brilliant markings of the male almost metallic in the sun. The little fellow was so bold and sprightly that he made Portia laugh. She reached into her pocket for a few crumbs, and scattered them at her feet. To Dithers' amazement, the creature came right up to her, its tail swinging from side to side as it pecked at the offering.

'I'm worried for the birds, Courtenay,' she lamented. 'This

battué could wipe out a lot of them.'

They walked back to the verandah, picking their way between piles of discarded kerosene drums, sheets of tin, and timber. 'I wish Chumley would get the men to clean it up,' Portia said, pointing to the debris. 'It attracts snakes, and I'm terrified of them. Especially with the baby coming.'

The *battué*, it transpired, was a major undertaking. Nets had to be put in place, beaters gathered from the surrounding stations, and invitations sent to the local squattocracy. Dithers found himself with time on his hands. But what pleasures there were in Abotomy Hall! He revelled in the leisurely mornings spent lazing in his double bed with its silk sheets and eider-filled duvet. Through the wide French doors he could watch the changing shades of the Australian landscape as the sun rose.

And Portia was, if anything, too hospitable. She would invariably bring him breakfast in bed, then perch on the edge of the mattress and chat with him as he sipped his coffee and ate his fried eggs. The cooking must have been a priority for her, he thought, for she would arrive in her nightdress and dressing-gown, from which her full breasts seemed determined to escape. They provided, Dithers secretly thought, the most splendid sight of the entire property.

'Courtenay, what's happening in Sydney these days? What are the fashions at David Jones?' Portia asked, her black eyes opening wider than ever. 'And *pleaase* tell me about the opening of the harbour bridge. Was it really as fabulous as the radio reports made out?'

Courtenay was so touched by her yearning for the city that he invented things to entertain her: the scent of a perfume he'd detected in the crowd at the bridge opening, and a visit by a foreign dignitary to the museum. He described in detail the dresses, entertainments and chatter of the big smoke.

'Oh, Courtenay, I miss it all so much,' Portia exclaimed after one particularly vivid account. Leaning against him, she seemed almost to swoon.

It was, unfortunately, at this precise moment that Chumley Abotomy sauntered past the French windows. Portia did not see him, but Dithers caught the steel in his eyes.

That evening at dinner, Abotomy seemed to be in the best of spirits. 'Early morning tomorrow, old chap,' he said to Dithers after the meal. 'Need your help with a job. Got to lighten off a horse.'

Dithers rose at dawn, and was a little surprised to find his shoes innocent of paper balls. He met Abotomy in the parlour, dressed in his work clothes. 'Delighted to help with the unloading, old thing,' Courtenay said, 'but don't you have hired help for that sort of work?'

'There are some jobs, Dithers, that the man of the house must do himself,' Chumly replied grimly as they walked towards the stockyards. 'Like defending a wife's reputation.' He looked Dithers straight in the eye. This alarmed the curator, who felt that perhaps Abotomy had read too much into what he'd observed through the French windows.

They were now at the stockyard, where a beautiful black stallion was tied to a fence post. Two workers sat on their haunches beside a small fire. As Abotomy approached, they jumped into the enclosure, and threw the horse onto its side.

'Come here, Dithers. I want you to see this.'

The men tied the horse's legs. Abotomy crouched beside the creature and grasped its silken black scrotum in his left hand. To Courtenay's horror, the squire took a blade from his pocket and cut deeply into the bulging purse. In a moment it was over. Two bloody spheres lay in the dust beside the screaming beast.

'First and only warning, Dithers. If I ever see you near Portia again, I'll take the greatest pleasure in slicing *your* balls out with this knife.'

Abotomy stomped off to breakfast, leaving Dithers stunned. A cur shot from the shadows, wolfed down the severed organs, and fled growling into the half-light.

Chapter 14

After this singular incident, Abotomy showed nothing but civility to his guest. But Dithers couldn't relax. There was the problem with Portia, and the problem with the dunny. His perpetually costive state left him in a sort of delirium, and whatever sleep he found was filled with bizarre dreams. He would often close his eyes only to find himself wandering an enormous toilet block, inside which was hundreds of cubicles. He'd enter one to find that there was no toilet paper. Another lacked a seat, while another had no toilet bowl at all. But worst were the cubicles filled with spiders, or those in which Abotomy crouched, grinning maliciously, knife in hand. Dithers would wake with a whimper, grasping his crotch and wishing desperately for relief. Somehow, most mornings, the newspaper would be there in his shoes. He had no idea how Abotomy got into his room without waking him. What had started as an odd practical joke began to take on a terrifying aspect.

One morning Dithers awoke in the predawn light to a peculiar sound: '*Faark, faark, faaaarkkkkkkk.*' Was it the dying cry of a foul-mouthed shearer?

'My feelings exactly, old chap,' he said as a large black bird flapped away.

Over breakfast he mentioned the strange call to Portia, who told him that it was the cry of the little crow.

'Oh,' said Dithers. 'I'd been told that the crow sounds like *Wagaa, wagaa.*'

'That,' Portia replied, 'sounds like the Australian raven to me. You find it further east. Our crows are not so civilised.'

She was secretly pleased to discover that Dithers was taking an interest in the feathered tribes.

The evening before the *battué*, men began arriving at Abotomy Park. The entire district had been invited. A few of the men (and the visitors were almost all men) wore suits of varying vintages and states of repair, but the majority were dungareed and check-shirted, their sartorial elegance extending at best to the occasional neckerchief. A beast had been slaughtered and an enormous roast sizzled in the oven. Cauldrons filled with boiled pumpkin and potatoes, and piles of tinned peas completed the feast. As the multitudes gathered on the verandah, beer, cooled in a Coolgardie safe, flowed freely.

'I hear you're a curator?' asked an arrogant-looking young fellow, who had already downed several beers.

'Yes,' replied Dithers. 'I'm here to assist Mr Abotomy with the preparation of scientific specimens. What's your name?'

'Duggerton, Denis Duggerton. We don't see your type out here too often. You can start your collectin' with the wild dogs. And the blacks, though the pioneers did a pretty good job with them in this district.'

'So I hear.'

'My family shot sixty bucks off the property. The does and pikininis got away, but we got 'em all later, with damper. The whole mob were feasting on stolen sheep.'

'That, sir, is murder. Foul murder.'

'It had to be done. Our forebears dealt with them and the wild dogs the same way. Shooting and poisoning. Just put the strychnine in a dead beast, rather than a sack of flour. If it hadn't been done not a sheep would be left alive. And our claims to the land might have been doubted.'

Dithers thought back on the prickly pear, rabbits and foxes that afflicted the country. It was as if the land itself had been poisoned and was vomiting up great plagues of bile in its distress. But these colonials were surely the most pernicious plague of them all.

'I am astonished that anything has survived your campaign of extermination,' Dithers replied.

'Not much has. Nowadays the wild blacks have been pushed back as far as the Alice, and the dingoes are pretty thin this side of the Darling. If it wasn't for do-gooders like you, we'd have finished off the lot of them long ago.'

Duggerton walked off in search of another drink. Bastion, who had been listening, caught Dithers' eye. He led him to a quiet corner.

'My grandfather always said the blacks shot by old man Duggerton were the bravest souls that ever lived. They stood their ground against nine armed whites on horseback, for well over an hour. They fell one after another, giving the women and children time to get away. The last man standing died facing the foe, a spear hafted in his woomera, ready to let fly. They were braver than the Spartans, Grandad reckoned.'

The dinner gong sounded, and the men crowded around a trestle table stacked with food. Each took a plate and stood where he could on the verandah, wolfing down the tucker. As the crockery was cleared, Duggerton produced a violin. The strains of 'The Lime-juice Tub' were accompanied by wild cries, clapping and stomping, and soon the men were dancing jigs and reels. Portia and Chumley even managed a round to one of the more sedate tunes, to the applause of all.

At ten o'clock Abotomy cried out, 'Men! Port and cigars in the smoking room!'

Dithers had no wish to follow. He went to his bed as guffaws and sniggers emanated from the room. The shooters were presumably admiring Abotomy's antiquities.

When Dithers woke in the morning, he knew he could not participate in the *battué* before emptying his bowels. And that meant facing the spiders. Perhaps if he closed his eyes, he thought, he could relax sufficiently to perform in that den of venomous, eight-legged horrors. He made his way towards the dismal structure, opened the door, shut his eyes, and sat down. With growing anticipation he remembered the need for paper. Was there any in the place? He opened his eyes a crack. An old newspaper, ripped into squares and hung by a string from a nail on the back of the door. He went to grab a sheet, just to be ready, when he saw, crouched on its reverse side, the most horrid, hairy spider he'd ever encountered. He leapt up, throwing the sheet to the ground. Then the outhouse exploded.

The sound was still ringing in Dithers's ears when he realised that he was painted with the contents of the can. Yet he was euphoric, for the shock of the explosion had finally loosened his bowels.

The door to the outhouse slowly opened—to reveal Portia Abotomy. She was dressed in her night attire, and was holding a shotgun.

'Oh, Courtenay!' she gasped. 'My dear Courtenay! What have I done?'

Dithers found himself following Portia, trying to raise his fallen trousers with one hand and covering his bespattered privates with the other. She led him into a most splendid marble bathroom, where he showered. Portia fetched clean clothes. He was drying himself when he heard her call his name.

'Courtenay, I'm so terribly sorry!' she wailed. 'But I saw a black snake—a horrid thing as thick as your forearm—crawl into the hatch at the rear of the outhouse. It's been eating the chickens, I'm sure. So I took the shotgun that Chumley leaves at the back door, and fired at it. I had no idea that you were inside! I wouldn't mind at all if you used the main bathroom, whatever Chumley says.'

Dithers stepped out of the shower, a towel around his waist. 'Don't worry, Portia. Accidents happen. And, strangely enough, this one probably did me more good than harm.'

'But I could have killed you!' Portia wailed, grasping him in a terrific hug—just as Abotomy turned the corner.

'Say what? Portia, what was that shot?'

As Portia tried to explain things Dithers slipped away. Being trouserless in such circumstances left him feeling at a distinct disadvantage.

Dithers dressed in a state of high anxiety and walked to the verandah, where he pulled on his boots. He had never run from anything before, but he'd decided that as soon as the *battué* was over he would cadge a lift out of Abotomy Park. When in Sydney he would explain to Abotomy that he had been urgently summoned to the museum. As he plotted his escape a workman carrying a gunny sack dismounted from a swaybacked nag and walked up the steps of the verandah. He emptied the sack in a corner, revealing a pile of human skulls. Some had wet soil still adhered to them. Despite the dirt, Dithers could see round holes—bullet holes—in several.

Up until that moment the massacres Dithers had heard about were something abstract. But here was physical evidence of indiscriminate murder. If Britain had consumed her finest in the Great War, this revolting country had been born in butchery, in massacres so vile and craven as to defile all humanity. Massacres that were boasted of, even joked about.

The truth hit Dithers like a sledgehammer. Those skulls would not be given a decent burial. They were destined for a museum: his institution, to be labelled, studied and traded.

Studied, that is, for everything except forensic evidence of murder. The workman handed Dithers the bridle of the nag, saying, 'Here's your horse. For the *battué*.'

Stunned, Dithers mounted and rode away from the house to join the others at the gate.

The *battué* was itself a sort of massacre. Although it was not yet eight o'clock in the morning, several of the riders were dead drunk. They charged into the scrub as workers beat the bushes and clanged pots and pans, forcing all sorts of animals to flee towards the rabble, where they were gunned down en masse. Koalas and possums that climbed out of their trees to flee the noise were shot and shot again, or torn to pieces by dogs. Scores of wallabies and kangaroos were driven from their thickets into the arms of the shooters, and rare parrots fell from the sky by the dozen, bleeding as they landed in the dust—something Dithers resolved never to tell Portia about. As Courtenay watched from his horse, appalled, an excited yokel raced past, dangling a mangled body.

'What's this, do you think, curator?'

It was, Courtenay realised, the remains of a banner-tailed rat-kangaroo, the rarest of marsupials. Perhaps it was the last of its species. It could have been a valuable specimen, but it had been shot almost to pieces and so was virtually worthless.

As he looked at it, and at the drunken farmhand carrying it off, the *battué*, the dreadful business with the stallion, and the skulls all became too much. In an instant Courtenay Dithers understood that his sanity could be preserved only by immediate action. He turned his horse towards Abotomy Hall and did not stop galloping until he'd reached an outlying shed. There, an old bicycle leaned against a wall. He jumped on, determined not to stop pedalling until he'd reached the nearest town.

For several nights Dithers slept rough beside the track. He'd slept rougher in the trenches, he reminded himself. But by the time he arrived at Narromine, over two hundred miles away, he was more mud-spattered, and had a sorer posterior, than he'd ever imagined possible. He headed straight to the railway station, where, to his immense relief, he found a police sergeant on the platform.

'Sorry to bother you, old chap, but could I ask for a bit of assistance?'

'Bugger off. I'm not locking you up,' the policeman said. 'I can only take a dozen, and I reckon there'll be at least fifty on the next train.'

'What do you mean? Incarceration?' asked Dithers, taken aback.

'They come up from Sydney and I give them four days in the cells. After that they're on the wallaby, mate. Nothing more I can do for them. My wife cooks for them, and gets an allowance for it, too. These poor buggers won't have seen a square meal for weeks, so they'll be fighting to get into the clink, I can tell you.'

'Sergeant, I'm not requesting incarceration. Only a little assistance returning this bicycle to its owner. Do you think you might see it taken back to Abotomy Hall?'

The sergeant's demeanour changed. 'I'm sure one of the Sydney scrubbers will be only too grateful. Better than walking. Might even score a meal at Abotomy Hall as a reward.'

The train was now pulling in. Men in rags—some with rope holding up their trousers, others with singlets but no shirts, and some even lacking shoes—spilled out of the carriages. They began to besiege the policeman. 'Sergeant O'Reilly. Gov'nor. Sarge!' It was a cacophony of voices. 'Can you put us in the lockup for a few nights? I can cut and split wood,' said one man, who was little more than a walking skeleton and coughing badly. 'I'm good for as much work as you see fit,' he begged. The misery of the Great Depression in Woolloomooloo was nothing compared with this, Dithers thought. He purchased a ticket and boarded the train, vowing never to see Narromine, Abotomy Hall, or its owner again.

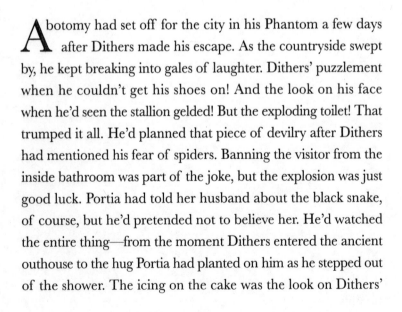

Chapter 15

Abotomy had set off for the city in his Phantom a few days after Dithers made his escape. As the countryside swept by, he kept breaking into gales of laughter. Dithers' puzzlement when he couldn't get his shoes on! And the look on his face when he'd seen the stallion gelded! But the exploding toilet! That trumped it all. He'd planned that piece of devilry after Dithers had mentioned his fear of spiders. Banning the visitor from the inside bathroom was part of the joke, but the explosion was just good luck. Portia had told her husband about the black snake, of course, but he'd pretended not to believe her. He'd watched the entire thing—from the moment Dithers entered the ancient outhouse to the hug Portia had planted on him as he stepped out of the shower. The icing on the cake was the look on Dithers'

face when Abotomy appeared. The poor fellow's tossle must have shrunk to the size of his little finger! How Abotomy had stopped himself from collapsing in hysterics, he did not know.

Neighbours had kept the squire informed of Dithers' travels. And when the swagman returned the bike, Abotomy knew the curator was safe. The jest, he reflected, had done a wonder of good. Portia had seemed to go off sex as the pregnancy progressed, but now she was positively kittenish—perhaps to appease him. And Dithers, bless him, *had* given him the name of that expert on antiquities. He hadn't entirely trusted Bunkdom. But before he visited Herringbone-Trout he must deliver his haul of specimens to Vere Griffon. And he wanted to beat Dithers back to the museum.

'Delighted, old chap, to have you back,' the director said. 'And even more delighted to see that you've succeeded in procuring specimens. I do hope Dithers proved useful?'

A thundercloud crossed Abotomy's face, the intensity of which alarmed Vere Griffon. 'Young whelp was sniffing around Portia. *And* he went missing without leave,' Abotomy growled.

'I'm shocked, Chumley. Deeply shocked. Dithers is no deserter. He was decorated in the war, you know. Highly decorated. And he's a Christ's College man, like myself. Are you sure there's no misunderstanding?'

'Portia did say it was all a colossal mistake. But then, she would. Still, if I so much as catch him anywhere near her again, I'll have his balls for breakfast. Make sure you tell him that, Vere!'

'I'll have a word,' said Griffon. 'But I can't believe that a man like Dithers would cause offence in any way, at least not intentionally. After all, he is so supremely grateful to you for funding his Africa venture.'

'Well, never mind that.'

'In any case, Dithers' absence has been a godsend. I've had control over the mammal collection and have selected three Tasmanian tigers for exchange with Giglione. Given the state of his office, I suspect it will be some time before Dithers misses them. They're in my safe, along with the Bathurst meteorite, awaiting shipment.'

'Splendid, old chap!' replied Abotomy, who saw they had almost everything required in exchange for the goats.

'Now, let's see what you bagged,' said Griffon, gesturing towards the crates that the storeman Gormley was stacking in the middle of the boardroom floor.

Chumley unscrewed the smallest box first. 'Rare parrots,' he said conspiratorially. When the top was removed, row upon row of salted skins were revealed. 'Alexandra parrots on top. Then paradise parrots. We only got two of them. Haven't been seen in years, you know—might well be the last pair in existence,' he crowed.

The director became solemn. 'Oh dear. Rare birds indeed, Chumley. But just look at the state of them. This one looks like it's been downed with No. 3 shot: great holes in it everywhere. And who did the skinning? The thing's been butchered! I expected better from Dithers!'

'As I said, Vere, Dithers did a bunk. But old Giglione won't care! He's a decent sort of fellow and will understand that one sometimes has to accept less than perfect specimens. Especially if they're rare. But he'll love the blackfellows. Got seven in the end. All ages and sizes.'

Abotomy opened the largest crate, revealing the skulls his workmen had unearthed. Vere Griffon took one out, noted the bullet hole in its forehead, and replaced it in silence.

Half an hour after Abotomy's departure, Archie's heart chilled. Dryandra Stritchley had summoned him, and once again he found himself in Vere Griffon's inner sanctum.

'Meek, I need eight native skulls. In perfect condition. Or as close as possible. Select them from the collection, and bring them to me.'

Despite his best efforts to mask his feelings, there was something in Archie's manner that revealed his loathing. He was clearly reluctant to act.

'Meek, you are a curator. Almost one, anyway,' Griffon said as he began to pace back and forth. 'A high priest of science. And I am your director. For God's sake, imagine where we'd be today if we returned to a mumbo-jumbo, superstitious approach to human anatomy? Just a century ago medicine was terrifically impeded by religious objections. Human bones must be studied, and sent to experts. As a museum employee, you will do your duty. Now go!'

At six o'clock that evening the train pulled into Central Station. Dithers had slept most of the way, but hardly felt refreshed. It was already dark by the time he reached his digs in Stanley Street. The door to his room swung open and Dithers, his hair matted and clothing torn, lurched in. Archie sprang to his feet.

'Thank God! Dithers, I thought you were dead!'

'I've no idea what you mean, old fellow,' Dithers said wearily. 'I left a note. But before I say another word, I must shower and change.'

Archie sat on the edge of his bed, waiting for what seemed an eternity. Dithers' note had hardly allayed his fears. On the contrary, its reference to departing urgently on director's orders had convinced him that his friend was in grave danger of becoming Griffon's next victim. As the days dragged by, Archie became more and more sure that Dithers was dead. Perhaps he wasn't too far wrong: the man looked like he'd just got out of a trench. Or a grave.

At length, Dithers returned in a clean set of clothes.

'I need a gasper,' he said. 'And a tot.' Dithers scrabbled under his bunk for a packet of black shag and a bottle, then rolled a durry in silence, lit up, downed his Scotch, and refilled the glass. 'Tell me, my boy, how have things been? With Beatrice, I mean.'

Archie, anxious as he was to hear about Dithers, divined that the man was not yet ready to talk about his absence. 'No progress, or very little, I should say. She's speaking to me, though not with much warmth.'

'Why, that's splendid, Archie! You've broken the ice.'

Dithers' enthusiasm meant little. Archie had pretty much given up on Beatrice becoming his lover. In the silence that followed he added, 'Perhaps. But something else has happened. Something odd. Griffon has asked me to bring him eight native skulls, from the collection. I've no idea why.'

'I think I can help there. Abotomy and Griffon are working

on an exchange. Abotomy is keen to secure a collection of goats—'

'Goats!' Archie broke in. 'Goats—for human skulls?' He could contain himself no longer. 'For God's sake, Dithers, where have you been, and how did you end up in such a state?'

'I've been to Abotomy Park. Things started out well enough. Then we stopped at Barrunbuttock where Horatio Bastion told me of the terrible history of the region and the role Chumley's grandfather played in it. I must admit, the horror of it shook me.'

'What do you mean?'

'The massacres, Archie! This country was born in blood and war. Thousands. No, tens of thousands were shot and poisoned by Australia's founding fathers. Out west they still talk about it.'

Until then Archie's view of Australian history had been all noble explorers and missionaries soothing the pillow of a dying race. His mind flashed to the museum's collection. Many skulls bore marks of injury. Could it be that all these years he'd been staring at evidence of systematic murder—and not recognised it? His head began to spin. He pulled back from the brink, forcing himself to concentrate on Dithers.

'But what happened to you?'

'A rum business, old chap. Chumley got it into his head that I was attracted to Portia.'

'Who is Portia?'

'His wife. She's pregnant. I tell you, Archie, she deserves better. The man actually threatened me.'

'Abotomy? Threatened you?'

'Yes. With a knife.'

'Good God, Courtenay! You mean he threatened your life?'

'Not quite, Archie. He threatened my manhood. To be frank, I'm damn lucky still to have my testicles.'

'I knew it!' Archie cried. 'Oh, the horror! Skulls, foreskins, testicles. The man's collecting organs. He's gone stark raving mad, and he's recruiting allies to do his dirty work.'

Courtenay gave his friend a questioning look, and then burst out laughing.

'You, my dear chap, are the anthropologist—the one with the collection of organs. Not our director.'

Archie felt ready to burst. 'Dithers. Don't you see it? Your life is in grave danger. He already has my foreskin. I sent it to Beatrice with my marriage proposal, island style, but Mordant stole it for him. And I have evidence that Griffon has murdered four of his curators for their skulls already. You are marked down to be the fifth.'

Dithers was stunned. 'Evidence. You say you have evidence. What is it?'

'The fetish, in the boardroom. Four of the skulls on it have been replaced. One, which has buck teeth, is Polkinghorne.'

A chill went down Dithers' spine. Griffon had been behaving oddly of late. That, at least, was clear. But Archie's ravings were over the top.

'Oh, I see I can't convince you until you discover things for yourself,' lamented Archie. 'But please, tell me that we'll look out for each other. We are both in grave danger, and we can't be sure where, or how, it will strike.'

The next morning saw Chumley Abotomy loitering at the entrance to the Nicholson Museum. The institution occupied one corner of the University of Sydney's famous 'quad', as the glorious sandstone quadrangle that lay at the heart of the institution was known. Chumley looked out of place in his country tweeds, holding a roughly wrapped statue under his arm and with a suspicious bulge in his trousers' pocket. Gaggles of bright young students drifted past on their way to their lectures, and one pretty girl so distracted him that he almost didn't spot the thin, long-nosed and short-sighted professor. Dressed in a dishevelled suit and brogues, Herringbone-Trout was bumbling along beside a line of glass cases inside the museum. His eyes, disappearing behind prodigiously thick lenses, were fixed on the vases behind the glass.

'I say, old chap, are you Herringbone-Trout, the antique expert?'

'Harvey Herringbone-Trout, professor of classical archaeology. You must be Mr Chumley Abotomy?'

'Abumley.'

'Quite so,' said the professor, peering at Abotomy's ruddy face.

'I've a couple of pieces I'd like your opinion on, Trout.'

'Herringbone-Trout, if you don't mind.'

'Hrumph. Double-barreller, eh? Now, what do you make of that?' asked Abotomy as he unwrapped the marble statue.

The professor examined it minutely, paying special attention to the feet.

'Copy. A poor one. Itself from a Roman copy, after a Greek statue of Aphrodite. Venus, if you like. That's the Roman name,' he said, without enthusiasm.

'Very good,' replied Abotomy, not entirely understanding what the professor was saying. 'And what do you make of this?' He groped in his trouser pocket.

The priapus came out head first, and was so lifelike that for an instant the professor averted his eyes. When he looked back, he was relieved to see that the object was bronze.

'Now, that's altogether more interesting,' he said when he'd regained his composure. 'A priapus. And a very good one at that.' Herringbone-Trout took the piece from Chumley's hand, drew a lens from his pocket, and studied it in detail. 'Remarkable. Remarkable indeed! It bears an astonishing resemblance to the one found in the House of the Gladiators at Pompeii. Could you come to my office, so that I can compare it with sketches I made in the Vatican Museum during my visit in 1923?'

The professor's office was high up in one of the towers bordering the quadrangle. It was filled with books and papers, among which were scattered fragments of antique pottery and statues, old coins and a few bones.

'Yes, here it is.' Herringbone-Trout pulled a large sketchpad from beneath a tower of documents. 'Look here, Abotomy. See that scratch? Looks remarkably similar to the one on your priapus, wouldn't you say? I very much fear, old chap, that the thing has been stolen from the Vatican.'

'Director, today's mail contains two items you must see immediately.' Miss Stritchley held the tray aloft.

'Very well, Dryandra. Would you mind reading them to me? My eyes are tired.'

'Of course, Director,' said Dryandra, trying to hide her satisfaction. She loved reading the correspondence to Vere. It made her feel so close to him. 'Sender: Dr Elizabeth Doughty. Postmarked: Ternate, May 15, 1933.'

> *Dear Director,*
>
> *Please find below the first, and most probably the final, report of the Doughty Spice Islands mineralogical expedition. I sincerely hope that you can see your way clear to table it at the next meeting of the board.*
>
> *The Dutch steamer Slachthuis made an excellent crossing of the Coral Sea, arriving at Ternate just fourteen days after departing Sydney. I made my way from the docks to the Dutch administrative offices and obtained the Surat Jalan, or travel document, necessary to proceed to the island of Tidore. There I based myself in the village of Pasir Hitam, from which each day I sallied forth up the volcano, seeking Count Vidua's caverns.*
>
> *On the seventh day, in a crevice on the eastern side of the crater, I located an outstanding Dickite. I'm afraid it's not quite as prodigious as the count boasted. Typical of the Italians, I suppose. But in colour and shape it is exquisite. My heart beat wildly when I saw it. And, when I took it in my hands, I became quite faint with excitement. I set to work and obtained eleven pounds of crystals, the largest weighing three pounds and standing seven and a half inches tall.*

*Obtaining that ultimate nirvana, Isleby Cummingtonite,
was more difficult. Vidua had reported it as outcropping
in a cavern high on the volcano's northern slope. The
mountain was in a state of eruption during my stay,
with the magma flowing to the north. After three
attempts—each time being driven back by a rain of lava
bombs and ash—I finally reached the cavern on April
26. My cowardly guides had fled at the foot of the final
slope, saying that they feared the wrath of the volcano
god. I carried on alone, while they wailed and hullooed
from below, before deserting me altogether. Unassisted,
I managed to fill my pack with twenty-five pounds of
specimens, mostly of excellent quality.*

*Regrettably, Director, I must inform you that I ran into
a spot of bother on the way down. The easiest route of
descent followed a recent lava flow. It was tricky going,
however, because the flow was just a few days old and its
surface was still rough and extremely hot. I'm afraid to
say that the weight of my pack told against me. My left
leg broke through the congealed crust and I was plunged
up to the mid-thigh in the molten lava flowing beneath. It
was only with the greatest effort that I pulled my parboiled
limb free.*

*A crust of solidified lava now encased my left leg,
to six inches above the knee. This proved to be both an
impediment and a godsend. The extra weight slowed me
down, but the rocky cast also kept my limb rigid, allowing
me to walk rather than hop. As I descended, the pain
caused by the baking eased somewhat, and I was able to
set a better pace.*

*When I reached Pasir Hitam, around four o'clock that
morning, I rather alarmed the villagers. They'd imagined*

that I'd fallen a virgin sacrifice to the volcano god, the rocky embrasure of my limb only serving to convince them that my maidenhood had indeed been taken by the deity. After they had marvelled at me for some time, prostrating themselves at my feet, or rather foot, they made all haste to convey me and my specimens to Ternate, from where I write.

I'm afraid, Director, that a considerable part of my already slender grant has been consumed in medical costs. For the last few weeks I've been in the care of Dr Siegfried Leggenhacker, a German ship surgeon who had sailed with me on the Slachthuis. Upon seeing the state of my limb, he urged amputation most vehemently. He was very neat about it—I'm rather proud of my little pink stump. And at my insistence he kept the rock impression of the leg, sawing it in half, so that it forms a rather splendid natural mould of my lower appendage. I'm bringing it home with me, as I thought it might come in handy if we were ever to mount an exhibition of the marvellous ruins at Pompeii, or on volcanism more generally.

Over the days of my recuperation, Dr Leggenhacker and I have become ever-more close. Two evenings ago, as he dressed my stump, he made a proposal of marriage, which I have joyfully accepted.

I'm now on my way to Kupang, accompanied by Siegfried, and we have secured berths on the next steamer bound for Sydney. If I'm to get my collections packed and secure I'd better sign off this report, and hop to it!

Yours sincerely,

E. Doughty

Dryandra folded the letter and replaced it in its envelope. For a while, she and the director sat in stunned silence.

'Remarkable,' Vere Griffon ventured. 'What a formidable woman. Most admirable.'

'I'm very happy for her, finding her Leggenhacker, I mean,' said Dryandra. She looked up at Vere, her eyes searching for a flicker of affection, or at least of personal recognition of his loyal lieutenant.

But Vere was lost in his own thoughts.

'I suppose the cast might be of some use to us,' he opined.

Wearily, Dryandra reached once more into the in-tray. 'Letter No 2,' she said. 'Sender: Herr Dr Mertens, Director, Statliches Museum, Stuttgart. Postmarked: January 30, 1933.'

Herr Doktor Director Vere Griffon,

Or my dear Vere, if you will permit me an informality most welcome in our student days, which I hope does not offend now; but I fondly remember when as a young Cambridge scholar you visited the Institut für Zoologié to examine our comprehensive collection of the fang-bearing Myriapoda—your area of special expertise. I was also a mere student then, but how dear to my memories is the time we spent in the tavern, eating sour pork lung and singing leider as we downed our lager! I was so touched that you named one of the most ferocious of the centipedes—a specimen you had collected yourself—in honour of me. I shall be forever grateful. Now we are both museum directors. How the world changes!

My esteemed colleague, I have a favour to request of you. We have a promising student here in Stuttgart by the name of Herr Hans Schmetterling. Like yourself, he is a devotee of the Myriapoda. He is visiting the old fatherland colonies in Melanesia, as well as your adopted home of Australia, to make a collection. He is a bright young man. For old time's sake, I hope you can take care of him while he is in Sydney.

    On a more personal note, do you keep your interest in Meissen? A colleague of mine has located here a unique Böttger Steinzeug and a most splendid chimney garniture once owned by the Duke of Saxony himself. They are yours, for a most modest price of £300 and £700 respectively, if you just say the word.

'Did you say the postmark was January 30?' asked Vere. 'That's over four months ago! Schmetterling must be arriving at any moment. It's a most inconvenient time to have a student about the place. The evolution gallery is running behind schedule and will require all my attention. But of course we must reply about the *Böttger Steinzeug*, don't you think, Dryandra? Could you contact Bunkdom, and find out what seven Hellenic gold coins might fetch?'

Chapter 16

When Courtenay Dithers walked to the museum the following morning, he half expected Chumley Abotomy or one of his henchmen to leap at him from every alleyway he passed. He slowed down and cautiously eyed the unusual-looking fellow loitering near the museum entrance. Slender, almost mouse-like, he sported a finely pointed and waxed moustache and a cowlick of hair over his high forehead. He clasped to his chest an oversized wooden box, with a perforated lid like a pepper pot and a large brass clip fastening it shut. From one elbow hung a bag that Dithers could see was filled with tin cans.

'*Guten morgen*—'

'Can I help you, old chap?' Dithers asked, fairly confident that the stranger didn't hail from Abotomy Park.

'I am looking for Herr Doktor Director Vere Griffon.'

'Don't think our director'll be in as yet. But come on through. I'm Courtenay Dithers, curator of mammals. Abotomy didn't send you, did he?'

'*Nein.* Herr Doktor Professor Mertens of Stuttgart me sent.'

'I see. Let's rouse up a cup of tea for you while you wait. What is your name?'

'I am Hans Schmetterling, student of the Myriapoda, and I am in Australien for the collecting expedition. I am looking forward to meeting Herr Director since so long. My weeks in the Bismarck Archipelago, on die route to Australien, have been most productive.'

By the time they had finished their tea, the museum was stirring into life, and Dithers judged the moment right to guide Schmetterling to the director's office. A rather surprised Miss Stritchley greeted the pair.

'Mr Schmetterling, we have been expecting you, but not quite so soon! I'll see if the director is available.'

'My God,' said Vere Griffon. 'That letter must have arrived by the same steamer as Schmetterling himself. Might as well bring him in. And Dithers too. He may be able to help.'

It was a distinctly nervous Herr Schmetterling who stood before Vere Griffon. He had heard great things about the man, and the office and boardroom were so imposing that the German's slender grasp of English seemed to desert him.

'Herr Doktor Professor Director, *Ich bin...*' He struggled before falling into an awkward silence. He reached into his bag. 'This lung of the swine, pickled as you like it, is a gift from Herr Doktor Professor Mertens. He was sure that such delicacies are not obtainable in the Antipodes—at least not those of the finest grade.'

Something about the hapless visitor roused Vere Griffon to cruelty.

'Dithers, thank you for delivering Mr Schmetterling into our hands. We could, of course, speak German if we wished. Most of us have a strong grasp of technical German at the least. But, Schmetterling, you will do no good here unless you master English. Dithers, would you be kind enough to find some bench space in the mammal department for our visitor? And Miss Stritchley, show Mr Schmetterling where the Myriapoda are kept. We will conduct a daily examination, in this office,' he said, giving the awe-struck German a penetrating gaze, 'to assess your grasp of the subject.'

Schmetterling detested examinations. He could not sleep for days before one, and inevitably emerged a trembling mess. The idea that Griffon would examine him was paralysing, but he managed to nod his understanding and follow Dithers.

'There you go, old fellow. Hope that bench space is enough,' Dithers said unconvincingly. 'The mammal department is rather crowded at present.' Bones, boxes, books and papers lay so thick on every surface that there was barely room to put down a pencil. 'Might be time for a tidy-up,' he added. 'We can at least move that walrus skull if it helps. But please do make yourself at home. And, by the way, what do you have in that box?'

'My myriapods. You would like to see them?'

'By all means, old chap. Be delighted.'

It took no further inducement for Schmetterling to loosen the bronze fastener. Inside were compartments, each one containing dozens of glass vials and jars, their tops covered with squares of muslin tied in place with string.

'This is my finest trophy,' Schmetterling said, reaching for the largest jar.

As the muslin was lifted Dithers glimpsed the coiled shape of a centipede, hiding among some dried leaves. It must have been the length of his forearm. The scarlet head, tail and limbs contrasted with the fluorescent green body, and a pair of wicked black fangs a centimetre long protruded from its head.

'*Sind sie hungrig, meine schönheit?*' Schmetterling murmured. Dithers cocked an eyebrow.

Schmetterling reached into a cloth bag and pulled out a tiny pink mouse. Dithers could hear its mother squeaking as the hapless infant was dropped into the jar. The monster roused itself and began feeling about. A leg touched the pink flesh, and instantly the centipede turned and plunged its fangs into the newborn. As Dithers watched, the mouse blackened and shrivelled.

'The toxin is…*sehr wirkungsvoll.*'

'Powerful indeed,' replied a shaken Dithers. He took a handkerchief from his pocket and dabbed at the corner of his mouth. 'Do you think, old chap, we might keep the box shut while you're here?

A knock at the door interrupted them. It was Miss Stritchley.

'Schmetterling, you'd best use your time wisely. Follow me to the collection.'

The museum's collection of myriapods was not large, but, as a result of donations from Vere Griffon, it contained some important specimens.

'Here are the Myriapoda. But don't go in there,' she added, gesturing to a bay of wooden shelves to the right. 'That's arachnids, and Dr Wrigley has a colony of funnelwebs under study. Most importantly, don't forget that the director has requested your presence in his office at three o'clock. Please be punctual.'

Schmetterling spent most of the day rapt in that sublime pleasure only a researcher ensconced in a collection can know. Seated before a white enamel tray, he peered intensely through a magnifying lens at the jointed legs, mouths and genitals of creatures new to him. He made pages of notes, drawings and measurements, and details of one new species after another began to accumulate in his mind. Species that he, Schmetterling, would have the honour of naming. The hours flew by, his concentration so deep that he didn't feel his muscles cramp or his joints ache. He didn't even hear the approaching footsteps echo in the corridor. So, when he felt a tap on his shoulder, he leapt from the bench. It was Miss Stritchley again.

'Schmetterling, your appointment with Professor Vere Griffon was for three. It's now ten past. The director is an extremely busy man. Follow me—and be smart about it!' She marched off along the narrow corridor. The young German was still placing articles in his bag as he followed.

'Unforgivable. To be so tardy,' Schmetterling mumbled once he was in Griffon's presence. On the splendid board table stood a solitary specimen jar.

'What do you make of that?' asked Griffon, looking down his aquiline nose at the specimen bottle. Schmetterling moved towards it and saw that it contained a gigantic centipede, its prodigious, pinkish-purple jaws jutting from its face like instruments of torture.

'*Ich denke*,' Schmetterling said, to buy time.

'Well, man, out with it. In English please. What is it? Come on!' Griffon barked.

'*Ja*, legs long. Fifteen leg-bearing segments. A scutigeromorph, I think. I guess that it is the *Scutigera coleoptrata*?'

Griffon rose from his desk and began pacing up and down.

'Schmetterling, you might be an intelligent young fellow, but you don't know your Myriapoda. This is no *Scutigera*! Look at the fangs, man! This is in fact the one and only specimen of *Horribilipes mertensi*—the rat-eating centipede of the Arabian Sea—which is named for your beloved professor! It is without doubt the most spectacular and, might I add, most beautiful of all the myriapods. And do you know who collected and named it? *Me*. Vere Griffon, during the cruise of the HMS *Sulphur*, sent to punish the pirates of Socotra. I went ashore as the howitzers blazed. It was under a coconut shell beside the village latrine that I found the *Horribilipes*, my greatest scientific triumph.' Drops of foamy spittle had appeared on Griffon's lips, and he was almost barking out his words.

A look of horror came across Miss Stritchley's face. Her gaze was fixed upon the professor's left shoelace. It had come undone. She rushed forward and bent before the great man. But Griffon was so fixated on his lecture that, before she could fasten the errant lace, he had marched up onto the podium once more. Miss Stritchley crawled after him.

Despite his terror, Schmetterling had to bite his cheek to stop himself laughing. Finally Griffon stopped long enough for

Stritchley to fasten the lace. He had not even noticed. 'If you hope for a job in a museum, Schmetterling, you'll have to do better than this. Now go back to the collection and study your Myriapoda. Until you have mastered them.'

'Might be time for a restorative lager,' Dithers suggested as the quaking Schmetterling returned to his office.

He collected Archie, and, on the way to the Maori's Head, the trio ran into Beatrice. She was not entirely comfortable in pubs—even in the lounge—but she did speak fluent German and so agreed to come along.

The men ordered lager, and Beatrice had a lemonade.

Schmetterling bolted down his first schooner and Dithers bought him another. The German grasped it in shaking hands, took a few gulps, and said, 'Oh, how I am unnerved! The ale will calm me, thank you.' As the drink worked its magic, he went on. 'But how wonderful to be in this young country of yours. The fatherland is terrible now. Destroyed by the war. On every corner you find the old soldiers—their faces just a mess of scars, a leg or an arm missing, or both—trying to sell matches or some other trifle. They are broken men, still frozen in terror, or men who want only to keep on killing. And the politics! Oh, how savage it is! There will be more blood. Yes, much more, before long. It is a country in which I can no longer live.'

'Medea,' Dithers mumbled. 'Not even kind enough to kill her children cleanly. And we were part of it. My God, what have we done?'

'What's that?' asked Archie.

'Nothing. Nothing. But damn all Kaisers. And all Churchills,' snapped Dithers angrily.

'Another beer?' asked Archie, looking at Schmetterling's empty glass. '*Ja, dankeschön.* I was hoping so much that Herr Professor Doktor Vere Griffon would give me a job,' Schmetterling continued. 'Professor Mertens remembers him fondly, as a good man and steadfast friend with a warm and generous heart. You know, my professor pulled every string to get me out of Germany. He has even given a little of his own money towards the cost of the collecting expedition.'

Schmetterling took a swig of beer. 'I fear I have disappointed Herr Director,' he concluded sadly.

'Hans,' Beatrice said, 'if it would help, I could ask my uncle if you could stay with him for a few weeks. My sisters Betty and Myrtle are boarding at his house, and are learning German at school. If you tutored them I'm sure Father would agree to pay your board.'

'Of course, old chap,' added Dithers, 'you'd have to leave your, er, specimens, at the museum. But you could set up in the mammal department, as a visitor, if you liked. Perhaps you could lend a hand with a tidy-up. Give you more space. And until Beatrice gets things sorted you could stay at the Maori's Head.'

'Mine good friends. It's been long years since anyone but Herr Doktor Mertens has shown me such kindness.' Schmetterling sighed. 'I hardly expected to find friendship in the Britisher colonies.'

'Who would like another lager?' asked Dithers, full of bonhomie. But as he regarded the increasingly merry Schmetterling, he was not sure that another drink was altogether a good idea.

Beatrice made her excuses and rushed for the five o'clock

ferry, and Archie accompanied her. When Dithers had finished his schooner he took Schmetterling back to the museum to feed his centipedes, then headed off to a meeting of the Society for the Preservation of Native Animals.

The following morning Dithers suggested to Archie that they walk into work together. 'Not that I'm nervous, Archie. But it's a beautiful morning for a companionable stroll.' Archie was glad to see that Dithers was taking his warning seriously, even though he knew Dithers would never admit it.

They walked to Dithers' office. The mammalogist had just seated himself at his desk, when he let out a bloodcurdling scream. Archie rushed back in to find Dithers staring fixedly ahead. As Archie neared he saw a scarlet head, attached to four inches of fluorescent green body, poking out from under a kangaroo skull that sat on a shelf at eye level. The vile black fangs that protruded from it palpated just inches from Dithers' nose.

'Abotomy's behind this!' cried Archie. 'I'm sure of it.'

'For God's sake, just help me!' wailed Dithers.

Archie searched frantically for something to knock the creature away with. He had grabbed a kangaroo leg-bone and was swinging it about wildly, when a pallid face appeared from behind the hippo skull.

'*God in Himmel. Meine Schönheit!*' squeaked Schmetterling. Clearly the worse for wear from his drinking the previous evening, he drew a pair of long tweezers from his pocket, grasped the beast by the head, and returned it to its jar. 'I was feeding my sweetie, and must have dozed. I am so sorry,' he said, looking at Dithers aghast.

When he had recovered, Dithers turned to Archie. 'I do think you are taking this conspiracy theory of yours rather too seriously. There is always a simpler, more straightforward explanation for such things, as you can see. I do think it best, Hans, if you and your menagerie stay at the Maori's Head until Beatrice sorts things out.'

Later that day an intense annoyance at himself settled over Courtenay Dithers. He, a man who had seen the worst of trench warfare, had survived a bayonet charge and stormed a Hun machine-gun nest, was scared. Scared to feel. Scared to act. Never again, he promised himself, would he run as he had from Abotomy Hall.

Chapter 17

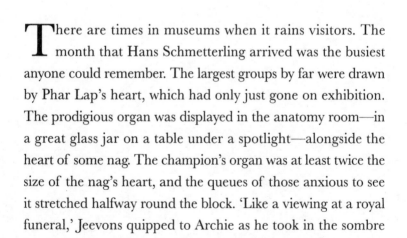

There are times in museums when it rains visitors. The month that Hans Schmetterling arrived was the busiest anyone could remember. The largest groups by far were drawn by Phar Lap's heart, which had only just gone on exhibition. The prodigious organ was displayed in the anatomy room—in a great glass jar on a table under a spotlight—alongside the heart of some nag. The champion's organ was at least twice the size of the nag's heart, and the queues of those anxious to see it stretched halfway round the block. 'Like a viewing at a royal funeral,' Jeevons quipped to Archie as he took in the sombre faces of those grieving the death of the champion racehorse.

A few days later Archie arrived to find half the Japanese navy in the staff entrance. He'd read in the newspapers about the arrival of Vice Admiral Nobijuro Iamaura and the Japanese Training Squadron, but had not expected them to visit the museum. Yet there they were, the neatest human beings he'd ever seen, in their white uniforms with not a hair out of place. They stood stiffly—almost at attention—in the foyer until Miss Stritchley came through the door carrying a splendid bunch of yellow roses. The flurry of waist-deep bows and presents emanating from the oriental gentlemen took her by surprise. She reciprocated by handing the roses, originally destined for Griffon's office, to an officer, and then led the group away.

For the next several days the Japanese sailors seemed to be everywhere, and almost always in the company of Dr Abraham Trembley, the museum's jellyfish expert. Pale to the point of vanishing, Trembley was of uncertain age—indeed, almost of uncertain physical form. Hitherto, sightings of him outside his darkened office were rarer than sightings of the Yeti.

Archie was astonished by the rumour that the naval visit was a sort of embassy from the Japanese emperor to Trembley himself. Apparently the emperor was making something of a name in the realms of marine biology and, through their common passion, he and Trembley had developed a more than passing acquaintance. From what the admiral intimated, the emperor regarded Trembley almost as a god in his field.

The Japanese sailors invited the entire scientific staff to a formal dinner aboard their flagship, the *Yamamoto*.

In his room that evening, Dithers produced the elegant invitation. 'I suppose you'll be walking Beatrice to the ship? The loo is not safe for an unaccompanied woman these days,' he said to Archie.

'Oh, Dithers!' Archie's throat tightened so he could barely speak. 'I'm not sure she'll want me to.'

'What do you mean, Archie? It's plain for everyone to see that the girl dotes on you. I don't know why you're being so stand-offish with her.'

'Mordant will be at her side, I'm sure.'

'Archibald Meek, has the green-eyed monster got total possession of you? I've never heard anything so ridiculous in my life. Beatrice flees from his very shadow. You should be ashamed of yourself for doubting the girl.'

Archie would not admit it, but he did feel ashamed. It was as if he'd caught himself in the mirror, a man acting like a child.

'Jealousy, Archie, may be an emotion you've had little experience of till now. As something of a professional in the field, let me tell you about it: its symptoms are precisely those of rabies. The stricken beast develops a raging thirst, so it goes to a waterhole. But when it sees the water, it becomes terrified of the very thing it desires. Frothing at the mouth, it bites at anything that approaches. Rabid dogs have been known to chew off their own legs.'

'Well…' said Archie, struggling with his feelings. 'For safety's sake, I'll escort her to the dinner. As long as that toerag isn't hanging about.'

Dithers could see no advantage in pushing matters further. He turned to the wall and fell asleep.

Archie found Beatrice sitting at her register as usual. Surely no girl was ever more beautiful. Her hair fell in golden tresses, her blue eyes shone, and her lips formed a perfect, ruby-red bow. Had Mordant really tasted their glory?

'Rabies, waterhole, chewed leg,' muttered Archie. 'Beatrice, I hope you got your invitation to the Japanese naval dinner?'

'Oh, Archie, I'm so looking forward to it! I bought a new outfit for the occasion.'

'Woolloomooloo is a bit rough at night. Someone should accompany you to the vessel and back.'

'Nobody has offered.'

'In that case I'll do it. Walk with you, that is. For your protection.'

'Thank you, Archie. That is very gallant.'

The *Yamamoto* was moored at the navy dock, beside Cowper Wharf. The night was warm, and the vessel was gloriously lit. The ship's band was playing jazz as Archie and Beatrice approached. She slipped her hand into his. As they walked up the gangway a great moon peeped through the clouds.

They were greeted by a splendidly dressed lieutenant. Beatrice felt sure he was the tallest and most handsome oriental she'd ever seen. As he reached to take her wrap she couldn't stop blushing. The officers lined up to greet them. Bottles of French champagne were poured into long-stemmed glasses. Archie and Beatrice wandered the deck, looking at the cannon, the immaculately coiled ropes and the sailors who doubled as waiters.

Holding her glass delicately, Beatrice flashed her eyes at Archie. 'Isn't this the most immense fun?'

He said nothing. It was as if a hard stone blocked his heart. The thought of Mordant would not leave his mind.

The jazz ceased and the band struck up 'Hail to the Chief'. After a few bars, Vere Griffon, in the company of Dryandra Stritchley, appeared at the top of the gangway. Archie was immediately on guard. The admiral gave a low bow, then handed the director an elaborately wrapped box.

Champagne and canapés circulated once more, and the jazz recommenced.

Dryandra caught Archie's eye. He warily left Beatrice's side and approached her.

'I see things are not going smoothly with your girl, Archie.'

'Hmm. That's an understatement.'

'Come to my house after work one afternoon, for a cup of tea. I'm pretty full bottle on young girls and their ways. I might be able to help.'

Archie was stunned. He had assumed that Dryandra was part of Griffon's cabal. Now he was not so sure.

Archie returned to Beatrice just as the '*Kimigayo*' sounded out. Griffon looked up sharply, wondering who was being so highly honoured. The governor, perhaps? There was a moment of suspense as the last strains of the notoriously brief anthem died away. Still, nobody had appeared at the top of the gangway.

After what seemed an interminably long silence, the flabby and puffing form of Abraham Trembley began to materialise out of the darkness. He was pulling himself along, using the boarding rails of the gangplank. The embarrassing silence in which he approached the admiral was finally broken by the assembled naval officers, who led a round of applause.

Trembley smiled and gave a bow so low that it astonished all who saw it. The admiral's bow was even lower, causing Beatrice to catch her breath in fear that he might tumble over. A subaltern handed the admiral a long, thin package, which he placed in Trembley's outstretched hands. Inside was a samurai sword. The museum staff watched in amazement as the curator gave a long speech in fluent Japanese.

Trembley hailed Griffon as the crowd headed below decks for supper. 'Director, this is a most splendid reception. Perhaps we should present the emperor with something in return?'

'Splendid idea, Trembley. Could you find out what might be acceptable?'

At 10.30 p.m. precisely, the dinner broke up. As promised, Archie walked Beatrice through the streets and laneways of Woolloomooloo towards Circular Quay. The air was still warm and scented, but there was the hint of danger, both in the loo and in the museum. Archie felt more alive than he had since leaving the islands—all his senses were heightened. As they negotiated a narrow lane, the touch of Beatrice's breast on his arm shot through him like an electric shock.

In an instant he remembered the Venus Islands woman who had drawn him into the shadows of the coconut palms at the conclusion of his last yam festival. She'd placed his hand on her naked breast and moved it gently. Archie repressed the memory at once.

They walked on through the Domain and paused under a fig tree. Archie moved towards Beatrice, wanting to kiss her, but she stepped back from his embrace.

'We shall be friends, Archie. Friends and nothing more. Now, will you walk me to the quay? I must catch the last ferry or my uncle will be mad with worry.'

Archie felt at sixes and sevens as he lay in bed that night. Perhaps it would be as she said. They would be friends, nothing more. Perhaps she would marry Mordant. But he wanted her to be his. 'Rabies, waterhole, chewed leg!' Archie repeated under his breath.

The next morning, Abraham Trembley puffed his way up to the director's office.

'Director, the admiral has expressed a wish—an imperial one perhaps—to obtain a complete set of the jellyfish species of Sydney Harbour, along with a detailed map of the waterway showing the contours of its bottom and the locations of the jellyfish finds.'

'Sounds like a job for you, Trembly. Shake a leg then!'

Miss Stritchley accompanied Trembley to the cartographic section of the library. 'I hope we're never at war with them,' said the librarian as she hesitantly handed over a large naval map of the harbour, prominently stamped 'secret'.

'Oh no. Never,' Stritchley replied. 'They're far too civilised!'

Later that day Archie, too, visited the library, and was accosted, in excellent English, by a young Japanese lieutenant. He'd heard that the anthropologist had recently returned from the islands to Australia's north and was keen to learn all he could about the region. After explaining the local religion, forms of wealth and governance of the Venusians, Archie went on to describe the islands themselves and their fringing reefs. The sailor presented him with a beautifully wrapped package in thanks, and a half bow.

Inside was a bottle covered in Japanese writing. Mystified, Archie took it to Dithers, whom he found standing in the museum courtyard, contemplating the carcass of a pygmy sperm whale which had been found washed up on Cronulla Beach. It was not entirely fresh.

'Sake, old fellow. Japanese wine,' proclaimed Dithers, after sniffing the contents.

'Phew, tastes like preserving liquid!' said Archie, reliving the bad memory of finding Sopwith, as he spat out the mouthful.

At that moment Henry Bumstocks appeared, dressed in a leather apron. In his hand was a large flensing knife. He was unsteady on his feet. Archie saw that he was drunk and flinched as Bumstocks wielded his blade.

'Nothing to worry about,' said Dithers. 'Henry's teetotal, mostly. But when he's called upon to deflesh a whale I have to supply a bottle of Scotch. Says he simply can't face the job without a stiffener. And I don't blame him. Whale oil carries the taint of rotting flesh into every pore. The chap stinks for weeks afterwards.'

Bumstocks slashed into the abdominal cavity of the whale and a great gush of gas and greenish liquid burst forth, causing the two curators to reel. Bumstocks soldiered on, hauling out yards of intestines. Giles Mordant came around the corner trundling a deep wheelbarrow. Archie stood by stonily while he shovelled up the stinking mass and took a load away. The pair worked with such efficiency that it struck Archie that they must have dismembered countless bodies together, both great and small.

While the disembowelling of the cetacean was proceeding, Vere Griffon sat at his desk, his head in his hands. The faint whiff of decay did not brighten his mood. That morning he'd been summoned to the Department of the Arts—by Cedric Scrutton. Griffon had a feeling in his waters that the meeting was going to be particularly nasty.

Griffon was kept waiting a long time in the antechamber. When he was finally let in, Scrutton fixed him with a gimlet eye. 'Sit down, Director. I'm afraid I have some bad news for you. Treasury has revisited the budget for the current financial year, and finds that urgent cuts to expenditure are required. As a result, your museum budget will be cut by twenty per cent.'

'What!' gasped Griffon. 'That's completely impossible. It's June already. The financial year is almost gone, and we've spent the money.'

'I'd love an excuse to sack you, Griffon,' said Scrutton, smiling. 'In my opinion, you and your institution are bloody parasites on the body of this state. If you run one penny over budget, I'll make sure you leave New South Wales in disgrace.'

'It is utterly impossible,' continued Griffon, 'to make such a large cut in a few weeks—without sacking staff or selling collections. And that I will not do.'

'Cut, Griffon. Deeply and quickly. And don't wave your bloodied stumps at me! Get rid of some of those useless curators of yours. They do nothing except spend, as far as I can see. Now get out of my office and on with your job. I'll expect a full budget acquittal in six weeks.'

Vere Griffon had never felt so diminished. Threatened and shouted at by a third-rate colonial bureaucrat like that. What utterly absurd demands. What a dreadful place this was! Yet he could not give up or back down now. He was getting his curators into order, and soon the institution would re-establish its reputation on the world stage. He would find a way to outwit Scrutton.

Chapter 18

Archie was still in love with Beatrice, and he longed for her company. But when he was with her his pain only increased. The mere sight of her was enough to rouse his jealousy to fever pitch. So he was often aloof in her presence. Peace of mind would only come, he realised, when he could accept things on Beatrice's terms. But what should he do about Mordant? He was sure the vile man was in cahoots with Griffon. He wondered whether he should confront him, but could only see an encounter ending in a punch-up, and that would give Griffon the excuse he needed to act against him. For the moment, avoidance was the only option. And to make matters worse, Archie just could not bring himself to select the skulls that Griffon had requested. That, he felt, would be soul-destroying.

Instead he would wait for a second summons.

Beatrice had now got over the shock caused by Archie's love token. Her affections were as warm as ever. But something between them had changed. She wondered whether she was the cause of Archie's strange behaviour. Or had his experiences in the islands affected him? She wondered what might help her to understand him better.

'Would you like me to read your fieldwork report?' she asked as they sat in the winter sunshine in Hyde Park eating sandwiches.

'Well, Beatrice, it *is* an anthropological study, and it contains some matters that are not discussed in polite company.'

'Oh, Archie, you can trust me. I know it's scientific. I'd only read it for grammatical errors. I presume you'll want to publish it one day? Really, I wouldn't be shocked by anything in a report.'

When they returned to the department, Archie handed Beatrice a bulky manila envelope full of handwritten pages. Perhaps, he reflected, if she read them she might understand why he had sent the foreskin. He was disappointed that she had not even made the token effort of deregistering it.

That night Beatrice went to bed early. Archie's handwriting was not the neatest, but as she turned the pages she became more used to it. Leafing through the chapter headings, she came to one called 'Love and Courtship'. She put aside the rest of the manuscript, and started reading.

Among the Venus Islanders, foreplay and sexual intercourse are seen as entirely natural and expected activities. Following puberty, both males and females indulge in sex frequently, without embarrassment and with the utmost pleasure.

Beatrice gulped. What had Archie seen among the islands?

Virginity is usually lost at the first annual yam festival following the onset of puberty. This occasion, which coincides with the yam harvest, is marked with much feasting, dancing and social licence. On the first night of festivities, boys and girls clean and oil their bodies with the greatest care, arranging their hair and dress, which for girls consists only of a short grass skirt, and for boys a woven belt. The boys rub charcoal into the coconut oil they use to anoint their skin, which blackens their already dark complexion. The girls use ochre to give their bodies a rich reddish sheen. They dance late into the night to the throb of the kundu drum.

The feast is held at the full moon. As its orb dips into the ocean the dance breaks up. The young people form couples and make their way to the beachfront. There, among the low bushes and beneath the coconut palms, they make love until dawn, at which time they return to their families. Custom dictates that by day they ignore their sexual partners; nonetheless many a furtive glance and shy smile are seen in the village at this time. By night they are free to dally in each other's arms for as long as the festival continues—a period of three weeks in all. It is a remarkable sight to see the dreamy youths returning from the beach at dawn, the girls with black smudges on breasts and groin, the boys ochred wherever they've been caressed.

Marriage is not connected in any way with the festivities, but follows the initiation of the men, which is reported upon in detail in chapter seven. Suffice to say here that a couple who have enjoyed each other's company through several successive yam festivals are likely to become

man and wife. Marriage proposals are conducted through
delivery of the initiate's tattooed foreskin to his sweetheart.
Her acceptance of the proposal is signified by her rolling it
into a ring, which she wears on her fourth finger.

Beatrice was breathing shallowly when, in the early hours
of the morning, she put the manuscript down. So that was it.
Archie's foreskin was not some obscene act of tomfoolery, but a
sincere offer of marriage. If only she'd been born in the islands;
she sighed.

Beatrice could see the near-full moon through her window.
As she dropped to sleep she could feel a salty, tropical breeze on
her skin. She was surprised to find that she was naked. Then she
saw Archie. Tall, muscular and draped in a loin cloth, he walked
across the beach towards her, took her in her arms, and under a
graceful coconut palm kissed her passionately.

Archie pulled his trousers on next morning and absent-mindedly
thrust his hand into his fob pocket. He felt a small object—the
incisor that he'd found on the floor below the Venus Island Fetish
on the day of his return, nearly six months earlier. Somehow, in
the excitement, he had misplaced it. Had it really been hidden
in that small pocket all this time? His suit had been dry-cleaned
a couple of times, but somehow the tooth had survived intact.

As Archie rotated the incisor in his fingers, a thought came
to him. Griffon had said that Henry Bumstocks inspected the

fetish regularly. Perhaps Archie could use the incisor to strike up a conversation with him. The only reliable way to meet the famously antisocial taxidermist was to venture to his office, but there Archie was likely to run into Giles Mordant. Then it struck him. Perhaps Mordant kept the foreskin hidden in his locker in the taxidermy department. He changed out of his street clothes and into his work outfit every day. He was often busy running errands in the afternoon, and if Archie took the incisor to Henry while Mordant was out, he could search for his foreskin while Bumstocks reattached the tooth.

That afternoon Archie adjourned to the Maori's Head. He needed to kill some time and thought it worth asking Nellie if Giles had shown her anything unusual—such as his love token. He propped himself against the bar and downed a beer.

'Gentlemen,' called the publican, 'who wants a ticket in the duck raffle? A shilling each. Just a shilling for a duck.'

'What's this about a duck?' Archie asked Nellie, as the publican announced that the raffle would be drawn at five o'clock.

'Oh, Archie! I didn't want to, but I can't make ends meet,' she replied, red-faced. Then she added brightly, 'Would you buy a ticket? Please? For me?'

'Nellie, I'm no gourmand. I wouldn't know where to begin cooking a duck. If I was still in the Venus Islands, of course, I could *mu-mu* it in a stone oven. But I'm staying with Dithers and we've got no facilities at all.'

The publican drew a ticket out of his hat. 'Number 14, gentlemen. Who has the lucky number?' A lanky young fellow missing his front teeth let out a whoop and made a dash for the door. Once outside, he ducked into the back of a removalist's van.

'It's hard times, Archie. I'm sorry,' Nellie whispered as she followed the youth into the van's darkened interior.

Archie sat in stunned silence. Nellie returned amid the chaos of the six o'clock swill. She poured Archie a gratis beer on the sly, then another. He couldn't raise the issue of the foreskin now. The poor girl evidently had her own worries.

It was a decidedly unsteady Archie who made his way to the taxidermy workshop. The place was already steeped in preternatural gloom. He groped his way in. The stench was distinctive and subliminally revolting—a cloying, decomposing organic stew that lodged in the nostrils and pores.

Bones, dried organs, and bits of skin covered every surface and packed every nook. Even the ceiling was used—a half-stuffed gibbon swung from an overhead pipe and a human skeleton hung in a corner. In the middle of the room stood a frightening figure. Naked apart from a loincloth made of animal skins, it held a fearsome, knobbed club. It must be the model of Piltdown man, Archie realised, the prize exhibit of the new evolution gallery. It was ugly: a cross between human and gorilla, its face twisted in a terrifying scowl.

Archie edged around it towards the taxidermists' offices. The nearest one belonged to Bumstocks. It was a small space running off the back of the workshop with a dim light in the far corner. The narrow passage forced Archie's face uncomfortably close to the terrible visage of the Piltdown man. Unnerved, he backed away, and knocked a huge bone off the shelf behind him. It fell to the floor with an explosive crash.

For a second Archie was startled into stillness. Then a terrible roar erupted from the nearest office. It was Henry Bumstocks, wearing a long, bloodied butcher's apron and waving an enormous knife. Even in daylight Bumstocks was a frightening figure, but as he lurched forward in the gloom he resembled an animated version of his own monstrous recreation of Piltdown man. And now he was crashing towards Archie, intent, it seemed, on murder.

Sheer terror gave Archie an agility he usually lacked. He leapt from the taxidermy lab in a single bound. Once out of the line of Bumstocks' sight he slowed to what he hoped looked like a leisurely walk, and made his way to his office.

He was recuperating at his desk when Jeevons appeared at the door. Archie snatched up a book—Professor Hooton's classic *Apes, Men and Morons*—which he pretended to be absorbed in as he granted Jeevons entry.

'All in order this evening, Mr Meek? You're working late, I see. But I suppose you've a lot to catch up on?'

'Much to do, Jeevons. This new exhibition will take my every waking moment for the next little while, I expect.' Archie waved his hand in an awkward twirl meant to dismiss the guard.

Jeevons doffed his pillbox hat, gave a broad smile, and was gone.

Archie was flabbergasted. Surely the guard must have heard Bumstocks' rampage? And surely Bumstocks had reported the intruder in his office? If not, why not? If he had reported an intruder, then a search of the institution would surely be conducted. But, judging from Jeevons' reaction, nothing unusual had occurred.

Chapter 19

D ithers was out at yet another meeting. Archie lay in his bed, his eyes fixed on the yellowing ceiling, trying to make sense of the events of the evening. Why had Bumstocks tried to knife him? Could he be involved in the murders of the missing curators? Jeevons' reaction made no sense. Could he be involved too? It was as if the whole world was mad, and only he, Archie, saw the truth. As he drifted into an exhausted slumber, the Great Venus Island Fetish danced around the edge of his consciousness. He saw it advancing at him out of the gloom, and found himself awake, screaming. He knew that he needed a new perspective on things. After the episode with the centipede, Dithers clearly thought he was paranoid. He would not do as a confidant. But what about Beatrice? She said she would be his friend. Perhaps together they might make sense of things.

Archie found Beatrice hunched over an Aboriginal shield, inscribing a registration number on it. It was work she enjoyed immensely: first finding the spot where the number could be clearly read but not visible to the public if the object were ever put on display, and then forming those minuscule figures with the sharpest of nibs. Archie waited until she pulled the pen away and straightened herself.

'Beatrice, it's such a glorious day. Would you care for lunch in the botanic gardens? We could take a picnic.'

'Oh, Archie that would be wonderful,' Beatrice gushed, before checking herself. She did not wish to seem too forward. She sat impatiently for the rest of the morning before the great register, filling in line after line, until the clock struck midday.

Archie and Beatrice walked down Macquarie Street, past the lawn bowls club and the cathedral, and on to the gate of the gardens. Then they strolled through the ornamental plantings towards the harbour foreshore, and sat by the duck pond.

'Beatrice, there is something I have to tell you.'

'You can tell me anything, Archie,' Beatrice replied.

'On the day I returned to the museum, I was shocked to see that the Great Venus Island Fetish had been installed in the boardroom. Vere Griffon has no right to expose one of the institution's most precious relics to such a hostile environment. And it has started to deteriorate. Bits are dropping off, and some of the skulls have lost their patina.'

'What do you mean, lost their patina?' asked Beatrice.

'Well, they're not quite the colour they used to be. I became very familiar with the fetish before I left for the islands. The skulls are stained dark brown by the smoke of cooking fires—perhaps lit when food was sacrificed to the fetish. But four of the skulls I saw the day I returned were more orange than brown. They'd changed colour, somehow.

'At first I thought it could have happened through exposure to sunlight, so I carried out an experiment. I put some smoke-stained bones on the windowsill in the anthropology department. One end of each bone was exposed to the sun, while the other remained shaded. They have been there for about six months now, and their colour hasn't changed. I don't think it's possible that the skulls on the fetish have faded due to sunlight. And I can't think of another reason they would have changed colour. Unless they're not the skulls that were originally attached to the fetish.'

Beatrice was silent, taking in the implications of Archie's words.

'I noticed that one of the orange skulls was terribly buck-toothed—every bit as bad as Polkinghorne—and his was a severe case, as you know.'

'As bad as Polkinghorne?' Beatrice echoed.

'You don't think it was Polkinghorne's skull, do you, Beatrice? Could the original skull have been taken off, and Polkinghorne's put in its place? I know this sounds totally mad, but it *was* one of the orange skulls. And I can't think of how the original skulls could have changed colour.'

'But why would anyone do that? Exchange the skulls, I mean.' Beatrice was shocked at the gruesomeness of Archie's thoughts.

'The day I returned, Vere Griffon raved about "his collection" of curators. How he wanted the best museum in the empire. Maybe he is getting rid of those who don't perform. In any case, he is definitely collecting body parts. I'm convinced that Mordant stole my foreskin at Griffon's request. And I think that Chumley Abotomy, Henry Bumstocks and maybe even John Jeevons are involved somehow, too.'

Beatrice was becoming frightened. Archie's thoughts were almost unhinged.

He sensed her fright, and backtracked. 'Polkinghorne drowned, his body was never recovered. It's not possible that his skull ended up on the fetish. Tell me that's right, Beatrice, please.'

'That's right, Archie.' She knew that she had to hear him out, as distressing as that might be, and that now was the time to do it. 'But go on. What else has upset you?'

'Oh, Beatrice! So much has gone wrong. I still feel dreadful about poor Eric. Never in my wildest dreams did I imagine that he'd drink preserving alcohol from my collection! And I swear, hand on heart, that I was extraordinarily careful with the specimens and labels. I was tired that night, I'll admit that, and there was much unpacking to do, but I can't believe that I switched the trout for the toad fish. The value of the entire collection relies upon having the specimens correctly labelled.'

He took a bite out of a ham sandwich. Beatrice was eating cucumber.

'Archie, whatever happened that night, you can't take responsibility for Sopwith's death. It was an accident.'

'I'm not entirely sure about that.'

'What do you mean?' Beatrice shifted so that she could look

Archie in the eye.

'I didn't switch the fish and labels. But someone else might have. Somebody who knew that Sopwith was drinking preserving alcohol, somebody who wanted him out of the way.'

'Why would anyone want to kill Eric? He was a harmless old soul who was loved by one and all.'

'Just after I returned, Sopwith told me that there was something suspicious about Polkinghorne's death. And he said that Griffon was selling off the collection.'

'Do you think it's possible that Sopwith's mind had become clouded with drink, Archie?'

'There is one more thing. A few days ago I went down to Bumstocks' office. It was late. The office was gloomy, and I thought the place was empty. When I entered the workroom I knocked a bone off a shelf. There was an awful bang and Bumstocks emerged with a great knife in his hand. He was roaring, Beatrice. I feel sure he'd have killed me if he'd caught me.'

Beatrice wondered why Archie had gone to the taxidermy department. Was he trying to retrieve his foreskin from Mordant? She felt that to ask would risk inflaming Archie further. He was already in quite a state.

Archie tossed his crusts to a duckling swimming behind its mother in the shallows. A dark shadow lay in the water underneath the birds—perhaps a piece of pond weed, he mused.

Beatrice was turned away from the water, concentrating on Archie's face. Suddenly she felt immensely tired. 'The real world just isn't like that, Archie,' she said.

The dark shadow revealed itself to be an enormous eel. In

a single gulp, both the duckling and the crusts vanished. The mother duck turned, gave a single sharp peep, and started swimming in circles, looking for her chick.

Archie couldn't speak. Beatrice took his silence as a sign that quite enough stressful thoughts had been aired that day. 'Dearest Archie, I'm sure that there's an innocent explanation,' she said in the kindest, most sympathetic voice she could muster. 'You are home now. And I still…like you,' she trailed off.

But Archie wasn't reassured by Beatrice's words. They walked in silence back to the museum. Beatrice understood that in all this mystery there was one thing she could do for Archie. She could get his foreskin back. Perhaps that would ease his mind.

Chapter 20

Giles Mordant couldn't hide his pleasure. 'Come in, sweetie! Come in. What can I do you for?' he said in the dulcet, mocking tone he adopted with Beatrice.

Beatrice did her best to hide her distaste as she seated herself at his desk. She would have to go carefully, she told herself, if she were to succeed in her mission.

'What's that, Giles?' she said, by way of making conversation, pointing to a sponge-like growth in a jar of brownish liquid.

'Oh, that. It's the skin from the hand of a bloated corpse,' he said provocatively. 'A fisherman saw the body floating in the harbour and tried to pull it into his dingy. But it was so rotted that the skin of the hand came away and the corpse sank to the bottom. The police brought it to me to tan. They're hoping that fingerprints can be taken. It's their only chance of an identification.'

Beatrice told herself that she should not feel so revolted. After all, the collection she cared for included some gruesome objects. She thought of the dried pudenda war trophy from the Gulf of Papua that she had registered a few weeks earlier and the pile of chewed human bones from Fiji. But, despite herself, there was something about the object that filled her with revulsion.

'We do quite a bit of work for the police here,' Mordant went on. 'Cleaning bones, tanning skin. That sort of thing. Sergeant O'Toole's a close friend nowadays. A favour done…you know the saying. So if you're ever in trouble, Beatrice, you know who to turn to.'

'Giles, *I am* in trouble, which is why I'm here,' she replied. 'That love token you stole from the collection. It must be returned. At once.'

'Oh, you mean Archie-boy's foreskin? I'm having far too much fun with that to give it back just yet!' he said with a leer. 'Besides, I've got plans for it.'

'Where is it, Giles?' Beatrice demanded sternly.

'It's in my wallet, in that drawer,' Mordant said, gesturing teasingly towards a drawer in his desk. 'It's mine now. But I suppose we *could* trade for it.'

'Trade what?'

'Oh, I don't know. How about meeting me in Faucett Lane? At afternoon tea. So we can discuss it.'

'When?'

'How about today?'

Beatrice rose and turned to go. 'Very well, Giles. But you

better be serious.'

Beatrice was a little worried about the place Giles suggested for their rendezvous. She'd heard that the area was thick with women of the night and their thuggish boyfriends. Just being seen there could stain her reputation. But for Archie's sake she'd go.

She was surprised to find the air of Woolloomooloo filled with the smell of freshly baked bread. An old horse pulled the baker's cart, plodding along unguided, as the baker ran from door to door crying out, 'Ba-kerrr!' with his unmistakable upwards inflection. If no one emerged from the house he was delivering to, he just put the loaf down on the doorstep. 'Could do with a bit of paper around it,' Beatrice thought, as she glanced at the decidedly unhygienic stoops.

Another delivery was being made. A strong man, his muscles bulging under his blue singlet, was accompanied by a gangly youth. They stepped from an idling motor van that chugged up the hill, went to the back of it, and used a pick to cut up a great block of ice.

'Quarter of a hundredweight, Kenny. For Mrs O'Riordan,' said the man.

As he broke up the slab, splinters of ice sprayed into the street, drawing children who scrambled for the pieces and sucked them ecstatically. When the block finally split, the man put an old gunny sack on his shoulders and lifted a piece of ice onto it.

'Stray dogs hang around Mrs O'Riordan's place like flies at a barbecue,' he said, gesturing to the dog poo littering the footpath. 'You'll have to learn to do the Scottish sword-dance before you can deliver ice here,' he added with a laugh as he skipped between the turds, imitating the actions of a highland dancer.

The activity reassured Beatrice as she turned into Faucett Lane. The place was claustrophobically narrow and choked with rubbish. Giles Mordant was in his work clothes, leaning against a lamppost. He beckoned her to follow him into an alcove. Beatrice's self-confidence evaporated.

'Hello, girlie,' said Giles, who seemed to feed off her fear. 'How about a bit of trade. Lots of it going on round here.'

Before Beatrice could reply he grabbed her and kissed her. Beatrice was too shocked to react. She'd expected Giles to demand something—money, perhaps—but she'd never imagined this. She was too scared to move. But when Giles thrust into her groin the terror released her. She screamed. Her attacker grabbed her mouth and muffled her cries.

He was lifting her dress, when he suddenly fell back. Someone had him by the shoulder and was pulling him away. Then a fist landed with a thud. Beatrice looked up to see that Giles had turned around and was punching Archie, whose right eye was bloodied. She was sure that Archie was badly hurt, but he barely recoiled before throwing a fist at the taxidermist's nose. Mordant was not expecting pugilism from a scientist. Shocked, he grasped his injured organ. Then Archie struck again—with a blow to the jaw. Beatrice heard the crack of breaking teeth. Giles was writhing on the ground.

Archie lowered his fists. His battered eye was already closed. Beatrice took his hand. His knuckles were so bloodied it looked like he'd been gutting a chook. 'Are you hurt?' she pleaded. Archie didn't reply. He had astonished himself. All he felt was a primitive elation at seeing Giles lying on the cobbles.

Giles hauled himself onto his knees, and sat propped against the lamppost. The blood from his nose formed a long, foamy drip, which reached all the way to his blue-and-white work shirt.

'You'll pay for this, Meek,' he said in a low voice. 'I have friends who could get you sacked. Or see you at the bottom of the harbour.'

Archie remembered Giles' confidence when Vere Griffon interviewed him about Sopwith's death. A chill ran down his spine. He reached towards Beatrice and led her back across William Street.

Outside the museum, Beatrice hugged Archie. She didn't care who saw.

'How did you know where I was?' she asked.

'I saw you crossing into the loo, and thought I'd follow. Just to make sure you were safe, really. Did you go there to meet Mordant?'

'He told me that if I met him he'd give me back the foreskin.'

Archie slumped, the tension draining from his body. 'Oh, Beatrice. You never should have done that. You could have been very badly hurt.'

Beatrice said nothing. But she was more determined than ever to get the foreskin back. There was only one way to do it. Somebody would have to lure Bumstocks away from his workplace for long enough for her to sneak in and take it from the drawer where Mordant kept it. And it must be done today, before Mordant's return to work. There was only one person she could think of to help, and that was Courtenay Dithers. He was Archie's best friend, and she felt sure he could keep a secret. She ordered Archie to the doctor's, and then made for the museum.

Beatrice ran into Dithers in the foyer. He was engaged in an animated conversation with a red-faced woman who was wrapped in a large fur coat, which she kept clasped to her sides.

The curator was wearing a long white lab coat over his flannel suit and tie. He felt that it gave him an air of authority when taking public inquiries. And today he certainly needed it, for he suspected that before him stood that terror of all museum staff—a member of the public who believed she has a firmer grasp of a curator's area of expertise than the expert himself.

'But they're in there,' the woman wailed. 'With the snakes. And I know they're up to no good!'

'Madam, the Australian Microchiroptera—or insect-eating bats—are entirely harmless.'

'I can assure you that the bats in my roof cavity are doing the devil's work, young man. Them and the snakes.'

'What, precisely, madam, do you think they *are* doing?'

'Brewing concoctions!' the woman crowed triumphantly. 'Little puffs of smoke keep coming out of the cracks in the walls and the floor. They're mixing a witches' brew, no doubt about it! Now, sir, will you remove the evil creatures? You are the curator of mammals, and they are your responsibility. I can't stand it a moment longer.'

'Good heavens, madam. How could they be doing anything? Snakes have no hands, and bats only wings!'

'I don't know. But they are doing it. Constantly. And if you won't help me I'll go to the police! *And* I'll speak to your director about your lackadaisical attitude!'

'Madam, I'm afraid that snakes and misbehaving bats are

beyond my purview. I can only encourage you to enlist the assistance of our constabulary. Or if you wish, our director.' Dithers turned on his heels and fled.

In the corridor he collapsed against Beatrice. The pair of them bit their lips to contain their laughter.

'I'm sorry, Beatrice,' Dithers managed to blurt out, 'but sometimes inquiries from the public passeth all understanding!'

She accompanied Courtenay to his office holding his arm, giggling.

On the way, Dithers said, 'Don't worry about Schmetterling staying with your uncle at present. He's got a bit of a nervous problem, and has decided to lodge at the Maori's Head until he's over it. A good chap overall, I think. He's helping me clean up the office, as a sort of penance for letting his centipedes loose. Spends several hours a day at it.'

The encounter with the woman seemed to relieve Beatrice's tension. She explained about Archie's proposal of marriage, and all that had happened in Faucett Lane—omitting only the fine detail of Giles' transgression—without breaking into tears. She explained too, that she wished to take the foreskin from Giles.

'By Jove, poor you! And poor Archie.' Dithers exclaimed. 'No wonder he's been so on edge. That cad Mordant deserves to be boiled in a vat of his own lye! Don't worry, Beatrice. I think I can help you get access to the taxidermy rooms. I have a little job for Bumstocks. The zoo's warthog has died, and I'd like its bones. Transforming that mass of corruption into a clean, white skeleton will take some time.'

'Thank you, Courtenay. I shall await your signal.'

In her entire life, Beatrice had never experienced anything

half as dangerous as she had today. Or so exciting. Though she would hardly admit it, she felt strangely aroused. It had been thrilling to see Archie beat Mordant in order to protect her.

Beatrice waited impatiently in the anthropology department. Then, around four o'clock she heard from Dithers. She made her way to the taxidermy department and slipped into the workshop. There was a distinctive soapy smell—a bit like a glue factory, she thought.

The frightening reconstruction of Piltdown man dominated the space. The door to Giles' office was unlocked. She opened the desk drawer and took out his wallet. There, sure enough, wedged between two two-pound notes, was Archie's foreskin. It was a lot of money, she thought, for a taxidermist to be carrying about. She took the foreskin, and with a wicked flash of joy slipped it into her brassiere.

Beatrice replaced the wallet, closed the drawer, and shut the door to Giles' office. She was now back in the workshop. The door to Bumstocks' room was ajar, and on a bench just inside sat a large stoneware vessel filled with greyish liquid. Its rim was almost at her eye level, making it hard to see inside. A sign hanging from it said, in large letters, 'Do Not Touch'.

Ever since Beatrice was a small child such a sign might as well have read 'please do touch'. And today her excitement gave her the confidence to pry. Beside the jar was a long, hooked wire. Clearly it was used to retrieve whatever lay immersed in the liquid. She picked it up, and fished in the murky fluid, hoping to snag whatever lay below. The wire caught on something, and she gently lifted the object.

As it neared the surface she could make out that the thing was pale, roughly spherical, and surprisingly heavy. She bent close to the jar's rim to see. The object was only inches from her nose when she recognised it. A human head.

With a thrill of revulsion, she turned the rotting cranium around until the face was pointing at her. The gums were still there, as was a piece of lip. A small metal tag was attached to the cheek bone with a piece of twisted wire. Something was inscribed on the metal. She turned the skull to get a better view.

'Sop…Sopwith?' She screamed under her breath. Not Eric! She looked at the teeth, and instantly recognised the browning, crooked fangs. There was no doubt about it. She was holding Eric Sopwith's head.

She dropped the skull in fright, plunging it back into the liquid and splattering her hair with the soapy fluid in the process. A rising panic seized her. She rushed to find Archie, but remembered he was at the doctor's. Like an animal seeking safety, she fled home and to bed, where she feigned illness.

Chapter 21

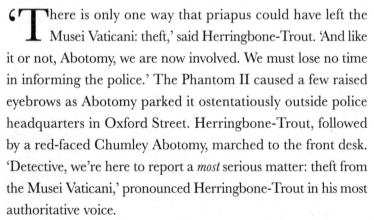

'There is only one way that priapus could have left the Musei Vaticani: theft,' said Herringbone-Trout. 'And like it or not, Abotomy, we are now involved. We must lose no time in informing the police.' The Phantom II caused a few raised eyebrows as Abotomy parked it ostentatiously outside police headquarters in Oxford Street. Herringbone-Trout, followed by a red-faced Chumley Abotomy, marched to the front desk. 'Detective, we're here to report a *most* serious matter: theft from the Musei Vaticani,' pronounced Herringbone-Trout in his most authoritative voice.

Detective Albert Brownlow stood at a counter examining some papers. A fedora sat at a cocky angle on his close-shaven head. Without looking up, he said, 'Mate, I don't give a bugger about your amusing fatty army, or whatever it is that's had something nicked.' He was used to dealing with arrogant, upper-class twerps with their assumed right to immediate attention. 'Right now, we've got more murders and assaults on our hands than you could poke a stick at. So bugger off.' He ended almost threateningly.

'Detective, you don't understand. The Musei Vaticani are among the most important museums in the world. They house the great treasures of the Catholic Church.'

These last two words acted like a charm. 'Catholic Church? Has somebody stolen something from a church?' asked the suddenly engaged officer.

'Not *a* church, sergeant, *the* church. The Vatican, to be precise. I'm sure the archbishop will be delighted to hear that the police are assisting the Holy Father. The piece in question is an antiquity nearly two thousand years old, and it was fenced from an antique shop on Oxford Street, in this city. Mr Chumley Abotomy—I mean, Abumly—here, purchased it, not knowing that it was stolen, and brought it to me for examination.'

'Can I see the object?'

As Herringbone-Trout unwrapped the priapus he began a dissertation on its history.

'Looks like a job for you, Brownie,' the duty officer quipped as he eyed the bronze dubiously. 'Right up your alley, so to speak.'

A guffaw erupted from an overweight policeman behind the counter.

'Shut up, Slugger,' Brownlow said, anxious to get the thing out of the police station. 'Easiest to walk, by the sound of it. Doolan'—he gestured towards the guffawer—'you come with me.' The detective strode towards the door, and Slugger Doolan, Abotomy, and Herringbone-Trout, who was still hurriedly rewrapping the priapus, rushed after him.

Lord Bunkdom was at the back of his shop, a rather poor print of Caravaggio's *The Calling of Saint Matthew* propped up before him. In his imagination the bench on which he sat was the same one that supported the muscular thighs of the saint-to-be. He was about to lift the saintly tunic when he heard a knock at the door, followed almost instantly by the tinkle of broken glass and the forcing of a lock.

Bunkdom leapt to his feet. 'I say! What's all this about?' he gasped.

'We have a warrant to search these premises,' said Brownlow, who did not seem to find Bunkdom's compromised position in the least remarkable. 'We have evidence that this establishment is being used to fence stolen goods—objects stolen from the Catholic Church. Now, can we see your account books?'

Bunkdom gestured limply towards a desk. The detective unlocked the solitary drawer—the key was already in the keyhole—and took out a small black volume.

'Professor, we'll need your help deciphering this.' He passed the volume on to Herringbone-Trout, who began turning its pages.

'What a tale of perfidy and imbecility is revealed here!' Herringbone-Trout exclaimed in a rather too-dramatic way. 'Just look at this: "23 April 1929. Statue of Venus. Purchased L. Corbone £1.6.6. Sold Chumley Abotomy, 29 January 1933, £165.9.6!"'

'Let me see that! This, sir, is an outrage,' shouted Abotomy.

'You told me that the statue was an original, but for what you paid for it, it couldn't possibly be!'

'Actually, sir,' Bunkdom said softly, 'I told you that it was a Roman copy of a Greek original, which it is. It's just not antique Roman.'

Abotomy looked so infuriated that Herringbone-Trout feared steam would issue from the squire's ears.

'I'm afraid, professor, that making a large profit from, ah, shall we say, the uninformed is not against the law,' murmured Brownlow. 'You'll have to do better than that, or we could all end up with egg on our face. Where is the evidence for receiving stolen goods?'

'Here it is!' said Herringbone-Trout excitedly. '"Three March 1931. One priapus, purchased Giglione, £67.11.6. Sold Abotomy, 29 January 1933, £127.9.6." That's the object. I have sketches of it that I made myself at the Vatican. It has without doubt been stolen and fenced in the colonies, where nobody thought it would be traced.

'Bunkdom,' Herringbone-Trout said solemnly as he turned to the shop owner. 'Best to come clean. What is your connection with Giglione?'

'It'll go far easier with you if you turn over now,' added Doolan. 'Otherwise, mate, I'll take the greatest pleasure in kicking your arse into the next world, while the archbishop gives his benediction!'

After a prolonged sigh and much fidgeting, Lord Bunkdom rolled his eyes heavenwards. 'My name is Edwin Breech, and I was born in London's East End. It was my good fortune to have been apprenticed, aged thirteen, to Moses Weinstock, an antique dealer on the Portobello Road. He treated me like a son, and eventually trusted me to go on buying trips to the continent. It was on one such venture that I met Professor Virgil Giglione. What a fine specimen of a man he is! Immensely strong, and a hunter of the first water. He has true alpine calves, you know—a product, he told me, of a youth spent hunting ibex in the Tyrol. When I first saw him in his plumed hunting hat and lederhosen, I fell under his spell.

'It was he who told me that there was a tremendous and rather undiscerning market for antiques in the colonies. He promised that, if I set up shop there, he'd keep me supplied. And so he has. Some pieces, I'll admit, are nothing but clumsy forgeries, but others are truly beautiful antiquities. I never for one moment imagined that any had been acquired by theft!'

'Well,' said Herringbone-Trout, 'I'm afraid that some almost certainly have. The priapus you sold Abotomy, for instance. It bears an uncanny resemblance to the specimen I sketched in the Vatican—right down to that scratch on its shaft. I very much fear, sir, that the treasures of Rome are being pilfered, and sold through your shop.'

Abotomy had taken up Bunkdom's account book to see for himself how badly he'd been diddled. Bunkdom finished his confession, and Abotomy abruptly shut the covers, looked up, and turned to Herringbone-Trout. 'Professor, you say that the priapus is stolen. But can you be certain?'

Herringbone-Trout was taken aback. A few seconds ago Abotomy had been baying for Bunkdom's blood.

'One can never be 100 per cent certain in such cases, but I've seen a plethora of priapuses, so to speak, in my time, and this is most likely the same specimen I saw in the Vatican in 1923.'

'A photographic memory—for pricks, professor?' said Detective Brownlow, getting his own back for his embarrassment at the station.

'Old chap,' said Chumley, 'that scratch—I fear I made it myself. The road to Abotomy Hall is rough, and both of my antiques took a beating on the drive out there. I'm not sure that this case warrants the use of any more valuable police time. Detective, I suggest you leave this matter with me—as a member of the museum board—at least until more evidence is forthcoming.'

'Sounds reasonable,' Brownlow said. 'But before we go I'd like to have a look at that book,' he gestured towards the black ledger sitting in Abotomy's lap.

'Really?' said Abotomy. 'Nothing exceptional in it…'

Brownlow's instincts were finely honed. He snatched up the volume and began reading. An entry caught his eye: '20 April 1933. Purchased: seven Hellenic gold coins, £350.00. G. Mordant…9 May 1933. Sold: Meissen figurine, £275.00. D. Stritchley.'

'Do the names G. Mordant and D. Stritchley mean anything to either of you?' He looked at Abotomy, then Herringbone-Trout. Abotomy was silent.

'Stritchley,' Herringbone-Trout said. 'An unusual name. The only D. Stritchley I know is Dryandra, secretary to Vere Griffon, the director of the museum. A good man. Cambridge, you know. I think a fellow named Mordant works there too, but I can't be sure.'

'Sarge,' said Slugger. 'A cove of that name turned up in the loo last week. Beaten black and blue, he was. Said he worked at the museum. But I couldn't get anything more out of him.'

'Thank you, gentlemen,' Brownlow said. 'I don't believe there's a great deal more we can do here. We will be in touch if we have questions.'

Chumley knew he had to act quickly. That night he dined at the Union Club. After a sumptuous repast shared with a member of parliament, he retired to the billiards room, where he smoked a cheroot, mostly for the sake of stubbing it out in the rather splendid ashtray—a ram's head on wheels, complete with horns, inlaid with a silver bowl. Then he retired to his room and penned a letter.

> *Dear Professor Giglione,*
>
> *I trust that by now you've received correspondence from Dr Vere Griffon agreeing to the exchange you proposed. We are most anxious to proceed with the acquisition of your splendid collection of goats in its entirety, and are hoping that you can dispatch it as soon as possible, in the knowledge that the requested specimens will be received by you in the fullness of time.*
>
> *I realise that this is a rather unconventional request, but matters have transpired here that must be weighed in the balance. A police investigation is underway in Sydney into certain thefts from the Vatican museum—your institution. Lord Bunkdom, who sells antiquities in this city, has*

privately told me that he received some of the supposedly stolen objects from you. I of course believe none of it, and I have some sway with the authorities in New South Wales. So I hope, my dear fellow, that you can see your way clear to shipping the goats. If we receive them within sixty days I'm sure that things will turn out favourably for your good self.

Yours sincerely,
Chumley Abotomy Esq.

Detective Albert Brownlow didn't like loose ends any more than he liked the whiff of a cover-up. He had no proof of wrongdoing, but something stank in that antique business, and he sensed that the source of the odour lay in the museum. It really wasn't his bailiwick, but, to tidy things up, he took a stroll down to Macquarie Street to have a word with Cedric Scrutton in the Department of the Arts. He'd worked with Scrutton years before, when a painting by Constable was stolen from the art gallery, and he liked the fellow.

'Detective Brownlow, what a surprise! Good to see you again. How can I help?' Scrutton warbled.

'It's nothing really, Mr Scrutton. Just a minor investigation. Some antiques, possibly stolen. And an assault. Can't say much more at present, but I wanted to pass a couple of names by you. Apparently these individuals have been making rather large sales and purchases on the antiques market. Hundreds of pounds, in fact. And one of the individuals ended up pulverised black and blue down the loo.'

'I see. Who are they?'

'G. Mordant and D. Stritchley.'

Brownlow, who was studying Scrutton's face, knew he'd struck gold.

'Inspector, you have delivered them into the palm of my hand,' exclaimed Scrutton.

'Delighted to be of service, old fellow.' Brownlow tipped his fedora as he strode off.

Cedric Scrutton could hardly believe his luck. He'd long felt that Vere Griffon was playing with him—indeed laughing behind the board's back at how easily he manipulated them all. Moreover, the man seemed to be wriggling out of the latest trap set for him. Griffon had written to Treasury, claiming that he needed more time to finalise the museum's accounts, in light of the twenty per-cent budget cut. He was doubtless busy shifting expenditure into the new financial year, hoping to defer his fiscal doomsday.

But now, this most unexpected information had fallen into Scrutton's lap. It was not possible that Stritchley or Mordant could afford expensive antiquities. Was Vere Griffon behind it? If so, where was he getting the money? A full investigation was warranted.

The firm of Descrepancy, Cheetham & Howe had served the Department of the Arts in all matters financial for decades. It was trustworthy, discreet and sharp as razors in all aspects of audit. When the firm's principal, Hardy Champion Descrepancy, picked up the phone Scrutton explained that he had good reason to suspect fraud at the museum.

'The museum! Mummies and that sort of stuff? By Jove, that could be fun!'

'Yes. Antiquities. And an assault. Can't say too much more though, just now.'

'I love a bit of cloak and dagger work, Cedric. This office gets stuffy at times, I can tell you.'

As he put down the phone, Scrutton looked forward to a great adventure with his old friend.

Chapter 22

'My God, sir, what's happened to you?' Jeevons was looking at Archie's battered face and bandaged hand. It was the day after the scrap with Mordant.

'It's nothing really. Just a bit of bother down the loo.'

'You must watch yourself down there, sir. I make it a rule never to go north of William Street these days, and *I* carry a baton,' the guard said, indicating the truncheon hanging from his waist.

'I'll be all right, Jeevons. A minor mishap, really.' Archie passed swiftly through the museum entrance and into the sanctuary of his office. The fewer people who saw his black eye the better. News of fisticuffs between employees was bound to spread. And to cast both parties in a bad light. Archie was expecting to see Beatrice, but as the hours ticked by she'd still not arrived. Visions swirled in his head of Mordant or one of his associates harming her. When the clock ticked past eleven, and he was about to begin a search, he received a note from Jeevons. It was in Beatrice's impeccable copperplate.

'Harris Tea Rooms. Midday.'

At ten minutes to the hour Archie made his way onto the street, pretending to be buried in a newspaper, and headed to the Strand Arcade. It was posh, and Archie felt doubly unworthy of being there on account of his bruises.

The tea rooms were abuzz. Fox furs and hats bedecked with birds of paradise were the order of the day. Customers filled every table and crowded the counter, standing as they drank. Archie found Beatrice hunched at a tiny table in a corner.

'Oh, Archie! It was awful!' Beatrice sobbed, clutching his arm.

'I've been so worried about you! Tell me what happened, from the very start. Let me get you a cup of tea—Earl Grey?'

When the elegant china cup and saucer on its silver tray, accompanied by a small silver teapot, was sitting before her, Beatrice stopped sobbing.

'Oh, Archie, I wanted to get your foreskin back. Don't worry, it's safe. I read your report and I know now why you gave it to me. Anyway, I waited for Bumstocks to go out. Mordant had shown me where he kept it. I opened the drawer and picked up his wallet. The foreskin was in it. I took it and went into the taxidermy workshop. It's a strange place, Archie. Frightening. But I was so curious. There was a stoneware jar on a shelf just inside Bumstocks' office, with a big sign saying "Do Not Touch". I couldn't resist. I fished in it with a wire hook, and it grabbed onto something—and out came Eric Sopwith!'

Archie found it hard to keep up. 'You're making no sense, Beatrice. How could Eric be in a jar?'

'It was *his skull*, Archie! With bits of flesh still on it,' she wailed, alarming the pair of shoppers at the adjacent table.

'Beatrice,' Archie whispered loudly. 'How do you know it was him?'

'It had his name on it, Archie. On a metal tag.'

'Could it have been a joke…or something?'

'No!' Beatrice wailed. 'Those teeth. I'd know those teeth anywhere! And the bad gums. Oh, it's so awful. You were right all along, Archie. The director has gone mad. He is collecting his curators. And Bumstocks is helping him do it. Thank God we didn't let him collect your foreskin too!'

'So, it really is true,' Archie whispered to himself. His worst fears were no yangona-fuelled hallucination, no paranoia resulting from five years in the tropics. Vere Griffon *was* collecting his curators. He was probably a murderer as well, and Bumstocks and Mordant were his accomplices. Dithers, his dearest friend, was surely next in the firing line, and the poor man had no idea.

But what, he suddenly thought, if Beatrice was wrong? Could she possibly have been mistaken?

Archie had to see the skull for himself. After his last encounter with Bumstocks, he was not looking forward to returning to the taxidermy workshop. But this time he would be more careful. The opportunity came two days later. Dithers told him that in a few hours the Piltdown man was going to be installed in the new evolution gallery and that most of the staff would be assembled there to get a glimpse of the terrifying reconstruction.

Archie loitered in the public exhibition space until he saw Bumstocks and Mordant, who had a large sticking plaster on his nose, struggling along with the wooden case containing the figure. The taxidermists would be some hours settling the exhibit in.

The door to the workshop was open and Archie went directly to the stoneware jar. The grey liquid it held looked revolting, and the 'Do Not Touch' sign was still in place. Archie lifted the wire hook off the nail, and dipped it gingerly into the grey liquid. Almost immediately it snagged something, and Archie's heart began to race. As he pulled it towards the surface he squinted in terror. An eye socket appeared above the slime. Archie's hand began to shake. But he had to go on.

'Sopwith?' he said softly as the skull emerged into the air. But there was something wrong. The forehead was almost flat, and the canine teeth huge. Even though the precise shape of the cranium was obscured by half-rotten slabs of flesh and sinew, Archie could see that it was not human at all. It belonged to a chimpanzee, and was doubtless destined for the new evolution gallery. He replaced the wire on the nail and strode towards the light of the corridor, feeling an immense sense of relief.

That afternoon he walked Beatrice to the ferry.

'Are you certain that it was Sopwith's skull you saw? The thing is, darling,' he added patronisingly, 'I went back today and looked myself. All I found in the jar was the skull of a chimpanzee. Do you think that the gruesomeness of the place might have triggered your imagination?'

Beatrice stopped, furious. 'How dare you, Archibald Meek.

How dare you doubt my word. I *know* what I saw! It was Eric's skull. I'd recognise those teeth anywhere.'

The look of hurt and betrayal on her face was more than Archie could bear. But one thing was undeniable: the evidence of foul play had vanished, if indeed it had ever existed.

Despite the skull incident, their adventures had drawn Beatrice and Archie closer than ever. Beatrice realised that she had fallen hopelessly in love with Archie. Yet she would not admit this to herself. Instead she remained stand-offish, except in her dreams. She could not have explained, even to her sister Betty, the full cause of her reticence. But she felt that things should be done properly. Archie owed it to her to propose, formally. Why didn't he seem to understand this?

Archie, meanwhile, had accepted Beatrice at her word. He and Beatrice should be nothing but the best of friends. On other fronts, however, his sense of perplexity was increasing. Griffon had said nothing about the fight. Had Mordant not told him? Perhaps Mordant had his own reasons for not spreading the news. When they passed in the corridor, Mordant now avoided Archie's gaze, which gave the idea some credence, Archie thought.

Despite these developments, Archie was half-expecting each day to be his last at the museum, anticipating that he'd be met at the entrance by a couple of policemen with handcuffs, to be arrested for assault. It was partly this fear that led to his dithering over the fetish. He really needed to examine it again. But how could he do that without alerting Griffon?

His ruminations were temporarily eclipsed when he picked up the phone in the anthropology department. It was a shipping clerk from Burns Philp.

'A group of savages has arrived on one of our steamers, sir, and they have a letter saying that you'll be responsible for them while they're in Sydney.'

Archie had quite forgotten that he'd written to the islanders, care of a missionary, requesting a dance troupe to perform at the launch of the new gallery. He grabbed his hat and dashed out the door. None of the islanders spoke English, or had ever left their homeland before. He'd been expecting advance notice of their arrival, but something must have gone wrong. They'd be as helpless as newborn babes. As he dashed down Macquarie Street it dawned on him that looking after them would be a full-time job.

Archie found the Venusians huddled on a bench in the shipping clerk's office. There were six: Uncle Sangoma, Cletus and his brother Polycarp, and their cousins Pius, Arenga and Barup. All except Polycarp, who had managed to cadge a blanket, were wearing nothing but bark loincloths. Sangoma sat impassively, a little distance from the others. A great boar's tusk pierced his nasal septum, and the head of a rhinoceros beetle ornamented his nose-tip. Horizontal scars running across his muscular chest marked him as an tribal leader, and in his left hand he grasped the conch shell trumpet of an island big man.

The younger boys and men, in contrast, looked miserable. Arenga and Barup, who must have been barely fourteen, were shivering, and sat with their arms wrapped around their chests. Archie noticed that Polycarp, wrapped in his blanket, wore a pencil, rather than a boar's tusk, in his nose piercing.

'Uncle, brothers! Welcome to my village,' Archie said in Venusian.

Instantly, the islanders became as happy as condemned men who've received a pardon. There was a long round of ecstatic hugs.

'Polycarp, why are you wearing that pencil through your nose?' asked Archie.

'A sailor swapped it, and this blanket, for my boar's tusk. I thought I might learn to write with it.'

'That could take some time—like you teaching me to climb a coconut tree.' The group laughed. 'Oh well, I suppose that we can get you a new tusk, from the collection. For the dance, I mean. And what happened to Father Clement? I'd arranged for him to accompany you—and send advance notice of your arrival.'

'Couldn't come,' Sangoma said, as he mimed a drunk man swigging from a bottle. Archie had heard the rumours, and mentally ticked himself off for trusting the missionary.

'Have you eaten?'

'Not a thing, for days,' said Sangoma. 'That stuff they call bully beef stinks. Cletus reckons it's preserved human flesh!'

'Well, the first thing to do is to get you a good feed. There's a cafe nearby that does the best steak and chips in Sydney,' Archie said, catching himself. 'Steak and chips', he realised, meant nothing to his friends.

The islanders clung to Archie's side like leeches as they walked up George Street. A passing lorry caused Cletus practically to leap into his arms. 'It's all right,' Archie kept repeating, but the sights, sounds and smells of the city were overwhelming for the islanders, as were the stares of the crowds.

They finally reached the cafe, and they calmed a little. They watched Archie carefully as he wielded his knife and fork, then tried valiantly to eat with the implements themselves, but to no avail. In frustration, Uncle Sangoma picked up his steak in his hands, and began chewing on it. Cletus, Polycarp and the others soon followed. The pretty waitress serving them fled into the kitchen, and moments later a burly cook with a thick black moustache emerged. 'What do you fricking cannibals think you're doing?' he thundered.

Archie decided that the best form of defence was attack.

'Look here! These fellows are members of the Tongan royal family, and they're in Sydney on an official visit. They're about to see the governor, and I'm sure you wouldn't want any trouble from his chargé d'affaires.'

The cook backed off. 'Well, just eat and get on your bloody way as quick as you can.'

Soon the T-bones were picked so clean they almost glowed, and Archie decided to take the islanders to the relative quiet of the museum. The domain was almost deserted, and he managed to get them there without incident. At the museum he installed the islanders in the guard room, under the watchful eye of Jeevons, and went to see Dryandra Stritchley about an allowance to cover their expenses. Then he walked to the hostel across the road and secured rooms in a boarding house. They were basic, to say the least, but the budget would extend no further.

By the time he'd gone to the second-hand clothing shop and bought half-a-dozen ex-military greatcoats, Archie knew that he couldn't look after the islanders alone. So he turned to Beatrice. She was excited by the prospect of meeting the exotic visitors, but was alarmed for their safety.

'What if Griffon wants to add them to his collection?' she asked in horror.

'I'd rather die than see harm come to my family,' Archie replied. 'I'll defend them with my life.'

Reassured, Beatrice helped Archie sketch out a rough plan. She felt certain that they would love to see where European goods came from. She promised to speak to a dressmaker she knew and an uncle who worked at the Eveleigh rail yards, to see if visits could be arranged. And she was fairly sure that Sir Halward Edmonds would be willing to show them his refrigerator factory as well as Taronga zoo, where he was director. Archie, on the other hand, felt they might enjoy a visit to David Jones, and the new mouse-trap factory in Mascot.

Later that morning Archie introduced Beatrice to Uncle Sangoma.

'This is your wife?' Sangoma asked.

'No, Uncle.'

'Ah, I see now she's not wearing your skin-ring. Still saving up pigs, eh? It took me years to get enough to marry your Auntie Balum. This woman looks pretty strong. Should be good for at least three gardens, and lots of kids.' He flashed a brilliant smile at Beatrice.

'What a gentleman!' Beatrice beamed.

Archie decided that a translation wasn't required.

They devoted the afternoon to a tour of the museum. As the islanders wandered through the great halls they scrutinised the contents of every cabinet. Those containing artefacts or objects from their region were observed with particular interest: the arrangement and labelling of sacred objects in particular were minutely examined. They also took careful note of the skeletons and stuffed animals—particularly the totemic ones like the whales and sharks. When the closing bell rang, it was only with the greatest difficulty that Archie got them to break off their studies.

As they were filing out, Archie found their way blocked by a knot of visitors. Predictably, they were gathered around Jeevons. The guard's face was turned heavenwards, the very picture of anguish.

'When you found Sopwith, Mr Jeevons, was he dead or alive?' a man asked.

'Alive,' croaked Jeevons.

'Did he say anything?' a matronly-looking woman asked in trepidation.

'Yes, yes,' the museum guard almost whispered, before pausing dramatically. 'He looked up at me with them terrible eyes, and pointed with his claw, all bent up with the poison, and whispered, "The golden cowrie."'

Archie hurried his visitors away. 'Who is that great man?' Sangoma asked, looking back in awe. 'Is he the chief of the museum? I can't understand a word he is saying. But what a powerful orator! And so well dressed.'

It was not without misgivings that Archie left his friends at the boarding house. It wasn't just the bedbugs and the cold he was worried about—there was nobody there who could understand them. And they understood nothing at all. He showed them the toilet, but was far from sure they properly understood what purpose it served.

'Just don't drink from it. The water is here,' he said, turning a tap in the common washroom. The sight of the water spurting from the wall had twelve eyes growing to the size of dinner plates.

When Archie arrived at work the next morning and found Uncle Sangoma standing in the foyer, handcuffed to a sturdy policeman, he was not entirely surprised.

'Constable Doolan,' Archie said, reading the policeman's badge. 'What is this about?'

'This savage is charged with theft. And resisting arrest. He practically dragged me here.'

'Uncle, what happened?' Archie asked.

'Well, I got up with the birds and went looking for food. I saw a man with a pile of fruit. He was giving it out to people, holding a feast, just like we do in the islands. So I joined the line, sure to receive my share. But when I took a banana and started to eat it, the man went mad, and called this chief,' he said, pointing to the policeman.

'I'll handle matters from here, officer. And I'll see that the fruiterer is paid,' said Archie.

'If I so much as see either of you again, in any circumstances,' Slugger Doolan said as he unlocked the handcuffs, 'you'll learn how to behave the hard way.'

Archie took Sangoma to his office and told him to stay there until he returned, but not before he issued a stern warning. 'Uncle, this is a dangerous place. Far more dangerous than the Venus Isles. Please, no matter what, do not leave your rooms without me. It's a matter of life and death.'

Archie found the fruiterer at his usual location.

'That bloody blackfella took the banana, and he smile like a bloody thief! Mista Mik, it's not right.'

'Joe, Sangoma comes from a place where there's no money. He doesn't understand. But if he and his family can have breakfast here every morning, I'll pay for the fruit. Okay?'

'If you say so, Mista Mik, I give the fruit. But they betta bloody well eat it over there,' Joe said, pointing to a park bench at some distance from his fruit barrow.

'I'll tell them,' Archie acquiesced. He could see how Joe's coterie of female customers might be scattered to the four winds by the presence of the swarthy islanders.

Later that day Archie and Beatrice took the men to the Eveleigh rail yards. They wanted to demonstrate the power of the industrial process—to show the islanders where the wealth of the white man came from. But the machinery, noise and glowing metal seemed not to impress. The islanders walked through the noisy sheds, their hands clasped behind their backs, looking at the faces of the workers and avoiding even peeking at the machines. A visit to the dressmakers and the department store got the same response. Only when they got back to the hostel, and Sangoma once more saw the running tap, did they become lively.

That evening, Beatrice suggested that they take the islanders for a walk through the neighourhood. On the corner of Palmer and Liverpool streets an elderly man, dressed in a nautical cap and jacket, was pushing a pram that looked as though it dated back to Queen Victoria's time. 'Oysters. Buy the lovely fresh oysters from Jimmy!' he was shouting. And indeed the pram was full of Sydney rock oysters scattered with lemon slices.

'*Karang, muli*,' Sangoma said, smacking his lips.

'Oysters, lemon,' Archie translated. He could see there was no helping it. He stopped and ordered three dozen from Jimmy, who opened them on the spot. They were gone in a instant. Archie dipped into his slender reserves to buy three dozen more.

'We better move on before they bankrupt us,' said Beatrice with a laugh. They walked towards Darlinghurst Road, where Archie caught sight of Nellie. She was walking beside a short, nuggety Italian man, and seemed reluctant to meet his eye. But a meeting was unavoidable.

'Hello, Archie. This is my husband, Guido Galetti. Guido, Archie works at the museum.'

Guido observed Archie through narrowed eyes. 'So you know my wife?'

'Yes, from the Maori's Head,' replied Archie.

'And who are these fine gentlemen?'

'My friends from the islands. They don't speak English.'

'Well, my friend, you think these fine men want a woman?'

Archie was shocked.

'Just five bob here for Nellie. We call this the stock-market special,' Guido said with a smirk.

'I'm sorry, Nellie, we must go,' Archie stammered.

He had expected Beatrice to be horrified. Instead she said, 'It's hard times, Archie. I don't blame Nellie for making ends meet any way she can. Better than starving. Or dying of TB.'

It was Sangoma who summed up Archie's thoughts. 'My son, that short, strong man is a bad man,' he said in Venusian. 'A very bad man. We should stay away from him.'

Beatrice suggested that they stop at a cafe on William Street. The islanders enjoyed the buns that Archie bought, but the tea was another matter. Sangoma took a great swig, unaware that the liquid was scalding hot. He pouted and tossed the cup away, then sat in embarrassment.

'Uncle,' Archie said, seeing Sangoma's humiliation. 'Don't worry. Do you remember when I first tried to eat sweet potato from the ashes, and burned my tongue?' The islanders broke into laughter at the recollection.

The next day they made a trip to the zoo, across the harbour at Taronga Park. The islanders enjoyed the ferry ride: the sea breeze in their faces gave them some of their old confidence back. And Beatrice and Archie were relieved to be away from the tension of the museum. Sir Halward was a model of hospitality. Now rotund, balding and mustachioed, in his younger days he'd traded round the Pacific, and he retained a great interest in all things Melanesian. He was anxious to show the islanders his magnificent collection of birds of paradise. He also took them to see the New Guinean wallabies, which he'd collected himself. He told them, through Archie, that the young kangaroo was born from the teat of its mother.

'The great man is wrong,' Sangoma said. 'The young kangaroo is born from the vagina, and climbs into the pouch.'

Archie thought it impolitic to contradict the bombastic industrialist. So he merely translated that Sangoma was impressed by Sir Edward's biological knowledge.

On the ferry trip back across the harbour Sangoma said, 'Arciballe, you have shown me many things. But not the fetish. Is it truly here in your village?'

Archie explained that it was in the museum boardroom—a place where only the most senior men could go. Sangoma said nothing, but he lifted the shirt Archie had lent him to reveal the horizontal scars on his chest that marked him as a fully initiated elder.

Archie weighed up the consequences of showing Sangoma the fetish. Would it expose him to greater danger? Perhaps there was a way. Hamlet, Archie recalled from his school days, had forced his uncle to confront his crimes by putting on a play. Could Griffon be forced to reveal his perfidy if Sangoma recognised that some of the skulls on the fetish had been substituted?

When they returned to the museum, Archie called the director's office. 'Miss Stritchley, Uncle Sangoma wishes to meet Dr Griffon.'

'I'm sure the director would be most interested,' Dryandra replied. Then, after a moment's silence, 'Can you come up now?'

When Archie explained what was happening, Sangoma said, 'Only me, Arciballe. These young men cannot see such a sacred thing.' So Archie asked Beatrice to take charge of Cletus and the others until he returned.

Dryandra looked on with fascination as, outside Griffon's office, Sangoma stripped off his shirt and puffed out his scarred chest.

She opened the door, saying, 'Director, your visitors.'

Sangoma appraised the fetish before entering the room. In a moment, he took everything in, then strode determinedly ahead, avoiding any further glances at the monstrous object. Archie trailed Sangoma, as if their relationship as it had been in the islands was re-established.

'Welcome!' Griffon said to Sangoma. 'Care for a cup of tea?'

'Perhaps water,' Archie replied.

'The fetish is altered,' Sangoma declared, staring at Griffon. 'The white men, whose great canoe foundered on our islands, were as easy to kill as flying foxes caught in the surf. We always feared they were not strong enough to contain the evil. But now I see that your big men have obtained substitutes—real champions no doubt—for the weakest of them. Congratulate your chief for me,' he said to Archie.

Things were not going as Archie had anticipated. Miss Stritchley passed a glass of water to Sangoma, and Archie fixed Griffon with a defiant look.

'Sangoma believes that four of the skulls on the fetish are not original.'

Griffon looked astonished. 'Meek, is this why you came here? Your obsession with the mask.'

'Sir, I am merely translating what Sangoma said.'

The director became agitated. 'I'm not sure I believe you. But whatever the case, you can tell your Mr Sangoma that if he is implying that we are not caring for the fetish, he is quite wrong. You should add that the mask is now the property of a museum. It will never be returned.'

Archie was flummoxed.

'We expect a great performance from our island dance troupe, Meek. Now, Dryandra, please show our visitors the door.'

Archie could not understand how things had gone so badly wrong. He had not anticipated Sangoma's response to seeing the mask. And Griffon had become agitated, all right. But he had not divulged his crime.

'I see now where the power of the white man comes from,' Sangoma declaimed as they walked towards Archie's office. 'You have collected all the sources of power in the world—the sacred animals, objects and the great mask—and gathered them here. The rail yards and other factories are an illusion. This spirit house is the true source of your power. The museum is the factory of the white man—the source of his cargo. And at its heart is our fetish.'

Archie was disturbed. Cargo cults were beginning to spring up all over the Pacific. Yet he knew that Sangoma was right in one thing. The fetish had become the centre of a cargo cult, a cult which worked through fundraising, and which was overseen by Griffon.

That night Archie was unable to sleep. The second he closed his eyes, the fetish came towards him. Should he risk his career and steal it? Give it to the police as proof of Griffon's perfidy? He understood now that he could no longer dither. He would have to discover the truth, with all its dark mysteries, that dogged the museum and his life. But before that, he needed to take care of his island friends, and ensure that they were prepared for the night of the gallery opening.

Chapter 23

John Jeevons stood beside Beatrice in the anthropology store, watching Sangoma rehearse his dance. Beatrice had retrieved some decorations and masks from the collection that she felt might be suitable. Sangoma donned a great headdress depicting a hammerhead shark. Painted black, white and red, and made of a framework of light timber and cloth, it was at least nine feet long, with jointed tail, jaws and fins, which were animated by the dancer's slow rhythmic movements. The headdress moved to the slow beat of the kundu like a shark on the hunt, making one forget the dancer below. As Sangoma approached Jeevons, the guard seemed transfixed. It was only when the snapping jaws were an arm's length from his head that he leapt aside.

'By the Lord Harry, that's a doozy of a contraption!' Jeevons exclaimed. 'It'll have the old girls at the opening quaking in their shoes.'

Sangoma stopped, looked at Jeevons and flashed a broad, toothy grin. 'I can see the chief likes it,' he told Archie in Venusian, before turning to his tribesmen. 'Cletus, you lead the headhunting party. Put on those grass anklet decorations. They hide your feet, and if you vibrate your ankles and walk in small shuffling steps, it looks like you're walking on air. You'll look really spooky.' The young islander did as instructed, and the others lined up behind him in single file and started to move in a similar manner.

'No!' interjected Sangoma. 'You look like you're going out to find girls, not heads. Come on! Look fierce! And Archie, can you get a boar's tusk for Polycarp's nose, and a man-catcher for Cletus? We need one to make this look authentic.' Archie translated for Beatrice, and she soon returned with the requested items. 'Right lads, on my beat of the drum, shuffle forward, and look fierce,' Sangoma continued. 'You're going to cut off some heads, remember! And look out! There's an ambush on your right! Some defensive action, please!'

Cedric Scrutton and Hardy Champion Descrepency marched in lock step up Macquarie Street. Sharp-featured, smartly dressed and as keen as hounds on a scent, they made a pigeon pair. An element of surprise, they felt, was essential. In the foyer they met Dryandra Stritchley.

'Miss Stritchley,' Scrutton commenced. 'This is Mr Hardy Champion Descrepency, the department's auditor. We'd like to examine the museum accounts, if you please.'

'Gentlemen, have you made an appointment?'

'No, we have not. The accounts, please. Now!'

Sensing danger, Dryandra demurred. 'One moment, please, gentlemen.'

She returned hastily to the director's office. 'Vere, ask no questions! Make yourself scarce. Go! Now! And don't come back until you hear from me.'

Vere Griffon was entirely unused to being addressed by his Christian name, let alone ordered around by Dryandra Stritchley. But something in her voice warned him not to cavil. 'I'll be in the library if you need me,' he said.

Dryandra ushered Scrutton and Descrepency into the director's office. 'Gentlemen, please be seated at the board table. I'll bring you the accounts books.'

'But where is the director? We need to speak with him,' Scrutton interrupted.

'I'm afraid he's fully occupied with preparations for our new exhibition. The opening is this evening. You are invited, Mr Scrutton. And you too, Mr Descrepency, if you wish. Now, please wait here while I retrieve the books.'

Miss Stritchley was in the director's storeroom, bent over the filing cabinet where the accounts books were kept, when she felt a hand on her shoulder.

'Mr Scrutton, how dare you! This is the director's private area!'

'What in heaven's name is that?' Asked Scrutton, pointing to an elaborate porcelain chimney garniture that lay on the table. 'And this?' He pointed to a large black rock shaped like a leg of lamb.

'That is the Bathurst meteorite. Part of an exchange, along with these birds and other specimens,' Dryandra said, gesturing at the boxes Chumley had brought from Abotomy Hall.

'Very well,' Scrutton replied. 'Bring us the books. And a pot of tea, if you would. You have a teapot, I see.' He pointed to a magnificent piece of Meissen.

The pair sat in silence for hours. As hard as they searched, neither Scrutton nor Descrepency could find the smallest irregularity in the museum's accounts. The director was meticulous. And modest to the point of miserliness when it came to his personal expenses.

'Well, Cedric, I've done my best,' sighed Descrepency at the end of the day. 'But these accounts are, well…exemplary. There's not the slightest discrepancy, so to speak, that we might use as the basis of a wider investigation.'

'But there *is* a rat here, Descrepency. I know it,' said Scrutton. 'And it's probably right before our eyes.'

Then it hit him. The coin collection. Donated by a Mr Marchant, he vaguely recalled.

'Stritchley!' he cried out. 'Come here! I want to see the coin collection bequeathed to the museum a few months back.'

'Mr Scrutton, it's 4.58 p.m. The public-service day ends at 4.56 p.m., and I have an appointment across town. I'd be only too happy to bring it to you. But you'll have to call again tomorrow.'

'It may be for the best,' said Scrutton as he accompanied Descrepency down Macquarie Street. 'We'll need a full list of the coins and valuations to make any sense of things. Would you like to come along to the exhibition opening, old chap? We've still got time to dress and return for the event.'

'I think I would. Need a wee dram or two after today. And we might pick up a fresh scent by observing Griffon in his element, so to speak.'

Dryandra Stritchley knew that she must tell Vere Griffon what had happened. It would worry him inordinately—not a good thing when he needed to focus on the exhibition opening. But, with an inspection of the coin collection the next day, she had no choice. She found Griffon in the library, reading a research article on centipedes. He seemed calmer and more content than she could remember.

'Director, I hate to disturb you, but this won't wait. Scrutton and Descrepancy want to examine the Marchant coin collection. Tomorrow.'

'I see,' said Griffon. He wearily put down the journal, and walked off. The pressure had been building on him for months. The stock-market crash, his useless curators, Scrutton and then the business with the Giglione goats. And now that damn interfering accountant Descrepency was scheduled to examine the coin collection! Well, there was no catalogue, so who could say if anything was missing? And the Meissen he had purchased by selling the odd coin. What of it?

As he'd planned his great evolution gallery Vere Griffon had thought again and again about what might epitomise the highest achievement of mankind. And then it had come to him: Meissen porcelain. Britain had the Hanovers (or Windsors as they now called themselves) on the throne, so something German was appropriate. And the cultured figurines of eighteenth-century noblemen and women were exquisite. They spoke to him of home. *Home.* The font of all refinement and progress in the world. There would be a small room, he'd decided, at the end of the exhibition. A sort of treasury where, in a soft light, the felonry of New South Wales could gasp at the beauty of Meissen ware, displayed in glass cases like precious jewels.

Griffon's mind drifted back to his present worries. Even if no impropriety were found, a departmental investigation could be disastrous, especially if it tainted the museum's reputation and so deterred donors. Scrutton's malice, and the gossip columns, might even see him sacked in disgrace.

'Think of Caesar drawing his toga over his face as the last, fatal blows landed. He endured the worst with dignity,' Griffon said to himself. It was, he realised, time to receive his guest of honour, Sir Arthur Woodward, who had travelled from London.

Archie had assembled the islanders in an antechamber off the main exhibition space. They had spent all day preparing. He felt confident enough to leave them, knowing they would appear on cue, and so returned to the main entrance to meet Beatrice. Jeevons was stationed at the door, directing visitors towards the reception. A small group was gathered round him, gawping.

'He tottered towards me, with them terrible eyes. Fixed on me, they was. And his mouth…my God. Great gollops of bloody slime were coming out of it. Oh! And that hand of his. I'll never forget that hand as long as I live. Like a mallee root, it was, all twisted up with the poison.'

'Jeevons, would you desist in telling such ridiculous stories about poor Sopwith! Our esteemed colleague deserves better,'

Archie said sharply.

Jeevons, open-mouthed—and for once speechless—watched as his audience scattered.

By six o'clock, the staff and guests had gathered in the foyer and the arrival of Sir Arthur Woodward was imminent. Canapés and drinks were circulating, and a jazz quartet played in a corner. Vere Griffon glanced around the room and, reassured that all was well, slipped out and made his way to the exhibition.

What he saw did not please him. Henry Bumstocks, a picture of anxiety, was daubing at the Piltdown man's face. Roger Holdfast was whizzing about like a dervish, a screwdriver in one hand and a hammer in the other, screwing here, hammering there, seemingly at random, while Mordant, his brow dripping with sweat, was wielding a paintbrush at the rear of a plinth.

'For God's sake, man, don't bother with the rear,' Griffon roared. 'I'll keep Sir Arthur to the front so he won't see the unfinished bit. And, Holdfast, the guests are sure to hear your hammering. I'll get the band to play a little louder, but for God's sake, keep the noise down!'

Griffon knew that museum artificers habitually worked up to the last moment on exhibits, but this had him shaken. Tonight of all nights he needed to look professional. And in control.

'Strike up something lively. Now.' He said to the band when he returned to the foyer.

The transition from lazy, background jazz to 'Ritzy Glitzy Mitzi' enlivened the atmosphere marvellously. Beatrice started to wiggle her hips. She looked up at her man, as she now thought of Archie despite the fact they had not even properly kissed. His eye was almost back to normal. But his right hand was still bandaged. She was so proud of him.

Archie had managed to get Joe an invitation—a sort of thank you for feeding the Venus Islanders. The fruiterer had turned up in an antique suit with a high-collared shirt that must have been inherited from his grandfather. Joe was a little overwhelmed. 'It's bloody wonderful, Mista Mik. Good onions,' he kept saying over and over. Then, to Archie's relief, Joe struck up a conversation with Hans Schmetterling. Already on his third champagne, Schmetterling was gabbling on in German, while Joe responded in Italian.

Beatrice was engaged in conversation with Mr Trembley, when Archie saw her mouth drop open. Her gaze was fixed on the foyer entrance. Roger Holdfast's son, Gerald, was making his entry. Dressed in a smart linen suit, he was walking hand in hand with Nellie. She looked radiant in a sumptuous ball gown of pink silk taffeta.

'He finally won the duck raffle,' Dithers said, beaming. 'But instead of dashing into the truck, he asked Nellie if she'd accompany him to the opening.'

'She looks beautiful. Her gown must have cost a fortune,' gasped Beatrice.

'That's Nev,' said Dithers with a knowing wink. 'Favour to a friend and all.'

The conversation lulled as a triumvirate strode into the room. Scrutton and Descrepency wore tuxedos, in distinct contrast with the trench coat–wearing Inspector Brownlow. Scrutton felt it appropriate that the detective should accompany them.

Abotomy greeted the three, but after a few words seemed anxious to get away. He fixed Beatrice with a lascivious eye, and slid across the room.

'Dithers, please introduce me to this delightful young lady.'

Dithers was confounded by the squire's bonhomie. 'This is Beatrice Goodenough,' he managed to say. He was about to add 'Archie Meek's girlfriend,' when Abotomy broke in.

'Not one of the Bombuggaree Goodenoughs, eh?'

'Yes, indeed,' Beatrice replied. 'My father is George Goodenough of Bombuggaree, nephew of Admiral Joseph Goodenough.'

'Aha! Holy Joe.' Chumley chortled. 'Died in the New Hebrides, didn't he? Bringing the good news to the savages?'

'My family is rather religious,' Beatrice replied, blushing.

Chumley caught sight of Mrs Gordon-Smythe, who Griffon hoped might fund a new gallery of Pacific cultures. His look, Beatrice felt, indicated more than a nodding acquaintance.

'Gladys, please meet Beatrice Goodenough. She works at the museum. And she's a Bombuggaree Goodenough—a relative of the admiral.'

'My dear girl. How delightful to meet you! My darling late husband counted Admiral Goodenough as a very close friend. But who is this? Not Archibald Meek, surely? Last time I saw you, you were a mere stripling.'

'I'm delighted to meet you again, Mrs Gordon-Smythe. I believe we met last when you came to examine your husband's collection at the museum. As you doubtless know, the reverend's memory is worshipped in the Venus Islands.'

A tear welled in the widow's eyes. 'We must do something, here at the museum, to honour his sacrifice. And we really must display the treasures you've brought back from the wilderness, young man. But what is that on your wrist?' She pointed to the frigate bird.

Archie flinched. 'Ah, it's just a small tattoo, madam. From the islands.'

'My husband bore one almost identical. He always felt that missionaries needed to understand the ways of the natives. He underwent initiation, you know,' she added with a wink. 'You remind me so much of him, when he was your age.'

Gladys Gordon-Smythe took Beatrice's left hand in hers, and examined it.

'Perhaps, my dear, in time…'

Beatrice could not speak. She had glimpsed something that had struck her to the heart—a parchment-like ring on the widow's fourth finger.

Abotomy sensed that Gladys Gordon-Smythe had been deeply affected. With surprising solicitousness he shepherded her to a quiet corner and consoled her with a hug and a glass of bubbly.

'What a nice man. He reminds me of my cousins,' Beatrice said, regaining her composure. 'And what a lovely lady. I can see she's mad on you, Archie.'

Dithers was perplexed by Abotomy's civility. Best to say nothing, he told himself.

A silence was falling on the crowd nearest the entrance, and a loose guard of honour was forming. At the very front of the line was the museum's chairman, the Very Reverend Sir Crispin Jugglers, who seemed to be practising a bow. Behind him was Vere Griffon. As Sir Arthur entered the room Jugglers sprang forward, giving the impression that his brilliantined body was about to topple over. As those about held their collective breath, he bowed deeply, from the waist, until his wizened torso was horizontal, his left leg stretching forward and his right bent elegantly behind. Sir Arthur was somewhat taken aback at the low obeisance—a form of prostration usually reserved for royalty. Then, at the lowest point of Jugglers' bow, the silence was broken by the strident trumpeting of a strangulated clerical fart.

'Very pleased to meet you, too,' said Sir Arthur, trying to make the best of things.

'It is an honour. A high honour indeed, Your Serene Highness, to have you visit these colonies.' Jugglers seemed to have confused Sir Arthur with the Prince of Wales, who had visited some decades earlier.

'Sir Arthur!' Vere Griffon broke in. 'How very good of you to come halfway round the world on our behalf! Welcome, welcome, welcome to our humble museum.'

In the silence that followed, Archie gave a low whistle, and the Venus Islanders danced into the foyer. With spears and man-catchers in their hands, they looked so ferocious that gasps and stifled screams rippled through the crowd. Griffon took the opportunity to lead Jugglers to the guard's office, where a cab was called for him. The director then returned to watch what he later called a magnificent performance of savage theatre. Sangoma led, dancing his shark mask hypnotically to the beat of the kundu drum. As he recreated the movements of the hammerhead sharks that seasonally visited the lagoon, he seemed to transform the mask into a living creature. The crowd made way for him like sardines before a marlin.

Then the entire troupe simulated a headhunting raid, the finale of which consisted of placing a man-catcher over Archie's head. When Cletus stalked onto the floor with the device in his hand, it looked like he was carrying a tennis racket. Though innocent in appearance, the man-catcher is a most devilish thing. Instead of strings, a spike projects from the point where the handle meets the frame. When placed over Archie's head, its horrible purpose became apparent. The spike sat where the spine meets the cranium: the slightest push would sever the spinal cord. Native people rarely waste energy; the purpose of the contraption was to force the victim of a headhunting raid to walk to his fate. So much easier than carrying a corpse. Archie found that he didn't need to mime terror as he was led off, the islanders whooping and pointing spears at his chest. He felt it in the pit of his stomach.

The Venus Islanders danced out of the foyer to the beat of the kundu and to riotous applause. The museum's supporters had, said one elderly matron, never been treated to anything quite so excitingly savage.

As the drumming disappeared down the corridor, Vere Griffon called for quiet, and speeches followed. Then the entire party walked to the new gallery. Griffon led the way, and entered the hall just in time to see Holdfast's left foot disappear behind a display case. The smell of paint hung a little strong in the air, but nothing else was amiss. With Sir Arthur Woodward by his side, Griffon stepped towards a blue ribbon strung between two chairs, on one of which sat a large pair of scissors. Sir Arthur cut the ribbon, and the warmed-up crowd erupted in applause.

There were *oohs* and *ahhs* as the guests entered the exhibition and took in the magnificence of it all. The skeletons of a giant sloth and a tyrannosaurus formed the centrepieces. But most attention was paid to the Piltdown man. He looked so brutish that one woman fainted, depriving her of the chance to hear Sir Arthur expound on the discovery of the Piltdown bones and their place in human evolution.

Vere Griffon found himself bailed up.

'Director! Let me introduce my husband, Dr Siegfried Leggenhacker.'

It was Elizabeth Doughty, dressed in a tartan skirt and highlands blouse, and a tam-o'-shanter on her head. Her one leg looked splendid in a tartan stocking, while her newly fitted peg of black ebony was striking, to say the least. At her side was a stout, blue-eyed, walrus-moustached gent, peering at the world through a monocle. Dr Leggenhacker was, Griffon thought, Teutonic to his bootstraps. Even his pot belly, loosely constrained behind his blue-striped shirt with its low collar, seemed unmistakably German.

'*Guten abend. Herzlich willkommen, sehr geehrter Herr Doktor Leggenhacker. Ihre anwesenheit heute abend ist uns eine ganz besondere ehre!*' said Griffon.

'How kind of you to welcome me in my native tongue, Director. It's a rare thing in the far-flung colonies,' Leggenhacker replied.

'Have you met your countryman, Herr Schmetterling? Let me introduce you.'

Griffon grew less certain as he approached Schmetterling. The man was somewhat the worse for wear.

'*Guten abend, Herr Schmetterling.* Meet your countryman,

Dr Siegfried Leggenhacker.' Griffon's presence had reduced Schmetterling to a trembling mess. It was Joe who responded.

'Good onions, Dottore Leghacker! Is a good party, eh!'

'*Ja*. But the best is yet to come, I think.'

The Japanese sailors, meanwhile, had gathered beneath an exhibit titled 'The Ladder of Progress'. It consisted of skulls, arranged in a pyramid whose bottom rung was labelled 'Australian Aborigine'. Then came layers of Africans, Papuans, Islanders, Chinese, Arabs and finally, at the apex, a single skull with 'Caledonian' written in ink across its brow.

'Director!' cried Admiral Iamaura. 'Very excellent. British on top. But next should be Japan. Why no Japanese?'

'Oh…well, Admiral. Quite simple, really. Couldn't get the skulls.'

'Ah so.' Iamaura bowed as Griffon moved on.

The director was intending to visit the bathroom, but at the far end of the hall he felt a tap on his shoulder. He swung around, and came eye to eye with Cedric Scrutton. Behind him was Hardy Champion Descrepency.

'Griffon, you vile thief. We're onto you!' Flecks of foam appeared on Scrutton's lips.

'Really, old thing. No idea what you're talking about. Perhaps we could discuss it tomorrow.'

'Oh, that we will,' Scrutton spat back.

'You've met your Golgotha now, Director,' added Descrepency.

'*Gol*gotha, please!' Vere Griffon insisted with an emphasis on the first syllable, as if he were correcting an ignorant child. He found mispronunciation intolerable.

The director was standing at the urinal with the faintest echo of satisfaction at the launch having gone off so well, when he heard a tremendous crash. He cut things off as best he could, buttoned up, and returned to the hall. A crowd had gathered around the soaring tyrannosaurus skeleton, which he could see now ended at the neck.

An ashen-faced Cedric Scrutton was holding his shoulder. Brownlow, notebook in hand, stood beside him. In front of them lay a shattered saurian cranium. Roger Holdfast was looking up in horror at the abruptly terminating neck.

'I just can't understand what happened. Gerald checked all the bolts this afternoon. It's impossible that they could have come loose.'

Scrutton woke as if from a trance.

'Griffon, I knew that you were a low life, but I had no idea that you were a murderer as well. There will be an investigation into this, I swear. There will, indeed! I'll see you hang!' He cried as he stormed off.

The museum guards soon erected a temporary barrier around the fallen skull. More music, and a fresh round of drinks and canapés, restored gaiety. Archie, however, could not relax, and did not trust himself to have a champagne. He was on the lookout for Dryandra Stritchley, who was nowhere to be seen. Tied up with officework, he thought. Just as the guests were getting over-jolly she marched into the hall, looking about as if in search of someone.

Archie slipped out and made his way to the boardroom. To his shock, the door opened as he approached. Elizabeth Doughty and Dr Leggenhacker stepped into the hallway, Leggenhacker's jacket was wrapped around what looked like a leg of lamb.

'Meek. What are you doing here?' hissed Elizabeth.

'I could ask you the same question,' he replied. Seeing the steely look in her eyes, he added, 'Err, I've come to replace the tooth in the fetish.'

'The what!'

'The tooth. On the day I returned from the islands I discovered that an incisor had dropped out of one of the skulls of the Great Venus Island Fetish. I haven't had a moment to replace it until now.'

The Leggenhackers seemed not to care for his explanation. They moved swiftly down the corridor towards the exit. Archie entered the darkened boardroom. The great fetish hung in the eerie twilight. Its eyes seemed to be staring at him, their manic spirals drawing him closer.

He was soon face to face with the beastly thing. He struggled to lift it from the wall, but his damaged hand lacked strength. It was as if he could smell the smoky fumes of hell itself emanating from the monstrous oral cavity. The fetish was far heavier than he'd imagined, and in his battle to lift it he found himself leaning repeatedly into the tooth-lined cavern. He felt like he was being consumed by it.

Then something broke. An object crashed to the floor and split in half. It was a skull—one of the orange ones. Archie stared at it in petrified silence. Then he looked at the gap in the skull ring.

The next few moments would always remain confused in his mind. His clearest memory was of a tremendous roar, as if the hobnails of hell had been let loose. The air about him turned into an inferno, the flames of which licked at him like the tongue of the devil himself. He knew that to save his life he must drop the mask, yet now it seemed to be holding onto him. Then the sleeve of his coat burst into flames, and he found himself running down the hall, screaming, 'Fire, fire,' at the top of his lungs.

Almost instantly Vere Griffon was at his side, acting with the resolve of the captain of a sinking ship. The director seemed to be simultaneously organising an orderly departure of the guests, a bucket chain of museum staff to pour water on the fire, and directing the newly arrived firemen towards the blaze. It was, everybody later agreed, the man's finest hour.

Chapter 24

The following morning Griffon learned that the fire brigade had been alerted by a tip-off. The fire chief quizzed him about the caller, but the director was unable to help. Examination of the scene revealed that the blaze had started in the old walk-in safe at the back of the director's office. It had smouldered there for some time before the heat blasted out a window in the adjacent corridor. Then the influx of fresh air had caused the flames to explode.

While inclined to arson as an explanation, the fire department could not rule out other causes. The electrical wiring of the museum, for one, was antique. Coming to a firm conclusion would be hampered, the chief explained, because the fire had almost completely consumed the director's office, destroying vital evidence. As Griffon examined the ashes, he realised that not only had the museum's financial records perished, but also his collection of Meissen porcelain and the Great Venus Island Fetish. All the exchange material he had accumulated for Professor Giglione had also gone up in smoke, though thankfully the rest of the museum had survived unharmed.

While Vere Griffon was pondering the previous night's events, Cedric Scrutton marched into the office of the premier's secretary, Winston Spencer. 'We have an emergency on our hands, Spencer. A full-blown emergency. The fire at the museum last night is highly suspicious, and I damn well know it was lit to cover up gross malfeasance, including a colossal misuse of government funds. If the premier is to avoid becoming besmirched, he must order an inquiry immediately.'

The following day it was revealed that a special commission would investigate not only the fire, but also the entire administration of the museum. It would be headed by that hammer of evildoers, Sir Harbottle Grimston, retired chief of the premier's department. Mentor and close friend of Cedric Scrutton, Grimston was renowned for his dogged ferreting-out of crooked public servants. It was whispered in the corridors that he always got his man.

The commission's first hearings, Grimston announced, would be held forthwith, in the Parliament building itself.

In the aftermath of the fire, Archie made his way to the boarding house to organise the Venus Islanders for their return. How, he agonised, could he tell Sangoma that the fetish had been destroyed?

'Uncle,' he began. 'The dance you performed last night was a triumph.'

'Thank you, my son. I had no idea that we had been invited to perform at such an important ceremony. When we islanders come to the end of a great ceremonial cycle—one lasting many years—we burn the spirit house that the ceremonies took place in. We see that your tribe follows a similar custom. When the fire started we followed the museum clan outside. Then your enemies, the men dressed in red, arrived, and tried to put out the fire so they could steal the sacred things and shame you. We were ready to join the fight and drive them away, but your great war leader Jeevons was not vigorous. He did nothing to protect the cleansing flames.'

'Uncle, I can't explain things now. But I do have something important to tell you. Last night I tried to take the fetish.'

Sangoma's eyes widened. He held his breath as Archie went on. 'I tried to pull it from the wall, but it was too strong. Then the fire came, and it was burned to ashes. I'm so sorry.'

'By the bones of my ancestors, I thought at first that you had succeeded,' gasped Sangoma. 'What good fortune that you did not. It was you—your power—that destroyed it.

There is no danger in ashes.'

'But it was a great work of art,' Archie lamented.

'Such things can no longer be fashioned, I admit. Its age is past.' Archie was beyond astonishment at Sangoma's pragmatism. There were, he concluded, many things about the Venusians he'd never understand.

On the docks Archie produced his old sea-trunk. It had been delivered to the steamer that morning, and was full of gifts. Clothes, drawing paper for the children, axes, bush knives. And a tap. He'd purchased it at the hardware so that Sangoma would remember the water coming from the wall. Archie placed five shillings in Sangoma's hand. 'This is from the director. It's payment for your performance,' he said, unable to look Sangoma in the eye. Then he watched as the islanders walked the gangplank. He knew that he would never see them again.

Only the director's office and boardroom had been damaged in the blaze, so most of the staff returned to work the following morning. After work Archie made his way to the Harris Tea Rooms, where Beatrice was waiting for him. As he walked he began to feel better, stronger. The fetish was gone. Future anthropologists would doubtless curse him for the loss. But he felt stronger and could finally see clearly. He saw a last chance to bring his director's murderous spree to an end.

He found Beatrice seated at an elegant marble table, surrounded by gold fixtures, sipping tea from a china teacup.

'The fetish, Beatrice. I tried to take it, but something happened. I just couldn't seem to free it from the wall.'

'Now who will believe us about Polkinghorne, Sopwith and the others?' she asked.

'We should go to the police, though I'm not certain that they would get to the bottom of things. Vere Griffon is very well connected. He'd probably get warning of an investigation, and do away with any remaining evidence,' said Archie. 'We need more evidence, and only Henry Bumstocks can provide that. He can't have done all his dirty work at the museum. Otherwise somebody would surely have noticed. I think we need to find out where he lives, and search his house. I remember Mordant saying that he lived in Balmain. Do you think that we could follow him home?'

With the assistance of the police, Grimston secured several witnesses to the fire who were not associated with the museum. This, he felt, was invaluable. Staff were not to be trusted. His prize witness was rather unlikely: an urchin who had been playing on William Street and told the police that he'd seen smoke belching from a window. The boy stopped to see what would happen. As the fire grew he observed a one-legged Scotsman and a butcher emerge from the museum, and vanish into Hyde Park.

Vere Griffon knew that he'd be called to testify, but he did not expect to appear on the first day. Dryandra Stritchley had not come to work since the blaze, and Griffon felt distinctly vulnerable without her. The inquiry was held in a large office used for state receptions. Below a portrait of the monarch a grand desk had been installed, upon which was a marble nameplate that proclaimed in gold lettering 'Sir Harbottle Grimston, Knight Bachelor, KBE', then below, 'Chief Investigator, Museum Inquiry'.

Vere Griffon stood to attention as an overweight and puffing Grimston waddled in, preceded by two secretaries. He was dressed in a black robe. Small, round, wire-framed spectacles obscured his bloodshot eyes. He took his seat and, without looking up from his notes, began.

'Dr Vere Griffon?'

'Yes.'

'You've been director of the museum since, let's see, 1923, have you not?'

'Yes, sir.' Griffon was determined to face Sir Harbottle with a stiff upper lip.

'And do you know of any reason why anybody might set fire to the institution under your care?'

'No, sir. None at all.'

Sir Harbottle fixed Griffon with a basilisk stare. 'Do you have any one-legged men in your employ, Director?'

Griffon smoothed his hair in bewilderment. He had not expected this. 'Well, no, sir, not that I can think of.'

'Have you, or have you not? Answer plainly!' roared Sir Harbottle, the veins in his forehead bulging.

'No, sir. Though we do have a guard with a gammy leg, if that's any help.'

Sir Harbottle's veins looked ready to burst. He composed himself, and switched tack. 'Have you had any dealings with butchers recently?'

'Beyond purchasing meat for my own needs, no.'

'Details, details,' Grimston roared.

'Hmm, four pork sausages, a piece of silverside and a bung fritz last Thursday at Gordons in Darlinghurst.'

During the war Grimston was responsible for sniffing out traitors and spies from the New South Wales public service. The mention of bung fritz triggered something.

'*Pickelhaube* under the bed sort of chap, eh, Griffon? Do you speak German?'

'Yes, passingly. I'm finding your line of questioning somewhat difficult to follow. A one-legged man and a butcher?' Vere added cautiously.

'We have a witness, Director—a disinterested witness—who claims to have seen a one-legged man and a butcher carrying a leg of lamb fleeing the scene of the blaze. I can assure you, sir, that my commission will get to the bottom of this if we have to interview every meat-vendor and amputee in the city.'

Discharged at last from the inquiry, the director returned to work, exhausted. He'd hardly slept since the fire. Without Dryandra to support him and to attend to the day-to-day details, the pressure was becoming almost unbearable. He'd even begun to wonder whether it was all worth it.

Later that day Vere Griffon sat in the museum library, where he'd temporarily set up office. He had received a letter.

October 25, 1933. MV Prinz Wilhelm, 2nd Class
Dear Vere,

I hope that you will protect me by never revealing the contents of this letter. If you cannot promise me that, then please reduce it to ashes at once.

The official purpose of this correspondence is to inform

you of my resignation as your secretary. Please forgive its abrupt nature, but my choices are limited. I intend to relocate to Malaya, where my cousin manages a rubber plantation. As you read on, please understand that all I did—even the destruction of our illicit child, if you could call the Meissen that—was done for love of you.

When I saw your face collapse as I told you about the visit of Scrutton and Descrepancy, I knew that things had gone too far for you to straighten out. I realised there was only one way forward. A cleansing blaze, and that it was I who must light it. As you always said, there's no time like the present, and that evening the entire museum staff were at the opening of the evolution gallery. It almost broke my heart, as I know it will break yours, to see all that irreplaceable Meissen perish in the flames. Please forgive me, dearest Vere, if you will let me call you that just once. The accounts books, that horrible mask—the office where we worked together so happily. I knew that it had to be cleansed.

At the last moment I faced a terrible crisis. What if the fire spread undetected? It might destroy the entire building and its priceless collections. It was a dreadful risk. But even as I weighed things up my hands were busy accumulating the kindling. The accounts books, the Marchant coins and the precious Meissen soon lay in a pile in the middle of the drinks pantry. I looked at the glorious porcelain one last time. How often had we sat in that small, windowless space gazing at it in perfect serenity, our minds elevated from the sordid business that is life in today's public service?

There was one thing which did not need to perish in the flames. Dr Doughty deserves better than to lose her precious meteorite, so I carried it to the board table and placed it there, in the hope that the fire brigade would arrive before the flames advanced that far.

I wanted the fire to take quickly, and wasn't sure that the single malt I'd poured on the pile had the alcoholic strength required for the job. Then I remembered the centipede in its jar of pickling alcohol. At 70 per cent proof it would go up with a whoosh. I knew, Vere, how much you would lament the loss of that unique specimen. But better lose it than being torn to pieces by the curs snapping at your heels. I unscrewed the jar and spilled its contents over the account books. I thought that you'd like to know that the *Horribilipes* flowed out with the liquid and draped itself atop the Meissen mantle garniture like a dead Viking chief atop his funeral pyre. Before striking the match I went to the phone and called the fire brigade, and then I walked out of the room.

Vere, you stole my heart as surely as Dr Leggenhacker took Dr Doughty's leg. But you did not know it, and my feelings were never reciprocated. If only things had been different.

Yours affectionately,
Dryandra Stritchley

Chapter 25

Vere Griffon had reached breaking point. An investigation into his administration, a burnt museum, and now he had lost forever the only woman who had ever loved him. He collapsed into his chair, hunched and grey, a defeated man.

He didn't know how much time had passed—he may have sat there for minutes or hours—when he heard a distinctive rumble. It was Mr Gormly, the museum's storeman, announcing his presence by respectfully clearing his throat.

'Seven large boxes have arrived. From Italy, sir, addressed to your good self. They're in the storeroom. Shall I have them brought up?'

Gormly took the dismissive wave as a sign of approval. 'Very well, sir, I'll only be a moment.'

The librarian, who was doing temporary double duty as Griffon's secretary, rapped on the pillar that acted as a door and said, 'It's Mr Abotomy, sir. He wants to see you, and won't take no for an answer.'

'What-ho, old fellow?' warbled Chumley Abotomy. 'Looks like you lost a pound and found sixpence. Come on, Vere! Cheer up. Things can't be that bad!'

'It's Dryandra. Resigned.'

At that instant the first of the Italian crates arrived.

'By Jove, I do believe these are the Giglione goats!' exclaimed Abotomy. 'What a treat. Let's have a look at them, eh.'

'Impossible,' replied Vere Griffon. 'We've not sent the exchanges yet. And now that the most important pieces have been lost in the fire, I doubt we'll ever complete the transaction.'

'Balderdash,' Abotomy shot back. 'More than one way to skin a cat. Giglione won't be demanding the exchanges. Open them up, Gormly. Let's have a look.'

As the crates were prised open and the stuffed goats removed from their wrappings, Griffon's heart sank even further. They were a motley lot, the majority bandy-legged, cross-eyed, or twisted of horn. 'My God, how much more debasement must I suffer?' he asked. But it was hard to hear anything he said, because Abotomy was laughing so loudly.

'Look at that one clenching its bottom. What a painful expression! That, my dear director, is Cardinal Corleone, famous throughout Rome as a martyr to the haemorrhoids. They say the fellow prays hourly to Saint Fiacre. Even takes confession from the throne, Giglione reckons. And that one with the crossed eyes, he's Cardinal Stefano. Head of the Roman Inquisition—and a famed self-abuser! And ah! See that big fellow over there,' he said, pointing to the Chilean mounteback, whose testicles hung almost to the ground. 'That, my man, well, that's the pope! Biggest lecher in the whole damn Eternal City according to Giglione. Tremendous fun, isn't it, Vere?'

Vere Griffon erupted. As he howled, he didn't know whether he was laughing or crying, but with Abotomy cackling alongside him he began to feel better. And this he could not understand, because things had definitely taken a turn for the worse.

'Giglione says he is a good Catholic, but he hates the hypocrisy of the Church. Really, as he told me himself, he's nothing but a naughty boy. Bit like me, I suppose,' said Abotomy. 'I say, Vere! Did you know that the premier is a great goat enthusiast? A breeder of champion cashmeres. I think he should get an eyeful of this. Let's call his office and see if he can come over.'

Vere was beyond caring. Would things get any worse if the premier saw these ridiculous ovine mounts?

Abotomy sent out for cucumber sandwiches and a bottle of the premier's favourite French champagne. With Gormly's help he arranged the goats into a sort of guard of honour in the foyer, lining them up from least to most grotesque.

He'd just finished when the premier strode in. 'This better be important, Abotomy. I cut short a meeting with the treasurer to be here. The government hangs by a pubic hair at present!'

Then he saw the goats. 'Great Caesar's ghost!' he exclaimed. 'Is that an ancestral cashmere? *And* a Syrian fat-tail! Never thought I'd live to see the day.'

'And here, Premier, is a Chilean mounteback. Almost the

last of his race,' Abotomy exclaimed as he poured a glass of champagne. 'Just look at those lips! It's the only beast on the pampas able to take on the prickly pear—and beat it! Eats it down to the stumps, they say.'

'Is that right, old fellow! The pear's devastating the grazing lands of the west as we speak. The graziers are in uproar. Chumley, I don't suppose this could be described as stage one in the fight against the pear, could it? If we could get some living examples of the mounteback and breed them up, in a few years we might have the dastardly shrub on the run! And what a handsome fellow! Proud, strong and virile. Answer to a maiden's prayer the beast is, surely. And to a premier's, perhaps. If we play our cards right, Chumley, that creature might just save my neck at the next election.'

'You mean there might be votes in goats, Premier?' said Abotomy gleefully.

'Vere,' the premier said, turning to the director. 'Well done. Always knew you were a good man. Was a bit worried at first that you were overly academic, so to speak, coming from Cambridge and all. But I can see now I was wrong. The Royal Agricultural Show opens in a week, and if you could arrange to have these splendid specimens displayed there—perhaps with the Chilean mounteback chewing on a prickly pear—along with a few words on its potential to rid us of the infestation, I'd be immensely grateful. After that we could get the whole lot out on tour in the west. I know finances have been tight lately, and you've had a terrible fire, which must have set you back. But for this, money would be no object.'

Vere Griffon felt like he was in a dream. He had expected the axe to fall on his career, if not his neck. But instead he was being feted as some sort of political Svengali. It was as if he'd entered another world. And perhaps he had.

'Do you think we should tell the premier that the Chilean mounteback is supposed to be extinct?' Vere Griffon asked after the politician had left. 'Giglione claims he shot the last one.'

'Politics, Vere, is all about expectation—and the management of it. What's required, in this moment of peril, is hope. Hope that the pear can be defeated. That and public confidence that the premier is doing his utmost to eradicate the vicious weed. I think we can leave any *practical* concerns on the backburner for the moment. But I tell you what, credit would redound on the museum if an expedition were dispatched to secure a few living mountebacks—whether it succeeded or not. Perhaps Dithers should delay his African safari and go instead to South America?'

'I thought your feelings towards Dithers were hostile,' Griffon replied.

'I was just having a little fun, Vere. Dithers is such a serious sort of fellow. Believes everything a chap says. A bit like you that way.'

'I see. Perhaps you could try to mend fences with him. Tremendous asset to the place, you know.'

Griffon thought he'd try his luck a little further. 'Chumley, despite my best efforts, and my—I mean our—considerable triumph with the Giglione goats, I find myself in a spot of bother. On a couple of fronts. There's the fire, of course. Blame could fall, entirely without basis I hasten to add, on me. Then there's that damn investigation of Grimston's. He's found nothing, but the very fact he's sniffing about the place is damaging. A museum director must, you know, be like Caesar's wife—above suspicion. Otherwise the great and the good will avoid the place.'

'Vere,' Chumley responded after a brief silence. 'The premier is so in awe of your perspicacity right now that I'm sure he won't want your reputation, or indeed that of the museum, tarnished in any way. I'll have a word in his shell-like. But now a word of advice to you, if you don't mind. You might want to see that Mordant fellow moved on. Could be a spot of bother if Bunkdom was ever rolled for his fencing. Perhaps the government pathologist has a suitable position for a man of Mordant's talents?'

Vere Griffon finally understood that he had met his match. 'I'll speak to Leopold on the morrow,' he said evenly—despite the fact that he had no idea what Abotomy was talking about.

Chapter 26

'It must be tonight, Beatrice. There's not a moment to lose. Bumstocks might be destroying the evidence as we speak.'

Archie and Beatrice were once more in the Harris Tea Rooms. Beatrice looked fiercely at Archie. 'Yes. Tonight. I'll be ready.'

Bumstocks was working late. It was the gloaming before he made his way hurriedly down Macquarie Street towards Circular Quay. Beatrice and Archie, who had been watching from the park opposite, followed at a discreet distance. The old fellow was remarkably fast on his pins, and Beatrice had difficulty keeping up. Why she had worn her new heels that evening she could not say.

Bumstocks boarded the Balmain ferry, followed by a furtive

Archie and Beatrice. After Bumstocks seated himself for'ard and inside, they moved to the open deck on the stern. Beatrice shivered, and Archie hugged her. He took her hand in his and warmed it. He was even considering a second experiment in maritime kissing when the ferry started reversing. They'd reached Balmain.

Bumstocks shot down the gangway with the speed of a man half his age, and proceeded up the hill at a cracking pace. Beatrice shed her heels, and was soon puffing. The taxidermist stopped at 88 Short Street, a worker's cottage with a tiny neglected front garden. He rummaged in his trouser pocket for a key, entered, and slammed the front door shut. After a moment a light went on.

'Well, we know where he lives. But how do we get a look inside?' asked Beatrice, still panting.

'I think he lives alone, Beatrice. The cottage was in darkness when he arrived. And nobody came to greet him. It might be worth hanging about for a few minutes. He was in such a rush, perhaps he's running late for something and will go out again. We can wait just round the corner, behind that picket fence.'

As they stood in the darkness Beatrice thrilled to feel Archie take her hand in his. But she refused to be distracted, and kept one eye fixed on the front door of number 88. Sure enough, a few minutes later Bumstocks emerged, an ornate apron tied round his waist and a briefcase in his hands.

'I say! A Mason. I would never have guessed,' whispered Archie.

'He locked the front door, Archie. I don't think we'll be able to get in.'

'Let's try the laneway at the back.'

In the dark space of the rear lane, Archie counted off the blocks: '100, 98, 96, 94.'

'No, that's still 96, Archie, it's a double block,' corrected Beatrice.

'94, 92, 90, 88. This is it.'

Archie stood beside a dilapidated paling fence. A crude wooden door a couple of feet square had been cut into it. It was used by the nightcart man to remove the can. Archie tugged on the latch. It opened easily.

'Thank God the can's been emptied,' Archie said as he lifted a malodorous old kerosine tin from the opening. 'I'll go through and open the front door.' Beatrice was grateful that Archie was such a gentleman. She really doubted that she could have followed him in through the toilet.

Beatrice walked to the front door. There was a creaking sound, and the door swung open. 'Hurry up. Come in,' urged Archie. 'We can't put the lights on. Someone might see us.'

Archie struck a match. The entire hall seemed skewed to the left, as if it was falling into the neighbouring block. Its floorboards were covered with a single threadbare runner that extended less than half its length. A naked light bulb, its upper half black with filth, hung by an electrical cord from a Bakelite socket. Paint was peeling from the ceiling and walls.

'I'm scared, Archie,' Beatrice whispered. 'Maybe we shouldn't be here.'

But Archie kept moving down the hall. When they reached the kitchen he struck another match. A wood stove—a Metters No 2, its face spotted with rust—stood in the fireplace. Beside it a pantry lay open, revealing a few mismatched cups and plates. On one of the plates was half a pork pie.

'Upstairs,' said Archie. He gingerly made his way up the narrow staircase. At the top was a closed door. For a second Archie hesitated. Moonlight flooded in from a window opening into the staircase. He touched the knob, and the door swung open. 'Must be the tilt of the house,' he said nervously as he stepped forward and struck another match.

'My God!' exclaimed Beatrice. In the middle of the room was a narrow, single bed. Its old striped horsehair mattress was falling apart. There was nothing else on the floor. What had caused Beatrice to gasp was the walls. Every inch of space was taken up with glass-fronted display boxes. Row upon row of them. And in them were the most varied scenes of domestic life imaginable. In one, a mother wearing an old-fashioned Mother Hubbard dress was busy frying sausages, her child playing at her feet while the father sat at the kitchen table, reading the newspaper and smoking his pipe. In another, a mother was bathing her children, and in yet another, mother and father lay together in bed, reading *Harper's Bazaar*.

The innumerable scenes had each been constructed with the greatest care: the furniture was so intricately wrought that it would not have been out of place in a dolls' house at Buckingham Palace. The tiny frying pan and other kitchen utensils were forged out of metal, and included every detail. They must have been made under a microscope, Beatrice marvelled. But what drew her gasp were the figures themselves. The mothers, fathers and children enlivening every scene were not human. They were cats. Kittens mostly, judging from their size. And they had been stuffed with so much care that the expressions of concentration, weariness, disapproval or joy they wore were almost human.

Archie and Beatrice stood for a long time in silence, uncertain of what to do next. It was Beatrice who heard the front door open. The hallway light came on downstairs, and their hearts froze. They were trapped.

Bumstocks' heavy footfalls moved along the hallway, and ceased. The clink of glass on glass was heard, and the pouring of liquid. A kitchen chair creaked under a heavy weight. And an unearthly mumbling began.

'Be still, my hands.' It was Bumstocks, in a reverie.

'It's not right, God damn, it's not right for you to arrive here in this bloody sack, dropped in the sink with such a thud. If only they had asked me, I would have done things different. Brought you here in a fine box. As fine as I could get. No help now, anywise.

'I must look at you. Forgive me, to uncover you in such a state. I keep the light low.

'Your eyes are not as kind as they were. Nor is your mouth. But the wee spots of flesh at the corner of your eyes—I know them. The sweetness of their memory pierces me to the heart.

'You are heavy, and slippery. I must sing as I go. And drink. To you.'

The clink of a glass was followed by eerie chant.

There was three men come out o' the west, their fortunes for to try,
and these three men made a solemn vow, John Barleycorn must die.
They ploughed, they sowed, they harrowed him in, throwed clods upon

his head, and these three men made a solemn vow, John Barleycorn
was dead.

They have let him lie for a very long time till the rain from heaven did
fall. Then little Sir John sprang up his head, and he did amaze
them all.

They let him stand till the midsummer day, till he looked both pale and
wan. Now they pour him out of an old brown jug, and they call
him home-brewed ale.

Yes, they call him home-brewed ale.

'I must take a wire and empty you. Grey you flow into the sink.

'And now I must put out your eyes.

'Then I'll put you to rest in your own brown jug. And tend you and clean and scrape you, till you're whole again.

'But how shall I put myself to rest?'

Archie took Beatrice's hand and they stole silently down the stairs. They could see the great hulk of a man hunched over in his chair, breathing heavily. A bottle of Scotch sat on the table beside him, and he held an empty tumbler in his hand. As they approached the open kitchen door, the figure stirred. A flash of reflected light revealed that Bumstocks' eyes, hidden so deep in their sockets as to be all but invisible, were open—and fixed on them.

At that moment, if she could have, Beatrice would have screamed. But she was paralysed with fear. Henry Bumstocks' stare seemed to pierce her soul. His gaze turned to Archie, and he began clasping and unclasping his free fist, as if he was reaching for something to club the pair with.

'Mr Meek, Miss Goodenough. What are you doing here?'

Archie was now beyond fear. He knew only one thing: that he must not let Beatrice come to harm. Their very lives, he felt, depended on what he said next.

'Ah, Bumstocks,' he began as if he were expecting to meet the taxidermist. 'We've come with a message from the director. There are some specimens requiring urgent taxidermic attention. As a result of the fire. He'd like you to be at work early, to attend to them.'

'But why are you standing here, in the dark, in my hall?'

'Well, we knocked, Henry, and thought we heard somebody upstairs call us. So we came in. But we couldn't find a light switch. We were just admiring your wonderful taxidermy,' Archie said.

'My little kittens,' Bumstocks said softly. 'I get them from the pound. If nobody wants them they drown them, you know. So I take the poor sodden things in. If I could afford to feed them, I'd take them in live, I would.

'Oh, it don't matter anywise, Archie, why you've come. I never get visitors, so it's good to see you.' Henry Bumstocks' face was transformed by the kindest of smiles. 'Can I offer you a cup of tea?'

'It's a lonely life the taxidermist leads,' he said as they sat at the table. 'Bit like being a funeral director. I was never much to look at anyway, but whenever I told a girl what I did for a living she'd run a mile. And the formaldehyde's not been kind to my hands, or my head. S'pose that's why I never married. Anywise, the kittens is my family now.'

'Henry, can I ask you something?' If Archie did not ask now, he knew he never would. 'There have been some strange goings on at the museum, and I'm determined to get to the bottom of them. When I returned from the islands I discovered that the Great Venus Island Fetish had been installed in the boardroom.'

'I know. I've been doing my best to look after it. The skulls started to sprout mould and I've had to bleach them to get rid of it. I'm afraid it's damaged some.'

'How many, Henry?'

'Four, so far. You can pick them because they've lightened off a bit, with the bleach.'

'Yes,' said Archie, 'they've turned from dark brown to orange. And bits have started to drop off—must be the corrosion caused by the bleach.'

'I'm sorry, Archie. But orders is orders.'

Archie slumped into his chair. His whole world was suddenly turned upside down, and he felt like a fool. Yet still it didn't make sense. 'What happened to Polkinghorne?' he asked.

'Oh, it was so terrible, Archie. Soon after you left, a new cadet arrived at the museum. His name was Peter White. White by name, and pale and delicate by nature. He was about sixteen, and fascinated with mummies and suchlike. Anywise, Polkinghorne took him under his wing, and they became very close. I saw them once, in the Egyptology collection. You know what I mean. Anyway, one day Peter didn't show up to work. Instead his dad came in, and he took Polkinghorne outside and flogged the poor bugger half to death in the park across the road. It was dark. Winter. They had words too: I know because I was walking home when they parted.

'Polkinghorne said he didn't want a doctor. Just to get home.

But he never got off that ferry.'

'Do you think he committed suicide, Henry?' asked Beatrice.

'Maybe. But I wasn't going to besmirch his name. Said nothing to nobody, 'cept Giles. Only told him I didn't see Polkinghorne get off the ferry. But I reckon he leapt off the stern with weights in his pockets.'

'One more thing, Henry,' said Archie carefully. 'We know that Sopwith's skull was in the taxidermy workshop.'

'Aye. What of it? What were you doing snooping around my work area?' Bumstocks said sharply.

'That's a long story, Henry. But why was Sopwith's cranium in your workshop?'

'He donated himself to the museum, Archie. Most terrible job I've ever had to do, cleaning him up. He arrived, skinned, in a hessian sack. No respect at all. But I did it for him. When he was alive he often complained that there were no Scots' skulls to compare with those of the blacks. And he loved the place. Seems he never wanted to leave it. The director had a wonderful plan for him too. Eric represents the epitome of human evolution in the new gallery: the British Race. His is a fine skull. Strong and masculine. I even fitted him with a new set of teeth. You might have seen him there already. Sitting atop the skulls of all the other races, with "Caledonian" written in ink across his brow, as he'd have wished. And, you know, the director showed me his will. Eric left five quid so the staff could drink a toast to him. We were going to organise a small celebration in his honour, let everybody know that he was still with us, so to speak, after we'd got the exhibition open.'

Bumstocks was becoming animated. Beatrice noticed a

dirty bandage on his left wrist.

'Henry, come to the sink. Whatever's under that bandage needs tending to.'

Archie went to the laundry for some Eusol and a fresh bandage while Beatrice gently removed the old one. Under it was a large festering cut.

'It's been so long since I've had that,' Henry said as Beatrice took his hand in hers and began gently to clean it.

'How on earth did you do it?' Beatrice asked.

'An accident. I was cleaning up Eric, and I suppose me nerves were on edge—not wanting to be seen doing such a job and all. But I owed it to my old friend to do it. Then a giraffe bone dropped from a shelf in the workshop. It broke into splinters with a tremendous crash. I'm sure it was dislodged by someone. Probably some poor homeless chap looking for a dry place to spend the night. Mordant often forgets to close the taxidermy entrance, and more than once we've come to work to find a poor waif sleeping among the taxidermy mounts. Anywise, the sound gave me such a fright that I gashed my wrist with the flensin' knife, and I rushed outside, yelling in pain and anger. But nobody came to help me. Nobody heard at all. So I just cleaned myself up, and came home.'

'Oh, Henry,' Beatrice said, resting her hand on his. 'I'm so glad we got to know you. You've set our minds at ease about so very much.'

Archie and Beatrice walked back to the Balmain ferry. A bright, full moon shone out over the sandstone city. They were in no hurry, and stopped to admire the moonbeams skipping over the waves.

It was, Beatrice felt, an impossibly romantic night. One on which a girl might swoon if she received a proposal. When Archie began to speak, her heart swelled.

'Beatrice. I've been thinking about things. I was wrong to propose to you as I did. As you foresaw, my foreskin belongs in the collection.'

Beatrice could think of no response.

'I wouldn't mind having it cared for,' Archie went on in the silence that followed, 'into the unimaginable future, by curators of anthropology. They're priests and priestesses, really—custodians of our human sense of ingenuity, belief and beauty. But for all their efforts they can't preserve the full meaning of things. One day my foreskin will be just a love token from the Venus Islands. But that's okay with me. Is it okay by you too, Beatrice?'

'Shut up, Archie! Actually, it's not all right by me. Not at all.'

Archie stood puzzled as Beatrice reached up and kissed him. As unexpected as it was, it was the sweetest moment of his life. She flashed her left hand, and he saw a brown parchment ring on her fourth finger.

'It was meant for you, Beatrice. I've only got the one.' Then he plucked up the courage to ask her. Again.

Chapter 27

Henry, Beatrice and Archie set to work organising Eric's final carouse. They spread the word around the museum that the following Friday informal drinks would be held in the evolution gallery, in honour of Eric Sopwith. Vere Griffon, uncertain about whether he still had any respect among the staff, debated whether to go.

'You really must do it, old chap,' Abotomy advised. 'Like going to the funeral of a colleague. Expected of us big men, you know.'

Vere was girding his loins for the event when he heard a knock on the pillar that served as his door.

'Dithers! Good to see you, old stick.'

'Vere, I've come because I'm worried about the museum. And

about you,' Dithers said cautiously. 'I appreciate tremendously the support you've shown me of late, but I must say that when I sing your praises I'm a voice in the wilderness. I'm afraid that the old European style of director doesn't work well here.'

To Dithers' surprise Vere Griffon listened. The director could tell that Dithers was speaking from the heart.

'You must understand, Vere, that the Antipodeans are a strange lot. I fought with them at the charnel house that was Pozières. They were the bravest soldiers I ever commanded, and they died like flies. In somebody else's war. I never saw one shot in the back for deserting the fighting. But they hated being ordered about. The worst day of my life came when I was commanded to assemble a firing squad to execute a young man for failing to salute a brigadier. He was the best soldier we had. Fearless. Refused a blindfold: just stood there staring at me as the squad fired, as if to say, "I'm every bit as good as you, mate". I was only twenty-one—just a year or two older than him—and not a night goes by when I don't relive it.

'I can't help but think,' Dithers went on, 'that if you trusted them a bit—mixed with the troops; that sort of thing—you'd find that you have the finest set of curators in the world. And a far easier job of it.'

Griffon thought that maybe, just maybe, Dithers had a point.

'I have my own problems, Vere,' Dithers continued. 'Abotomy is a queer sort of chap. Deficient, somehow. Lacking in character. He's convinced that I attempted to seduce his wife, a charge of which I'm entirely innocent. He has threatened me with, er, physical violence.'

'Yes, a most disagreeable type. But in this case all bluff and bluster. Though I do know what you mean about his character. I can't help but think that in a frontier country like this, men like Abotomy are considered great solely because they get things done. A conscience just gets in the way. If you want to find the truly great here, you have to dig. History buries them deep.'

'Thank you, sir. There is just one more thing. I have a manuscript I intend to publish. Could I leave a copy with you?

Griffon scanned the title page: 'The Role of Museums in a Nation Founded on Murder'.

'I see. I'll try to get to it…in the fullness of time. But, my dear chap, the subject is outside your area of expertise.'

Dithers knew what that meant. Obfuscation and delay, in the hope he'd lose interest in pursuing what Griffon doubtless saw as his latest craze. He slumped against the pillar. He had more sympathy than hard feelings towards his director. But the last few weeks had changed him. It was as if the shellshock and despair had finally lifted. He had discovered that there was something worth fighting for. He knew what he must do, and now there was no way but the hard way.

'Shall we be off to Sopwith's do?' Griffon asked. He took Dithers by the arm and led him from the room.

Archie and Beatrice were surprised at who turned up. Some board members came along, and even the museum recluse, Mr Trembley, put in an appearance. He was, Archie was surprised to see, wearing his Samurai sword.

Almost everyone had a story of Sopwith's kindness—and everyone arrived with a bottle or two and some food. With the five quid's worth of catering, they'd have a surplus to give to the street kids.

Henry Bumstocks, Archie and Beatrice were debating who should say a few words when Griffon and Dithers walked through the door. Immediately, the atmosphere chilled. Dr Doughty hopped forward, a determined look on her face. 'Director, I know you've done much to support me of late, and I'm grateful for it. But you should be ashamed of yourself, pilfering the Bathurst meteorite from the collection while I was in the field. It was a despicable act!'

Vere Griffon's jaw tightened. He looked at the faces around him and fought the impulse to be high-handed.

'Elizabeth, I knew that you would be upset, but please try to understand. These miserable financial times put the very existence of the museum at stake. And I do bear responsibility for the fate of this institution. Sacrifices had to be made. I can't tell you what a difference the acquisition of the Giglione goats has made to the finances of the place. I'm only sorry that the meteorite perished in the fire.'

'You're mistaken there, Director. On the evening of the blaze, my dear Leggenhacker assisted me in removing it from your office and returning it to the mineral collection. The Bathurst meteorite is a *most* precious celestial body. It has the power to reveal the mysteries of outer space, and I have no doubt that one day it will! But after wandering the heavens for millions of years it very nearly didn't get the chance. No thanks to you.'

'I see,' Griffon said, suddenly understanding why the urchin thought he saw a butcher and a one-legged man fleeing from the fire. 'That is good news, Elizabeth. And of course you are quite right. Quite right.'

Griffon drew himself into a directorial stance.

'I have an announcement to make. At the next meeting of the board I intend to propose an amendment to the rules. From now on, curators will be consulted, regardless of where they are, if specimens they're responsible for are required for any purpose. We will live with the delays entailed. After all, you curators are the backbone of the institution, and your authority needs to be respected.'

A murmur of surprise rose from the crowd.

'While I am on the subject of curators, I have another thing to say. This morning I received approval from the Public Service Board for the elevation of Mr Archibald Meek from the position of assistant to full curator in the anthropology department.'

A wave of jubilation swept through the hall. The efforts of an esteemed colleague had been recognised. And many dared believe that the sanctity of a curator's care for his collection was to be upheld. Nothing was more important to the museum men and women assembled there. Dithers, catching the emotion, led a huge 'hurrah'. He grabbed Archie and old Mr Trembley, and together they lifted their rather alarmed director onto their shoulders and began parading him around the room. It was Dithers who struck up the old tune:

> *Here's to the prof. of museology,*
> *Master of all natural history!*
> *Good man he, and good men we,*
> *that suu-ch—a one—our director be.*
> *Hip hip hooray, hip hip hooray, hip hip hooray!*

With each cheer the curators tossed an embarrassed Griffon into the air. *And* they caught him again.

When things calmed down Archie tapped his glass. 'Director, friends and colleagues. In an institution such as this, where we live and die for our science and our collections, it's not surprising that passions can lead to tension. And so it should be. But we must honour the spirit of this place. And there you see it,' Archie said, pointing to a skull mounted high on the wall. 'The last and greatest gift a curator can give to his institution is himself—whether in the field or in a will. Here's to one of the finest curators this museum has ever known. And I believe that I can discern a smile on him even now. Ladies and gentlemen. I propose a toast to our friend and colleague, Eric Sopwith.'

'To Eric,' the choir of voices rang out as all eyes turned towards the skull.

'May he not be forgotten,' added Henry Bumstocks, a tear in his eye.

'There's something I'd like to say.' Courtenay Dithers was tapping his glass. 'I'm sure that the entire staff will be most interested to learn a little secret. We have one more cause for celebration today. This morning Miss Beatrice Goodenough informed me that she has accepted a proposal of marriage from Mr Archibald Meek. So, here's to the happy couple. Long may they sail with us!'

This time it was Archie and Beatrice being carried aloft, with Chumley Abotomy leading the cheers.

As the drinking started in earnest, Abraham Trembley caught Archie's eye.

'I've seen things in the corridors, young man. Things that

cause me to carry my sword wherever I go. A word of advice. Look to your man-catcher.'

Archie barely caught the old man's words over the din. His man-catcher? Perhaps he was telling him to look after Beatrice.

'I certainly will, Mr Trembley. She's quite a catch herself, I think.'

Trembley raised a bushy eyebrow and a corner of his mouth, and transfixed Archie with a look of horror, before vanishing into the crowd.

Chumley turned to Vere Griffon.

'Must be off, old fellow. Portia's at the hospital. About to pup at any moment. I might even be a father by now. But walk with me a little. I hear that Professor Picinnini of Florence has the most tremendous collection of stuffed swine. Every wild and domesticated breed, and every type of boar under the sun. What say we grab them for the colonies? I understand that the treasurer's a keen pork man.'

'Perhaps, old chap,' the director replied. 'But I feel I need a holiday first. Might ask for some leave. Just a couple of months. Fancy I'd like to see Malaya.'

Chapter 28

Courtenay Dithers felt that he had done what he could for Archie. Now he knew that he must do something for all humanity. He took a copy of the paper he had given to Griffon and strode to Speaker's Corner in the Domain. A crowd of fifty had gathered around a cadaverous-looking fellow in a ragged black suit who stood on a fruit box holding a sign proclaiming 'Christ is Risen!' in handwritten capitals. A few yards away a nuggety man stood atop another box, shouting to a smaller crowd about the universal brotherhood of working men.

Dithers stepped onto a vacant box, and began to read.

'The Role of Museums in a Nation Founded on Murder. By Dr Courtenay Dithers.'

A few people drifted away from the cadaverous speaker, and approached.

'The continent of Australia was colonised by Britain less than 150 years ago. Prior to that it was the home of hundreds of thousands of black men and women. What happened to them? Many thousands died in a war. One of the bloodiest and most craven wars ever known. Men, women and children were indiscriminately shot, poisoned and bludgeoned to death—by colonial Australians.'

By now pretty much everyone in the Domain had gathered in front of Dithers. Even the nuggety man had got down from his soapbox to listen, while the cadaverous chap watched in silence from atop his. As he read on Dithers caught a glimpse of a man throwing something at him, and felt a sharp pain in his forehead. Blood dripped into his left eye. 'Liar!' shouted his assailant, a man in a slick green suit, as he began scrabbling in the dirt, adding to the stones he had already gathered.

'Who are you, sir!' demanded Dithers, brushing the blood from his eye.

'Ken Shuttlecrap. And I can tell you that the pioneers never massacred the blacks. We've been spending a fortune soothing the pillows of a dying race. They get better care on the missions than our unemployed do.'

Dithers folded his manuscript and placed it in his pocket.

'You see that grand memorial up there, in Hyde Park? We built it, by public subscription, to honour those who had fallen in the Great War. I was there, and I know. Nothing is as horrific as war. The civilised countries consumed the finest flower of their youth in the trenches of France. Brave men were shot in the back as they fled the insanity. The skeleton of the unknown soldier that rests in that sepulchre is symbolic of all the glorious fallen.

'But in the war I talk of, whole tribes fell facing an enemy whose armaments made them all but invincible. The bravery of their heroes merits a VC. But where is their monument? Do you see that building to the left of the war memorial? It's our museum. And it is filled with the remains of the unknown dead, including some of the finest soldiers this country has ever produced. Men who defended home and family armed with wooden spears and clubs, against horses and guns. Yet we do not honour them. Instead we study their bones, and trade them. We defile their glorious sacrifice.'

'Nigger lover. Nigger lover.' The chant started low, but quickly swelled into an aggressive howl.

'Who did the killing?' Dithers shouted above the crowd. 'Our bunyip aristocracy, that's who. It was the great and supposedly good of this country whose ancestors pulled the triggers. The Duggertons, the Abotomys…'

Dithers felt himself being pulled from his soapbox. His left hand was being shoved far up his back. The blue of a police uniform pressed against his face.

It was early afternoon before Griffon learned that one of his curators was locked in the police cells.

He arrived at Darlinghurst police station to find Slugger

Doolan slouched over the counter.

'You museum chaps do like a stoush, don't you?' he said as he led Griffon to the cells.

'Oh dear! My poor chap. What happened?'

Dithers was sitting on a concrete floor. The side of his head was caked in blood and his patrician nose was badly broken.

'Officer!' Vere shouted. 'Get this man out of here. He is doing valuable work for the premier. Now move it!'

Griffon hailed a cab, helped Dithers in, and headed for Dithers' rooms.

Dithers spoke from the heart. 'I know what I must do, Vere. Never again will I suffer an injustice of this kind to remain unchallenged. I am going to Alice Springs, where the last of the wild tribes roam. The war still rages there, and I will not allow the desert people to suffer the fate of their coastal neighbours. You have my resignation: I can be nothing but an embarrassment to you from now on. Now go, Vere. Your museum needs you. And the tribes need me.'

When Archie and Beatrice heard about Dithers they rushed to his rooms. They found him lying on his bed.

'Oh, Courtenay, what have they done to you?' cried Beatrice.

'Don't tell the truth in this country, Beatrice.'

'Dithers, old chap, did you really have to stand in the Domain reading your manuscript? The place is full of rough types.'

'No need to worry about me, Archie. I'm off to Alice Springs. The final frontier of the black war. There are still shootings going on out there, and I'm determined to stop them.'

'We must come with you, Courtenay!' cried Beatrice impulsively. There were tears in her eyes as she lit the cigarette he had fumbled into his mouth.

'No. No!' Dithers replied emphatically. 'I need to face this alone.' He turned to Archie. 'For God's sake, treat the remains of the fallen with the respect they deserve.'

Archie had never felt so utterly helpless. His friend had gone where he could not tread. As a newly minted curator, he had a duty to treat the skulls as specimens.

When Vere Griffon walked through the door of his apartment that evening he was surprised to see the wall of his sitting room alive with the dancing shadows of a fire. It was burning gently in his fireplace, and sitting in a lounge chair before it, her back to him, was Dryandra Stritchley.

'Dryandra, what a surprise. What a pleasant surprise, I mean.'

'I realised, after I wrote to you, Vere, that I couldn't leave. It would all be for nothing without you.'

Griffon stepped back.

'Surely you knew? How many times had you confided in me that you'd like to rid yourself of those appalling curators? I have a talent for carrying out orders, you know. And for looking after you.'

'Dryandra, are you mad? Tell me, for God's sake, what's going on.'

'Were you sorry to see that useless Polkinghorne, and Dolt, Hadley and Jones, vanish? I made it so easy for you, Vere.'

'But, Dryandra, how could you possibly make them leave?

Did you threaten them?'

'No, Vere. I was far more decisive. Dolt, Hadley and Jones were easy. Men are such simple, gullible creatures. They were all eager to come home with me. And I love cooking, especially fish. It was old Trembley who told me about fugu. It's such a common species, and I love the challenge of preparing it. Getting the dose just right. It's such a gentle death that it's almost a pleasure. And it makes candlelit dinners for two so very interesting, even when the company is more comfortable communing with a blowfly than a woman.'

Vere slumped into the unoccupied armchair beside Dryandra. 'You killed them?' he whispered.

'The bodies would have been a problem if it wasn't for my rose garden. I thought that those useless curators should be productive, in death at least. They did little enough in life.'

'Polkinghorne gave me trouble, I admit. I watched him fight with the father of that young man. He didn't want to come with me at first. He was scared of you, Vere. Of what you might think of him. So I followed him onto the ferry, and eventually I persuaded him to come back with me to Circular Quay, and to my home.

'But surely you agree that my greatest triumph was Sopwith. I did hope that I'd killed two birds with one stone there. And I didn't even have to manage the body. With the others, Mordant was always eager to earn some pin money. Carrying boxes, letting people in, administering a few drops of fugu here and there. But he never glimpsed the full genius of it all.'

'But the letters. They all sent letters!' cried Griffon.

'Oh, Vere, you simple boy! I'm an excellent copyist, and our files are full of paperwork bearing staff signatures. You never asked to see the envelopes. But the best trick is yet to come. I had to dig them up, of course. Couldn't leave skeletons in the garden. It was tremendously interesting smoking the skulls so they resembled the originals, and sewing them onto the fetish. I do believe I was a forger in a previous life!

'And don't worry, Vere dearest, the skeletons, along with the skulls I took from the mask, are safe in our collection. I even labelled the skeleton boxes with their state of origin. Dolt, with a switched skull, is now a "native of Victoria", while Jones and Hadley are natives of New South Wales. I don't worry much about the switched skulls. They always were wrong-headed anyway. Delicious—and rather funny—don't you think? Perhaps one day some super sleuth will discover my clues, and understand the genius of it all. But not for a very, very long time.

'I only slipped up once. My bone staining wasn't up to old Bumstocks and his bleach. But even that wouldn't have mattered except for that young man, Meek. I almost had him, you know. If Beatrice had played hard-to-get just a little longer, you would have received a letter from the broken-hearted Mr Meek. "I can find neither peace nor love here. I've returned to the islands," it would have said. But he never took the bait.'

Vere was staring at Dryandra, his eyes dark with horror.

'Our work's not yet done, my beautiful Vere. My poor, hard-working Mordant is now assisting with the roses. Those man-catchers really are most ingenious objects. Archie Meek was careless enough to leave one unattended after the opening. I don't know how I would have managed Mordant without it. But there are yet suspicious minds we must still. Meek and Goodenough at the least.

'We're two of a kind, Vere. Inseparable. Let's pledge on our better selves that we'll never part. Come with me to Malaya. After we've done our tidying up, that is.'

Sunlight spilled onto the old sandstone verandah where Beatrice stood looking out between the buildings at a tiny sliver of water glittering in the sunlight. A real estate agent might describe it as 'harbour glimpses'. As the warm sun dispelled the last of the winter gloom, Archie stood, looking positively Arcadian, in his gardening boots and gloves, and secateurs in hand.

'I'm so happy, Archie. I keep having to pinch myself to know it's real.'

'I can hardly believe it myself, Beatrice. I had no idea that Dryandra Stritchley thought so highly of us. To leave us use of her house until she returns. And with no real duties apart from caring for her roses. It was extraordinarily generous.'

'Such a lovely letter, too, wishing us well for our marriage. I never realised how similar her handwriting was to Griffon's,' Beatrice said absently. 'Strange that she was so emphatic about not disturbing the flower beds. But I suppose that her roses are like children to her.'

'And that, Beatrice, is the only dark spot thus far, on the glory of married life. No matter what I do, I can't get the things to bloom as gloriously as she did. I've read every book—put my everything into it. But still it's not enough.'

Beatrice was aware of a tenderness in her breasts. She thought she knew what that meant, but it was far too early to say anything.

'When do you think she'll be back, Archie?'

'Her letter gave no idea. But surely she'll write from Malaya, giving us time to find somewhere else, before she returns.'

'Darling, I'd be delighted if we could stay here forever.'

'Perhaps we will, my sweet. It all depends on Dryandra.'

END

END NOTE

While preparing the manuscript for publication I uncovered some remarkable facts pertaining to various incidents portrayed therein. A cult mask, known as the great Darnley Island mask, is strikingly similar to the fetish described in the manuscript. It was probably (though not certainly) destroyed in a fire that consumed most of the Australian Museum's ethnographic collection in the nineteenth century. The cause of the fire was never determined, but newspapers reported that a one-legged man and a butcher's boy were seen fleeing the scene shortly before the blaze broke out.

Even more remarkable instances concern Dr Doughty's adventures in the Spice Islands. A privately published journal reveals that a Count Vidua of Genoa had travelled to the Dutch East Indies. While climbing a volcano, his leg broke through a lava crust and was badly burned. A German surgeon travelling on the count's vessel urged the nobleman to have his limb amputated. But Vidua waited too long, developed gangrene, and died. That surgeon's name was Leggenhacker. Moreover, I was astonished to learn that Cummingtonite and Dickite are actual mineral species, and that Abraham Trembley was a world-renowned authority on the Medusae.

Less certain, but still intriguing, are the parallels between Courtenay Dithers and several anthropologists of historical note. George Augustus Robinson's experiences in 1840s Victoria are similar, as is the story of Sydney University anthropologist Olive Pink, who gave up her studies to live among the Aborigines at Alice Springs.

When I first worked at the Australian Museum in the 1980s, its collection included a most grotesque assortment of stuffed goats. They had been acquired ninety years earlier through an exchange with an Italian professor of zoology, who received in return an irreplaceable collection of now-extinct marsupials. Strangely, around the time of the exchange, the director, Edwin Pearson Ramsay, was made a *Cavaliere* of the Crown of Italy, though what services he rendered that country remain obscure. But here, I must emphasise, I rely on my memory. Many specimens have been de-accessed from the collection over the intervening years. I'm not sure that the goats still exist.

T.F.

AUTHOR'S NOTE

The *Mystery of the Venus Island Fetish* is my first work of fiction, and it was the product of one of the most stressful periods of my life. In 2010 I was appointed as Australia's first climate commissioner. The job was independent of government and purely educational in nature, involving informing the Australian public about the scientific basis of climate change and how people around the world were responding to the climate challenge. Myself and my fellow commissioners wrote reports and travelled the country, meeting with ordinary citizens and answering their questions.

When the government introduced a carbon tax, elements in the media fixed on the Climate Commission as the force behind the new tax, and by 2012 I found myself living in a state of siege. Photographs of my home and details of its location were made public, and media trolls obtained my e-mail address. The Australian Federal Police watched my house, I needed security guards to escort me to and from public meetings, and I was often abused by strangers as I walked the street with my family.

I knew that I had to continue with the work, but as things got nastier and nastier, what I really needed was a refuge. Leaving my job was unthinkable, and I realised that the only refuge available was an invented one. So it was then that I started to create an imaginary world that I could enter at will. The sense of calm and wonder I found as I wove my characters and their world into a plot was astonishing—like walking through a magic doorway into another life. I'd invariably return from it refreshed and revitalised—and ready to fight on for a better climate outcome for future generations. So I suppose I should thank all those climate deniers, media goons and trolls for giving me a new string to my writer's bow.

The decision to use a pseudonym when the book was first published in Australia arose from the idea to depict the story as coming from a lost manuscript. I've always been taken with the device used by Cervantes in *Don Quixote*, whereby the manuscript containing the story is discovered and translated before being published by Cervantes.

I have always been a museum man. I got my first paid job, aged seventeen, in a museum, but I had been volunteering there for years before that. Ever since, I've worked at pretty much every level in museums, even spending seven years as a museum director. I love museums and those who work in them, so it's hardly surprising that I set my first novel in one. Nobody can deny that they are infinitely strange, full of paradox, eccentricity and mystery. Nowhere is there a greater chance of making an amazing discovery than in a museum collection. Even in a new country like Australia, treasures have been accumulating in some museums for nearly two hundred years. And those who work in them live by a dictum: never to throw anything away. Bits of rocks, animals and people are arrayed or stored there for purposes only dimly understood by most. The truth is that museums, and those who work in them, are great and exotic machines used to catalogue and understand the world. Can you imagine what it must be like to have spent sixty years utterly absorbed in the taxonomy of, for example, upside-down flies? Museums are full of such people, with every division of the animal kingdom having its own expert.

Museums may sometimes seem timeless, but they do change. I decided to set my novel in the early 1930s, in Sydney's Australian Museum. Back then the museum found itself stranded on the edge of Depression-era Woolloomooloo and Darlinghurst. Located near Sydney's docks and the first home to many immigrants, both suburbs were bywords for lawlessness and sheer, starving desperation. How, I wondered, could a museum director possibly keep such an extravagance as a museum going while the streets surrounding it were filled with starving people?

The 1930s exert an irresistible attraction for me, perhaps because I am fortunate enough to be surrounded by parents and family members who were children at that time, and whose childhood memories remain razor sharp. My dear Uncle Lou grew up as a street urchin in Darlinghurst, his Italian immigrant mother having died when he was eight. Through his eyes, and those of my other relatives, I found I could experience the sounds, sights and smells of Depression-era Sydney with exceptional vividness. If you walk the streets and lanes of

Darlinghurst and Woolloomooloo, you'll see exactly where the action of the novel plays out. In fact, until very recently, Archie and Dithers' hostel was still operating as a doss house for single men down on their luck.

My own life experience also played a role in the development of my story. I am a member of the last generation of explorers and researchers who could really launch themselves into another world, right here on Earth. In the 1980s you could still cross that invisible line between the global civilisation we are now all part of and societies all but untouched by the outside world. Back then there were no GPS systems, no mobile phones. Just topographic maps of places like New Guinea made by aerial survey, with extensive blanks caused by persistent cloud and great areas marked 'uncontrolled territory.' Back then you set out on foot with fifty or so native carriers and slogged through jungle for days until you reached a distant mountain range, knowing that your contacts with the outside world were well and truly severed. In the 1930s, of course, that 'other world' was much closer. Uncontacted Aboriginal tribes still roamed Australia's inland, and cannibals and headhunters could be found in many places in the Pacific. My principal protagonist spent his formative years living with a largely uncontacted tribe on a remote Pacific island. How, I wondered, would long emersion in such a society change a man?

Writing fiction felt very different in my head from writing nonfiction, in ways that I cannot fully explain. Like exercising a new set of muscles after long use of a different set, I found it refreshing and revitalising. The act of writing fiction didn't feel at all like work, and it felt nothing like writing nonfiction.

Instead, it was as if I were resting my brain at the same time that I strengthened my working tools.

Why write a comedy, mystery and judgement on my country all rolled into one? Simply because that is how life is, at least to me. I started out writing my novel with a sense of control. As I went on, however, I found that my characters needed to do things—things I did not always agree with. But in letting them lead I discovered that a richer tapestry was being woven than I could ever have contemplated at the outset. I discovered, as well, layers of meaning in the business of museum curation that I had previously ignored or skated over. But my biggest surprise was the discovery that things can be said more directly and powerfully in fiction than in nonfiction. A novel is a very good place to start a revolution.

I had to invent very little, except character, as I wrote *The Mystery of the Venus Island Fetish*. Real experiences in museums provided almost all of the 'furniture' for the story, though just how the characters evolved as they peopled the museum stage had nothing to do with anyone I know or knew. One of the most difficult to control was Chumley Abotomy. He started out as a straight 'black hat' man, but he refused to stay that way. Instead he became more and more multidimensional as the book went on. In some ways, I think, he is the embodiment of 1930s Australia.

T.F.